JOSIE BONHAM

The Viscount's Convenient Bride

First published by Pitcheroak Press 2020

First edition

ISBN: 978-1-913856-02-1

This book was professionally typeset on Reedsy.
Find out more at reedsy.com

Chapter One

May 1800 Leicestershire

Kitty paused at the top of the library steps at the sound of a carriage drawing up. Oh no, was Sir Walter here again? The curtains were closed against the dreary, late afternoon rain, blocking her view of the drive. She took some calming breaths. What was the matter with her? He wouldn't return after the last time. It was probably one of the girls from the vicarage. She still hadn't adjusted to being on her own, apart from Nella Spencer, housekeeper cum cook and her husband, Robert, who did everything else. It was making her nervous.

She clung on to the pole at the top of the steps, unable to move. That wasn't true, it was the thought of Sir Walter making her nervous. She held her breath at the sound of the front door opening. Robert was talking to a man. She twisted so hard in an attempt to see the library door as it opened that the pole broke off in her hand. The steps toppled from under her.

Kitty closed her eyes and braced herself for contact with the hard, wooden floor. She stalled in mid-air. Her eyes flew open as a very human curse ruled out a supernatural cause. A pair of strong arms held her close to a greatcoat smelling of damp wool as her saviour staggered backwards. He managed to keep them both upright before juddering to a halt next to the mahogany desk in the middle of the library, breathing hard.

They stood with her locked in his arms. For some strange reason that felt a good place to be. His greatcoat tickled her nose as he caught his breath. She became aware of a delicious scent of tangy citrus with a hint of spice, so much more enticing than Sir Walter's stale wine and snuff. He wasn't Sir Walter! Relief flooded through her, leaving her legs too weak to hold her upright unaided. She slumped against him. The sound of footsteps made her look towards the door.

Nella Spencer rushed in, enveloped in a floury apron and holding a rolling pin. "I'm sorry I didn't come to the door myself." Her voice shook.

Nella's mouth dropped open when she saw them and she waved the rolling pin at their visitor. "Let go of her, you monster. Viscount Enstone will hear of it if you don't."

Kitty felt, as much as heard, a deep chuckle.

He held her away from him with his hands gripping her shoulders. "Can you stand unaided?" He gave her a quizzical look.

"Yes, thank you." She stepped back and caught sight of his heavy gold ring. Oh heavens, was he Viscount Enstone? A glance at his amused expression suggested he was.

"Nella put that thing down. Lord Enstone has just saved me from a hard landing." She frowned at him. "I'm grateful of course, but I would like to point out that I wouldn't have fallen if you hadn't distracted me."

Nella stood and stared at her. "Are you sure? He never said." She lowered the rolling pin. "We were expecting your new land agent, but not until next week."

The viscount bowed. "I apologise for not apprising you of the change of plan, Mrs?"

Nella flushed and dropped a curtsy. "Mrs. Spencer, my lord."

A smile softened his austere features. Shrewd looking hazel eyes studied them both.

"Well, Mrs. Spencer, would you mind drying this wet coat for me? A hot drink would be welcome too."

"I'll call Robert to you, my lord." Nella drew herself up to her full height. "It wouldn't be seemly for you to stay in here."

"It will be sufficient to leave the door open. I need to talk to Miss...." He hesitated. "Ah, Miss Davenport."

Kitty stiffened, he'd struggled to remember her surname, despite having met her brother, Edward, barely a couple of months ago. That didn't bode well.

"Nella, ask Robert to take His Lordship's coat to dry and then bring us some tea to the front parlour."

Nella dropped a slight curtsy and marched out. Kitty's gaze was drawn to Lord Enstone. He was an attractive man, in a stern sort of way. Probably not much older than her. Splashes of water dripped off his greatcoat on to the library floor and his faced was pinched with cold.

"You look perished. We can't afford to heat many rooms but there will be a fire lit in the parlour."

"I've dealt with much worse in my army days but a fire would be welcome." He rubbed his hands together. "It's so cold for the time of year."

Heavy footsteps sounded in the hall and Robert Spencer knocked at the open door.

"I've shown your man where he can rub down the horses and stable them, milord." He stepped closer. "Now to help

3

you out of your coat."

Viscount Enstone raised his eyebrows at Kitty but allowed Robert to take his coat. They stood in silence until Robert had gone.

"How many servants do you have?"

"Just Mr and Mrs Spencer, the two you have seen. Our funds don't run to any more."

Kitty winced inwardly. That wasn't very tactful since his father had been supplying those funds. With the old viscount dead, they needed this man's help. Edward's future depended upon it. If only Edward had been nearer to her in age, he would have finished his education by now and things would have been so much easier. Why couldn't Lord Enstone have warned them that he was coming in person rather than his agent? At least then she would have been better prepared.

Kitty moved towards the door. "Come, it's warmer in the parlour."

She sailed out of the room; head held high. Heat flooded her cheeks. Lord Enstone must think her shockingly fast staying in his arms like that. Exactly the impression she couldn't afford to create. If he heard about Sir Walter Greenough forcing his way into the house the week before, how would he react? Would he blame her? She tried not to think about the feel of Sir Walter's wet lips on hers before Robert had pulled him off and received a bloody nose for his trouble.

Why on earth had Sir Walter thought treating her like that was going to make her warm to his repeated offers of marriage? He had seemed angrier with Robert than her. Lord, had he been hoping Robert would spread the tale of the kiss abroad? That would make sense after his parting threat to tell everyone that she was free with her kisses. They reached the parlour and she forced her mind back to the present.

The parlour was the best kept room in the house and she had made it cosy with her embroidered cushions and tapestries. She walked across to the window and closed the drapes to cut out the late afternoon gloom. Lord Enstone followed her in and she indicated the larger of the two tan leather armchairs positioned either side of the fire.

"Please be seated."

He nodded and stood by the chair until she had taken the other one. At least he was treating her with respect, but it was his fault she was in this mess. Anger welled up but she stared at the floor and quickly doused it. He was under no legal obligation to them after all. He could throw her out today if he wanted to. She tried to steady her breathing. Her palms felt clammy and yet she was shivering. Why didn't he say something? She looked up to find him watching her with his head tilted and his lips slightly pursed. If only she knew what he was thinking. A tremor went through her.

"My father was ill for some time before his death and things have not been looked after as they ought, Miss Davenport. My new agent is struggling to make his way around all the properties to see what needs to be done. Your brother explained a little of your situation when I was called to his school but at the time it made little sense to me. I have been unable to come here personally until now, for which I apologise."

Kitty closed her eyes and counted to ten. Their situation, as he called it, clearly wasn't of much interest to him. Her nails dug into her palms. She forced herself to smile and open her eyes.

"Are you in full possession of the facts now, my lord?"

He gave her another appraising glance. "No, I don't think I

am, perhaps you would explain it all to me."

She pushed a stray lock of hair behind her ear. Nothing but the truth would do, shaming as it was. "Our fathers were old friends. My father died within a few days of gambling away our home and the investments that provided our only income. Since his death we have been living on your father's charity."

* * *

Luke stared at Miss Davenport and then at the fire. Such generosity didn't belong to the father he remembered. There must be more to it than that. He studied the young woman opposite and frowned as he tried to remember something her brother had said about Miss Davenport being on her own too much.

"That much I gathered from your brother, an admirable young man. He has promised to repay me every penny when he's older. There was something else. Oh, that was it. He was very concerned that your aunt had died. A sad occurrence but I'm not sure why Edward was so worried."

The girl gasped and her face turned a brilliant shade of red. What on earth had he said to upset her like that? Before he could ask, Mrs Spencer marched in.

"Begging your pardon, Miss Davenport, but it'll be dark soon and the weather is closing in. If His Lordship doesn't go now, he'll be stuck here all night which wouldn't be fitting."

Her point was emphasized by a loud clap of thunder.

Mr. Spencer joined them. "There ain't no way His Lordship will be able to drive in this, Nella. You may as well accept it and see if you can stretch the dinner."

Miss Davenport rose and walked across to a window. She

opened the drapes to reveal a solid sheet of rain. "Robert's right, His Lordship's horses can't go out in this."

Luke's lips twitched. He seemed to be low down her list of priorities, certainly below his horses.

She moved back towards her chair. "See what you can do about dinner, Nella. Robert, would you set a fire in the best spare bedroom."

Luke stood until she was seated. Another blush stained her cheeks. The smile she gave him didn't reach her eyes. He would say she was under considerable strain. The tense way she held herself reminded him of a young lieutenant the night before his first battle. But then she was in an uncomfortable situation, especially for someone who showed every sign of being an independent sort.

She was well-spoken and could have found herself a job as a governess or lady's companion, but of course she had her brother to worry about. He should have read all those letters before he came. At least then he might have had some idea of what they were doing under his father's protection. The whole thing made no sense. Father had never done things for people without getting something in return that Luke could remember. Good lord, she hadn't been Father's mistress, had she? She was too young for one thing. His father had been a hard man but would he have taken advantage of a young woman like that? Luke's jaw dropped open. Surely not.

As soon as he was seated Miss Davenport tapped a foot. "Well, my lord?"

She held her head high as she looked at him. Her greyish blue eyes sparkled and bright spots of colour decorated her cheeks, as if she knew what he was thinking. His first impression had been of a rather plain girl but there were signs of an attractive young woman under the camouflage of her shabby, well-worn clothes. His breathing quickened as his gaze lingered on her rosebud lips. What would it be like to kiss them? A flash of heat spread from his groin and it was his turn to blush.

He looked towards the fire. "I have to admit that my father and I weren't close. His secretary left in a hurry the day the household heard my return was imminent. My new man has found a lot of irregularities in the accounts. This estate wasn't the only one not to receive all the money that was meant for it."

She gasped. "I see, but what about the letters I sent you?"

"I was stationed on the continent when word reached me that my father was gravely ill. It took me months to reach home. I haven't seen any letters from you. The first I knew of your existence was when I was summoned to your brother's school."

Her face became even redder and she studied him intently. "So, what happened to all your correspondence?" Her voice was little more than a whisper.

"When my new secretary became concerned that the accounts didn't add up, he searched high and low for more paperwork. I expect your letters are in amongst the piles of correspondence he found stashed in various drawers and cupboards. Some of it is years old and he hasn't had chance to work through it all yet."

"I see. That explains a lot." She looked worried and rather embarrassed.

"My new secretary is entirely trustworthy. You needn't fear that he will disclose anything about your family to anyone but me."

"Thank you. I'm not worried for myself but my brother

might suffer if our indebtedness became public knowledge."

Luke nodded and decided not to tell her about the pile of personal letters to his father his valet had found tucked away in the master suite of the country home which was now his. At least he had brought those letters with him. They might throw some light on the affair.

"Doesn't your brother's school already know after he had them send for me?"

She lowered her head and her voice was so soft he could barely hear it. "I'm sorry about that. I don't know what came over him. I believe he told them you were his guardian and a trifle absentminded."

Luke laughed. "How very enterprising of him. I did make sure that the fees were paid and gave him some pin money, but until my new secretary found the missing ledgers, I didn't know the estate was making you an allowance. He will be contacting your bankers immediately." He hesitated. "It appears that the quarterly sum you were receiving was only a fraction of what my father had allocated for you."

"Oh!" She looked seriously discomposed now. "My aunt said more than once that I ought to query it with him but to do so felt impertinent. As long as Edward's fees were being paid, I thought it best to leave it. We did have her jointure until she died."

Luke sat back. "Your aunt was living with you?"

"Yes."

"Who is your companion now?" He frowned and looked towards the door, half expecting a flustered elderly lady to appear.

"I don't have one."

Damn, that must have been what her brother had tried to

9

tell him. He didn't know much about the niceties of female behaviour but he had a strong suspicion that a housekeeper wasn't considered enough chaperonage for a gently bred young woman like Miss Davenport.

The housekeeper walked in unannounced. "That's why she's troubled by the likes of Sir Walter."

Miss Davenport's hands clenched into fists. "Nella! That's enough." Her voice shook.

"It's nowhere near enough." Mrs Spencer turned towards him, her face a mask of belligerence. "I've worked for your father all my life, young man. If you put Robert and me out of a job after me speaking my mind, you do, but it has to be said. You should be ashamed of yourself leaving her like this. All the gossips in Shepley and every village for miles around have enjoyed themselves at her expense and it's your fault. Her reputation is ruined. What would your father have said?"

It was surprising that his father had anything to do with the matter at all. Mrs Spencer was pleating her apron in her hands and staring at the floor now she had said her piece. She must be devoted to Miss Davenport to risk her position. Miss Davenport stared at him with pursed lips. Luke rose and walked to the window. His father had got him into a sorry mess here but he was at fault for letting things ride for so long. It would be wrong to visit the anger he felt towards his father on a well-meaning servant. A muscle twitched in his eyelid as he fought for control.

"I'm not about to put anyone out of a job." Luke turned to face them. "I considered sending my secretary down when I heard about the Davenports living here but he was busy on other things, including finding me a new agent. I intended to send the agent but decided to come in person as it was a private family matter. I've had other things to attend to until now."

Luke kept a close watch on Miss Davenport. A mixture of relief and anxiety, even a touch of hostility, washed over her expressive features. Perhaps she was angry at being seemingly ignored for so long. Mrs Spencer's assertion that Miss Davenport was being gossiped about because of her lack of a chaperone would explain her embarrassment at being without her aunt as well as her brother being worried about her. He pulled back the corner of a drape. If anything, the rain was worse and thunder still rumbled around them. There was no help for it, he would have to stay overnight and hope his visit didn't become common knowledge.

"Spencer is correct that conditions are too poor to travel tonight. I accept your invitation to stay here. Perhaps you would direct me to my room, Miss Davenport?"

"Turn to the right at the top of the stairs and it's the first room you come to."

"Thank you." He bowed deep. "I will see you at dinner."

Luke found the room with no difficulty. Spencer was putting the finishing touches to a fire. At least the chimney wasn't smoking. The place was clean and tidy but there was a neglected air about it. It was a big house for one couple to manage all that needed doing. That was something else for his agent to sort out.

"There you are, milord. That should heat up the room nicely. Dinner shouldn't be too long. Nella has a chicken nearly roasted."

"Thank you, Spencer."

Spencer nodded and went out.

Luke pulled a chair in front of the fire and sat with his

elbow resting on his knee and his chin cupped in his hand. Underneath her anxious air, and who wouldn't be anxious when relying on the generosity of someone they knew nothing about, Miss Davenport seemed to be a spirited young woman. Her manners were pleasing and she had earned the loyalty of the Spencers. Despite his youth, Edward Davenport had impressed him. Why Father had helped them in the first place was a mystery but, whatever the reason, his father had accepted responsibility for the family and that responsibility was now his.

Spencer showed every indication of being an honest, reliable servant. On reflection he couldn't be sure of Mrs Spencer, who might be well-rewarded if she helped Miss Davenport to force an offer of marriage out of him. She had made quite a fuss about him talking to the girl alone. Perhaps that had given her the idea for her outburst later. Miss Davenport's brother was a baronet and such a marriage wouldn't be too much of a mésalliance on his part. It would solve all the family's difficulties as well as quashing any gossip about her. He should have trusted his instinct to let his secretary sort out the whole sorry mess but it was too late now. If he had walked into an ambush it was his own fault for not being prepared.

His mind in a whirl, Luke struggled into his evening clothes. He hadn't really expected to need them but Garner had insisted on packing them. A pity he hadn't brought Garner with him. He had worked for the family since he was a boy and would have known the Spencers if they had worked for his father. What a tangle he had got himself into. He pushed a hand into the secret pocket in his valise and pulled out two bundles of his father's personal letters, tied up with ribbon. With luck the Davenports would be mentioned in these.

He picked up the bundle with red ribbon and untied it. The first letter in the bundle was addressed to his father in a delicate hand. He opened it out and found Henry Davenport mentioned on the first page. The signature on the last page was Lucy Swift. In the body of the letter she announced the death of Henry Davenport and explained that the children were left with nothing. She couldn't keep her niece in her rented rooms indefinitely and she didn't know what she was going to do with her nephew when he was home from school. She appealed for his help.

Lucy must have been Miss Davenport's aunt, which tied in with what Miss Davenport had said. From the rest of the letter it sounded as if Mrs Swift, Sir Henry and his father had all been good friends in their younger days. Would that have been enough for Father to have bestirred himself to help the children? If so, his father had surprised him. He heard a gong ring downstairs. He flipped to the last letter. It was signed Kitty Davenport. Dinner would have to wait for him whilst he read it.

Miss Davenport gave his father the sad news of her aunt's death and asked if he could recommend a suitable companion for her. Presumably she hadn't the funds to engage one for herself and hoped he might find an indigent elderly relative, or some such, to send to her. It was dated a week or two before Father's death. The tone wasn't particularly affectionate but it wasn't formal either, which suggested that his father had been on good terms with the family. He stuffed the letters back into their hiding place and made his way downstairs.

Miss Davenport was waiting for him in the parlour. She didn't seem to be able to look at him but was that from embarrassment or guilt? She couldn't be too innocent to

13

at least suspect Mrs Spencer had tried to bounce him into making an offer for her to save her reputation. Then there was the possibility they had discussed such a strategy if the opportunity arose. It was hard to judge without knowing more about the exact nature of the gossip.

He held out his arm to lead her into dinner. She tucked her hand into it after a slight hesitation. He felt her shiver as they went out into the hall but that was probably the cold. Even with a shawl wrapped around her shoulders her dark grey gown didn't look warm enough for the rigours of Shepley Hall. Spencer had managed to find enough fuel to light a fire in the dining room and it was marginally warmer than the hallway. He handed Miss Davenport to a seat nearest to the fire and took the place next to her.

"Thank you, my lord."

Luke sighed. "I hate being called that. I was much happier in the army as plain Luke Bamford."

She gave him a shy smile. "I can hardly call you anything else."

He found himself smiling back. Either the girl was a complete innocent or a consummate actress. If she was an innocent then why had she lingered in his arms when he broke her fall from the library steps? She could have reacted in that way from shock, but it had certainly given him time to notice her exotic perfume and enjoy the feel of her in his arms. Had she guessed who he was from his dress and been throwing out lures to him? Possibly. He would reserve judgement. Indeed, who was he to judge? Her situation was difficult. At the same time marriage was something he dreaded at the best of times and he'd be damned if he would be trapped into it.

Mrs Spencer arrived with a vegetable soup. He tucked

into it with relish. He hadn't realised how hungry he was. Mrs Spencer might have a sharp tongue but she was a good cook. Conversation was stilted and confined to topics like the weather. The rest of the meal was simple but equally tasty. Roast chicken was followed by baked apple with cream. He sat back and smiled. It was amazing how a full stomach improved one's mood.

Miss Davenport gave him a half smile back. "Shall I leave you to your port, my lord?"

Luke hesitated; she was looking distinctly pale. "A glass of port might do you some good. You can't stop shivering. Why don't we go and sit in front of that fire in the parlour and enjoy a drink together?"

Miss Davenport hesitated but another shiver went through her and that seemed to decide the matter.

"It would be warmer."

"Good." He pulled back her chair and followed her to the parlour.

Spencer was stoking up the fire. "We've enough wood for a few days," he grimaced, "which is just as well."

"Why, Robert?" Miss Davenport sat in the same chair as earlier.

"His Lordship's man went for a quick walk to stretch his legs as soon as the rain eased off. The river has burst its banks. There will be no way out of here for at least a day or two."

Luke swallowed a curse as he sank into his seat. They had seen no one on the last few miles of their journey but the longer they were forced to remain the more likely that his presence here would become known.

He nodded at Spencer. "I hope we have enough food? That was an excellent dinner by the way."

Spencer eyed him with his head on one side. "Thank you, milord. I'll pass that on to Nella. She will be pleased. She was worried the dinner wouldn't be fancy enough for you. There's enough food for at least two or three days."

"Let's hope we'll be able to leave before then." Luke looked at Miss Davenport but she was studying the floor with fixed concentration. "After nearly six years of army rations Mrs Spencer's dinner was a feast."

Spencer smiled. "I'll fetch the port, milord. It's some that your father put down years ago."

Luke put up a hand to delay him. "It's strange but I don't remember coming to this estate as a boy. I can't even remember my father mentioning it."

"It's on the edge of some good hunting country, my lord. The old viscount came here regularly until your mother died. They met when he was staying here."

No one had ever mentioned that before. "What happened to it after that?"

"It was all closed up and we were left to look after it. His Lordship's agent stayed here two or three times a year on his travels. He was the only visitor until Miss Davenport and her aunt moved in three years ago."

Luke sat back. "I see, thank you."

He shot a glance at Miss Davenport who avoided his gaze. The hands resting in her lap were so tightly clasped her knuckles showed white. Luke grimaced. Once he had made his decision to continue to support them, he should have reassured her before they sat down to dinner. She was effectively destitute without his help, apart from any small sum she might have been left by her aunt.

Chapter Two

Kitty looked up when Spencer returned with the port decanter on a tray with two glasses and laid it down on a side table.

"Thank you, Robert." She turned to Viscount Enstone. "Port, my lord?"

He gave a brief nod. She picked up the decanter and willed her hands not to shake. Somehow, she managed to fill his glass without spilling any liquid. He accepted it with a muttered thank you. She filled a glass for herself. What was he thinking? He had seemed almost hostile since hearing he would have to stay for a night or two. What if he had heard the gossip and believed she had been his father's mistress? She gulped down her port and absentmindedly filled up her glass. Heavens, now he would think her a drinker as well as a Cyprian.

She knew nothing about him at all. Would he condemn her out of hand and expect her to leave straight away? Or was he considering offering her a carte blanche? Something her aunt had often warned her men might try since they couldn't afford a dowry for her. Why on earth hadn't she let Aunt Lucy's solicitor contact Viscount Enstone for her? For all she knew he would take her virginity and still cast her off. Why didn't he say something? She glanced up at him to find him studying her intensely. He didn't seem the sort of man who would ravish her but he did look angry. Kitty could bear the suspense no longer.

"What do you intend to do about us, my lord?" Her voice sounded shrill even to her own ears. Why didn't he say something?

Lord Enstone regarded her steadily for several moments. It was hard to read his expression but he didn't look particularly friendly. Kitty's heart skipped a beat.

"That depends." He was positively glowering now.

Something snapped. "What sort of answer is that? For goodness sake, stop toying with me like a cat with a mouse."

"The truth is, Miss Davenport, I am at a loss to know what to do in the circumstances."

The hazel eyes that had seemed warm when she first met him had taken on a hard, assessing gleam. She felt her cheeks flood with warmth. Her hands shook so much she clamped them by her sides.

"Have you heard the rumours then?"

"No, I haven't heard any rumours. I would like to know why Mrs Spencer considers your reputation is ruined." His eyes seem to bore into her. "Would you care to explain?"

Her voice came out as a whisper. "I don't want to talk about it."

He banged his glass down on the table between them and stood so quickly that his chair moved. He walked around the room in fast, jerky steps before returning to stand over her.

"Why mention rumours and then refuse to explain what you mean? There is no point talking any more tonight. I'm not in the mood for riddles."

He sounded so angry. Kitty raised her eyes to his and tried to say something but no words would come out. His expression seemed to soften.

"I am aware I have some sort of obligation to you. I will find a way to provide for you. Good night, Miss Davenport." He turned on his heel and marched out.

So, he did intend to help them. That was a relief, or was it? She shook with the effort of suppressing a sob. Had he been telling her the truth about not hearing any of the rumours? Perhaps, but what had Nella been doing by informing him her reputation was ruined? If he thought her a loose woman would he expect payment in kind for whatever help he gave them? She couldn't bring herself to become his mistress, even for Edward's sake.

Or could she? Would it be any worse than looking after a querulous old lady, like the one the vicar's daughter had ended up with? Her cheeks burned. Could she accept a carte blanche for Edward's sake? She dawdled up the stairs to her room. It wouldn't help Edward to have a sister who was someone's mistress. On the other hand, if he moved to a different part of the country to take up whatever profession he chose and she changed her name, no one need know. Kitty shuddered. It was no good, every feeling revolted at the prospect of accepting a slip on the shoulder. Perhaps she could bargain with Lord Enstone to finance Edward's education and help her find employment. She had lived very quietly, changing her name should be enough to hide her identity from any potential employer.

* * *

Luke found his way to the kitchen where Spencer was adding

wood to the fire. "Is my coat dry yet? I'd like to go and check on the horses."

"Yes, my lord. Let me help you into it."

Spencer helped him into his greatcoat and stood back. He appeared about to say something, before changing his mind.

"What is it, Spencer?"

"Don't take too much notice of my wife, my lord." Spencer took a deep breath. "She's been fretting herself to flinders over the young miss, what with Sir Walter Greenough and all."

Luke hesitated. "Sir Walter Greenough?"

"Ever since people found out that Miss Davenport didn't have a female companion, after her aunt died, the gossips have been spreading nasty rumours about her. Sir Walter has been pestering her for ages. I had to put him to the right about a few days ago."

Luke felt himself flush. It was months since Edward Davenport had tried to tell him about his sister's difficulties. He had completely forgotten about the family until his eager new secretary had found the missing ledgers.

"Did my father ever visit here after Miss Davenport and her aunt moved in, Spencer?"

Spencer scratched his chin. "He visited just after they came here. He and Lady Swift were childhood friends. We saw him a few times after that but the visits petered out a while before Lady Swift died."

"I see. I'm sorry my father's secretary was so dishonest. I had no knowledge my father was even supporting the family until a long time after his death. Don't worry about your position."

The army had taught him a lot about men and Spencer seemed a genuine sort. If Miss Davenport was a complete innocent, he had done her a grave disservice. But was she? Perhaps embarrassment had been behind her dissembling when they spoke about the rumours circulating. He went out to the stables in search of his new groom. Fletcher was shaping up well after two weeks in his service, which wasn't surprising considering what an excellent sergeant he had been. It would be interesting to see what he thought. The rain had stopped and he found Fletcher outside, leaning on a fence that separated some sort of paddock from the driveway.

"Evening, Captain. Sorry, my lord."

Luke laughed. "I prefer Captain. Life was so much simpler in the army. Tell me, what do you make of the situation here?"

Fletcher stood to attention and eyed Luke warily. "I know it wasn't your fault but the lady has been left in a bit of a fix by you not receiving her letters. They've had little money from your estate since your father died and her savings from a small sum her aunt left her are running out."

"I'm well aware of that." Fletcher looked uncomfortable. Did he know something more but didn't like to mention it? "If you know something I don't, you might as well tell me."

"Spencer thinks the world of Miss Davenport. He said it was about time she looked to her own interests instead of spending all her energy worrying about her brother." Fletcher hesitated.

"Out with it, man."

"There are rumours flying around the village that Miss Davenport was your father's mistress. Spencer says when Lady Swift was alive no one thought anything of them living here and it's probably been spread by that Sir Walter who's after her."

His guess was correct. What a damnable coil. "I wondered if there was something like that going on. Thank you for confirming it. What do you think of Spencer and his wife?"

"They seem a decent enough couple to me, my lord. That reminds me, Mrs Spencer asked if Garner was still with you but I wasn't sure."

"Garner is my valet and his father held the same position with my father."

"Sorry, I should have remembered your valet's name."

"Don't worry. I don't expect you to have memorised all the names of my staff yet. You've been most helpful, Fletcher. How are the horses?"

"Happily eating the hay Spencer found for them. They're a good team."

"Yes. If we're stuck here for a few days it's going to cost me a pretty penny to pay for their hire."

Fletcher stroked his head. "I'm sure we won't get out tomorrow but I'll have a better idea once I've checked out the route in the light. It might only be a couple of days."

"Is the road from Shepley open?"

"Yes, my lord, but it would be a huge detour if we went that way and we might find other river crossings impassable as well."

"True. We'll wait until we can go back the way we have come. Have they found you a room for the night or is it a bivouac in the stables?"

Fletcher laughed. "I would prefer the stables but they have given me a cosy room above the kitchen so it's quite warm."

"Excellent. I'll say goodnight."

Luke wandered along the drive, trying to collect his thoughts. Mrs Spencer had mentioned Garner which suggested that the couple were exactly what they seemed, two loyal old retainers, although they had transferred their allegiance to

Miss Davenport. He could definitely rule out any possibility that she had been his father's mistress. Not that he had entertained that idea for more than a moment. Although he hadn't been the only one to have the same thought.

With a rumour like that circulating, he could understand why Miss Davenport had been too embarrassed to elaborate. She had been very ill at ease all evening. Had she seriously expected him to leave the pair of them destitute? Conscience smote him, perhaps she had. Her inevitable worries for the future would have been enough to overset many a society lady. On top of that, since she had been having trouble with local men, she may have been afraid of him. He had been too busy being angry at the fix he had got himself into to think about it from her point of view. None of which helped him solve the puzzle of why his father had taken so much trouble to help the family.

The cold-hearted father he knew would surely have torn up what was essentially a begging letter. Her aunt had been Lady Swift. Could she have been an old sweetheart of his father? Perhaps the letters would throw some light on it. In the meantime, his best course of action would be to escort Miss Davenport to London and ask Aunt Theo to take her in. Aunt Theo was equal to anything and would know how to squash any whisperings of gossip that followed Miss Davenport to London.

As long as Grace liked Miss Davenport, having her to stay shouldn't be too much extra work. Aunt Theo and Grace would enjoy helping to make her presentable. What female didn't like frequenting modistes and such like. Miss Davenport was well spoken and seemed sensible. Her brother was a baronet. With Aunt Theo to guide her she would do very well and hopefully find a suitable husband. She would need a maid with her. Mrs Spencer would have to go with them.

Chapter Three

Kitty splashed cold water over her face. Sleep had eluded her until the small hours and now she was struggling to wake up properly. She splashed more water over her tired eyes. The sooner she went down to breakfast, the sooner she could talk to Lord Enstone, or should she call him Viscount Enstone? Despite her father being a baronet, they had never mixed a great deal in society and the niceties of such things were beyond her.

She would happily work as a paid companion if she could find a position but Edward was barely sixteen. If he was to earn a good living, he needed to finish his education. Edward had already made it plain to His Lordship that he would pay back what he owed. Surely Lord Enstone would agree to help him without attaching conditions? If the position had been reversed her father would have been only too pleased to help the son of an old friend.

A laugh escaped her. The chance that her scapegrace father had ever had those sorts of funds was negligible of course. They would have ended up in debtor's prison years ago, if she hadn't taken over their finances when Mama died, despite the generous income he had received from his investments. Why had he wagered his business interests as well as Davenport

Court? They could have managed quite well on that income and Aunt Lucy's jointure. She sighed. Her old home might be less than an hour's travel from Shepley Hall but it felt like a different world. There was a knock at the door and Nella came in.

"I'll help you get ready. His Lordship is prowling around downstairs and he wants to speak to you."

Nella was rifling around in her cupboards before she could stop her. Kitty smiled despite the fluttery feeling in her insides stirred by the description of Lord Enstone as prowling around. He struck her as an energetic sort of man, which could explain his impatience, but was he another predatory male like Sir Walter under his gentlemanly exterior?

Nella pulled out a soft lavender woollen gown that Aunt Lucy had bought her and held it up to the light. "The colour is a bit subdued but it's a stylish cut. It will have to do."

Nella helped her twist her thick, brown hair into a knot at the top of her head once she was dressed.

"You look lovely." Nella leaned forwards and pinched her cheeks. "There, you look even better with some colour in your cheeks."

Kitty took a step back and stared at Nella. "I feel like a cow being primped for market."

Nella smiled at her. "It never hurts to look your best when you have an important interview ahead. Don't you take any nonsense from His Lordship, he's a Bamford and he ought to know his duty. It's shocking the way he's neglected you."

"I can't afford to antagonise him. Edward's future depends on him."

Nella shook her head, hands on hips. "You're a babe in arms. Off you go and promise me you won't respond to anything he offers you without thinking hard first."

Kitty gasped. Surely Nella wasn't telling her to accept a carte blanche? She squared her shoulders and went into the dining room. If she was about to have an awkward conversation, she would at least have it on a full stomach. His Lordship could wait.

She hesitated in the doorway. Viscount Enstone was seated at the table eating a plate of ham and eggs. Nella gave her a gentle push from behind. His Lordship immediately rose to pull back a chair for her.

"Good morning, Miss Davenport."

"Thank you, my lord. I trust you found your room comfortable."

"Very comfortable indeed, thank you, Miss Davenport."

She settled down and accepted a cup of coffee from him. Spencer bustled in with a dish with more eggs and a plate of buttered toast, her favourite breakfast. She filled her plate and set about eating. She barely tasted the food but she was determined not to be rushed. She finished up with a second cup of coffee. The viscount was studying her over the rim of his own cup when she eventually looked up.

He laughed. "You are certainly a peaceful breakfast companion unlike my sister, Grace, who never stops chattering."

"Your sister lives with you then?"

"Sometimes, but at the moment she is staying with my aunt, Lady Grant, in London. She has only recently been presented at court, despite having reached the ripe old age of twenty last week. What about you? Have you ever been presented at court?"

He seemed to be watching her intently and she shuddered.

"You're cold. If you've finished your breakfast why don't we

27

go and sit in the parlour, where Spencer has a good fire going."

"It would certainly be warmer there, my lord."

Kitty kept her voice steady, glad of the interruption. Surely, he must have realised that they didn't have the money needed for her to have a court presentation. Was he toying with her again or just making idle conversation? He had the appearance of someone trying to elicit information. She met his glance squarely once they were both seated. He stuttered a couple of times and seemed less sure of himself all of a sudden.

"Have you ever had a season?"

Oh lord, they were back to that again. What did it matter? "No, I haven't. We lived in straitened circumstances for many years and my aunt's plan to give me a season with her in London, when my uncle was alive, came to nothing after my mother's death. My father wouldn't have coped with living on his own. Not that Aunt Lucy would have afforded things like court appearances."

There, if her poverty appalled him there was nothing she could do about it. "I've been very little out in society. My only claim to social success was my friendship with the vicar's daughter when we lived at Davenport Court."

"I see. Well I'm sure that can be mended. I believe my best course of action is to take you to London to my Aunt Theo. She will know how to help you."

He sounded impatient and he wasn't even looking at her. She closed her eyes and clasped her hands together. Could she trust him or was he another Sir Walter hoping to pounce on her when she was unprotected?

"Well, what do you say?"

Was that a question or a command? She studied his face but his expression told her nothing. "How long would it take to get there?"

"At least a couple of days. We will have to prevail on Mrs Spencer to come with you."

Relief swept over her and she slumped against the back of her chair. He couldn't have any dishonourable intentions if he was putting her under his aunt's protection and taking Nella to accompany her. What would his aunt say about having an unknown thrust upon her?

"That's very kind of you, my lord, but what about your aunt? Didn't you say she has your sister to look after for the season?"

"I'm sure she will be delighted to welcome you. You can keep Grace company." He gave her the smile of a man who had made up his mind. "Your brother's school and university fees will be taken care of and I'll help him find a suitable profession. Can you be ready to travel by the time the roads are clear?"

Edward's future was safe at last. She would travel to the ends of the earth for that. "Of course, my lord."

"Good. That's settled then. I'll go and consult my groom. He was a sergeant under me in the army and will know when it's safe for us to set off." Viscount Enstone gave her a fleeting smile and went out.

Kitty took some deep breaths. She ought to be happy now that Edward's future was secure but the prospect of being dumped on an aunt who would very likely think it a great imposition was daunting. At least she would have Nella's support to begin with. She rose with a sigh and went in search of Nella. She ran her to earth in the kitchens. Even the smell of newly baked egg custard tarts wasn't enough to lift her mood.

"Why the long face. Never say His Lordship has insulted you?"

Kitty shook her head. She tried to smile but it came out

lopsided. "He wants you to accompany us to London where he intends to put me in the care of his Aunt Theo."

Nella picked up a rolling pin and pounded away at the pastry for a meat pie. "That will be Lady Grant, his mother's sister. I'm sure Lord Grant was an earl." Nella stroked her chin. "That's right he was. She's the perfect person to look after you, so why are you upset?" Nella frowned. "Is it Edward?"

"No, he says he will fund Edward's education and help him into a career, almost as if he really was his guardian."

Nella dropped the rolling pin on the scrubbed pine table that took up a good part of the centre of the room. She put an arm around Kitty.

"That's just as it should be, so what has he done to upset you?"

"He hasn't done anything but his aunt is bringing his sister out into society. It's an imposition expecting her to bother about me. I don't want to be put into that position and I expect she won't be happy either."

Suddenly the prospect of finding a job as a companion seemed frightening. "What if she sends me to the first position that comes up to get rid of me? I'll be trapped."

"I remember the year the late master met His Lordship's mother. She and her sister, Lady Grant, although she wasn't called that then of course, were staying with friends in the area. I was a housemaid and had been brought along to help open up this place for a hunting party. Two lovely young ladies they were. I don't think you have anything to worry about. Lady Grant might even launch you into society."

"But she can't. I have no money for clothes and suchlike. All I can do is ask her to help me find a position as a lady's companion."

Nella grimaced. "Didn't you say that friend of yours is having a dreadful time as a companion? You would be better to use your time in London to try and find yourself a husband."

"Marrying someone I know nothing about would be risky. If I wasn't happy with the man there would be no way of escape." If she could find someone like Viscount Enstone it might be worth the risk of marrying. Kitty felt the heat rush to her cheeks. Where on earth had that thought come from? He was magnificent but he liked his own way. Any woman who took him on would have a hard time of it.

"I'm only going to stay in London for a short while until I find a way to become independent. I'm tired of always having to accept charity from people I don't even know."

"Your aunt told me your father and the old Viscount Enstone were firm friends. Lady Grant might be happy to try and get you settled."

Kitty shook her head. "Lord Enstone said that he and his father weren't close. He knew nothing of our existence. I'm sure he's only helping us out of a sense of duty. He won't expect his aunt to make too much effort on my behalf."

"Don't be in a rush to find a position that's all I'm saying." Nella smiled. "It sounds like you don't like the new Viscount Enstone above half. I'm surprised you agreed to go to London with him if that's so."

Kitty laughed. "I didn't have much choice in the matter. He's a man who's used to command." She sobered up quickly. "Besides with Sir Walter being such a nuisance and half the neighbourhood convinced I was the old Viscount Enstone's mistress I can't stay here."

* * *

31

Luke wandered down to the stables in search of Fletcher. He found him in conversation with Spencer.

Spencer touched his forelock. "I was just saying, my lord, how I miss the hunting parties. I don't have any horses to look after now apart from the one we use to pull our gig."

"I'm surprised my father kept this place on if he wasn't going to use it."

"I don't think he could bear to part with it, since he met your mother when he was staying here. We only saw him a couple of times after she died. I'd married Nella by then and he put us in charge of it. We've done our best but in recent years there hasn't been enough money to keep up with all the work it needs."

Luke swore under his breath. "My new agent comes well recommended and seems very efficient. He has taken on an assistant to help take stock of what needs doing. There will be some funds spent here."

Spencer rubbed the back of his neck. "Will you keep it, my lord?"

Luke opened his mouth to say no and then closed it. "I'm not really sure what I'll do. You have no need to worry about your employment. There will always be a job with me for you and Mrs Spencer."

Spencer broke into a beaming smile. "Thank you, my lord. I had best get on."

He hurried away.

Luke grinned at Fletcher. "That's one person I've made happy today. What are our chances of leaving anytime soon?"

"It's stopped raining and there is quite a wind today. I think we may get out tomorrow unless there is a lot more water to travel downstream."

"The sooner the better. I'm not even sure how much food there is in the house."

Fletcher laughed. "If it comes to it, I can always catch a rabbit or two."

"You always were good at filling the pot. My big worry is getting Miss Davenport away before the local swain comes around to cause her more trouble."

Fletcher lowered his gaze. "The Spencers are worried about that, my lord. They think the only way to save her reputation is to find her a husband who can protect her."

Luke stiffened. "They may be right. Which is something else to be laid at my father's door."

He turned on his heel and stalked back to the house. Lord, how was he going to fill the next day or two? Perhaps Miss Davenport could play cards? Then again did he want to spend too much time in her company? Her relief had been so obvious when he said they would have to take Mrs Spencer with them to London she must have suspected him of dishonourable intentions. Which wasn't surprising given the rumours about her. He winced. He hadn't been particularly kind to the girl and it was no more her fault than his that she was in this situation.

Even Fletcher had been hinting that he ought to offer Miss Davenport the protection of his name. Damn his impertinence. No doubt Mrs Spencer had put that idea into Fletcher's head. She was fiercely protective of her charge and was intelligent enough to know a bit about the fashionable world from her years of working for Father in their main homes. Now he had seen more of Miss Davenport he suspected her natural assumption of quiet authority made her seem more worldly wise than she was. She was probably unaware of Mrs Spencer's manoeuvring.

33

Aunt Theo would know how to dress Miss Davenport. She was an attractive young woman and if he provided a decent dowry, Aunt Theo should be able to bring a reasonable suitor up to scratch. Perhaps a sensible army man from a genteel rather than tonnish family, or some good-natured country squire. The prospect of Miss Davenport married to a bucolic country squire was strangely depressing. She seemed to be a cultured young woman with a love of reading but it was unlikely that Aunt Theo would want to risk a fashionable family for her with the stain on her reputation, however undeserved.

He ought to go and read the rest of the letters but it felt uncomfortable reading Father's private correspondence. Besides he was unlikely to find anything more to help him solve the puzzle of his father's involvement with the Davenports. Perhaps Aunt Theo would know something about it. The idea of his father helping a friend's children out of kindness was hurtful in a way. He hadn't shown much kindness to his own son! Heaven knew how he would have grown up without Aunt Theo's love and care. He'd be damned before he risked marriage, a state he dreaded, to tidy up the mess Father had left behind him.

Chapter Four

Kitty changed into an old gown in a drab brown colour that matched her mood and helped Nella with some household chores. She couldn't put off another meeting with Viscount Enstone indefinitely. Nella set the remains of the vegetable soup to warm up and sent her to fetch the butter.

"It's lucky I made another batch before the rain set in," Nella said, when Kitty emerged from the larder with the butter.

"That bread smells good." Kitty found a plate for the freshly baked loaf and set about slicing it.

Nella stirred the soup. "This won't take long to heat through. Go and change into a smarter gown and then find His Lordship, will you? By then the food should be ready. I'll put out some of the egg custards as well. He was up early for breakfast this morning so he'll be pleased to see a luncheon. We'll keep him in a good mood if we feed him well. There's beef pie for dinner."

Kitty did as she was bid but pulled a face as she left the kitchen. Why should they strive to keep Viscount Enstone happy? Oh well, Nella was enjoying herself having a bigger party to cater for.

Twenty minutes later Kitty found Viscount Enstone in the

library absorbed in a book. He couldn't be all bad if he liked reading.

"Luncheon is ready."

He looked up and grinned. "That's welcome news. In the army we ate when we could and I'm always glad to accept a meal."

Kitty led the way to the dining room. Viscount Enstone looked much younger when he smiled. A grin like that softened his features and emphasised what a handsome man he was.

Spencer was stoking up the fire. "There, that's a bit warmer for you. I'll go and fetch the coffee pot. There's some ale if you would prefer that, my lord."

Viscount Enstone grinned again and Kitty's insides did a somersault. Anyone would think that she had never seen an attractive man before.

"Thank you, Spencer. Some ale would be most welcome."

He pulled out a chair for her. Nella appeared with the soup tureen and he went across to help her with it before taking his own seat. She could feel quite in charity with him if she wasn't sure that he was much more relaxed now because he had decided what to do with her. It was horrible feeling as if she was nothing more than a burden. She liked to be useful. Viscount Enstone hadn't helped by being so obviously angry at having to deal with the problem of her future. She chewed at her bottom lip. None of it was her fault. If there had been enough money to pay for Edward and to keep her until she could become established in some genteel employment then she needn't have troubled him.

Spencer arrived with a coffee pot and poured her a cup. "I'll be back with your ale in a moment, my lord."

Kitty accepted a bowl of soup from Viscount Enstone with a

muttered thank you and set about buttering a slice of bread. At least then she would have been able to be selective in deciding on whether to accept a particular position or not. It would be awful if Lady Grant was angry at having to take charge of her. Just because she had appeared to be a lovely young woman to Nella it didn't mean she would be an amenable person now. The only countess she had ever had pointed out to her had seemed positively forbidding. A polite cough broke into her thoughts. She looked up to see Viscount Enstone studying her with raised eyebrows. Heat scalded her cheeks. How rude of her to ignore him.

"I'm sorry, my lord. I was thinking."

"I could see that. Was it about anything you can share?" He bit into a piece of bread. "This is delicious. Mrs Spencer can certainly cook."

Another wave of heat swept over her and she shook her head. Viscount Enstone laughed.

"I have rendered you speechless." He smiled at her, not unkindly. "Are you unhappy about going to London? I did rather dragoon you into it, but I truly don't see any other solution. We have to get you away from the attentions of your swain. What was his name?"

She lifted her head up high. "If you mean Sir Walter Greenough, he is not my swain."

The viscount laughed. "That's better. I feel much more comfortable with you ripping up at me. You can't deny he's a problem though, can you?"

"No of course not, but...."

The annoying man laughed again. "I apologise for making you feel that you must be polite when you are angry at me, with good reason. I admit I should have taken action as soon as your brother brought your situation to my attention."

Kitty pursed her lips. Now he had put her hopelessly in the wrong. What was she to say to that?

He reached out and laid a hand on hers. A jolt of awareness shot through her. He was a dangerously attractive man.

"Truly, I'm sorry. Even my groom is cross with me although he hasn't come out and said so. My best friend was in difficulties and I was helping him and it slipped my mind. It shouldn't have done."

He removed his hand and smiled at her. "I have no idea why my father took responsibility for the two of you."

He studied her from under hooded lids in the same way that had unnerved her when they first met. She lowered her gaze. There was something troubling him but what?

"Whatever his reasons I take my responsibilities seriously and I will make sure you are well provided for."

"Thank you, my lord."

Spencer arrived with a frothing tankard and laid it before Viscount Enstone. His eyes lit up when he saw it, giving him a positively boyish look.

"Wonderful. Thank you, Spencer."

Kitty made a determined effort at conversation. She even ventured a few questions about his life in the army and he surprised her with detailed answers rather than the usual inanities that passed for conversation at the occasional society event she had attended when they lived at Davenport Court. Nella arrived with the custard tarts and she absentmindedly ate two.

"Thank you for sharing some of your experiences with me, my lord. Before my father lost our home, I used to enjoy reading the London papers one of our neighbours passed on to us. I miss that."

"Where was your home?"

"Davenport Court is about ten miles from here. My father bred horses and was quite good at it. He told me that he was often invited to hunting parties here as a young man and he was asked to bring over his latest horses for sale. I believe he did quite well in those days."

Lord Enstone frowned. "I understood from you when we spoke before that your family's only source of income was your father's investments?"

"It was after Mama died. Father was a shadow of himself for some time and horse breeding was the last thing on his mind."

"Did you not even have a horse of your own? Spencer told me he misses his work as a groom now he only has the horse that pulls the gig belonging to the estate."

"Papa had started dabbling a bit again." She bit back a sob. "I really felt he had turned a corner. Then he was cajoled into joining Sir Peter Sewell's group for a few hands of cards and lost everything. I mean everything. The house and estate, my mare and his own horse and the handful of horses he was preparing for sale for the first time in years. We left with little more than the clothes we were wearing. I was so glad that Edward was at school and not there to see us thrown out."

She had his attention now. "What did you do?"

"I had enough money in the housekeeping fund to buy us seats on the next mail coach to Aunt Lucy's. Even the investment money stopped."

He frowned. "Are you sure it wasn't a case of them not knowing where to send the money?"

"Papa said it was included in what he had lost. Although he died before he could sign anything." She looked at the floor and hoped he wouldn't notice her wipe away a tear.

Lord Enstone pulled at his ear. "I wonder if that means they still belong to you, or rather to your brother I would imagine? What sort of investments were they?"

She gave a strangled laugh. "The investments were Mama's. Her family had interests in banking and insurance. Her shares were the main part of her dowry. Father's will bequeathed all of them to me and the estate, horses and any money saved to my brother. He must have made that will a long time before he died."

"I see. With your permission I'll have my secretary look into it for you when we're in London."

"Papa said debts of honour had to be fulfilled, even though he couldn't even remember staking anything. There were several witnesses. He must have been drunk but he swore to me that he wasn't." Familiar anger bubbled to the surface and she lowered her gaze.

"It's still worth looking into. They may have been in a family trust in which case they weren't his to stake."

"That's kind of you, my lord. Aunt Lucy's solicitor did write to the address we found in Papa's papers but he never received a reply."

"I wonder how hard he tried. I'm sure an enquiry from Viscount Enstone will elicit more response. Now, if you will excuse me, I'll go and finish my book."

Kitty inclined her head. "Of course, my lord." He was trying to be helpful but how arrogant of him, even though he was right of course.

He rose and bowed before leaving the room. Why did she have the feeling that he didn't entirely trust her? His conversation always seemed to go back to what amounted to quite detailed questioning. Did he wonder if she had done something to deserve being gossiped about? She raised her hands to hot cheeks. A spurt of anger carried her up to her room. She would have liked to find a book but the last thing she was going to do was follow him to the library, lest he thought she was trying to seduce him. They might leave as early as tomorrow so it would be as well to pack her belongings. A shiver ran through her. It wasn't Davenport Court but she had grown accustomed to this place and the cosy presence of the Spencers. Now she had to start her life all over again.

* * *

Luke threw himself into the worn leather armchair set in front of the fire Spencer had lit for him in the library. He looked around at the high shelves of books and a solid looking desk near to a window. With redecoration and some new furniture, especially a new set of library steps, this would be a comfortable room to entertain friends. He had certainly had an eventful introduction to Miss Davenport. The reaction of his body to an armful of woman suggested it was about time he found some female company. In better daylight she looked older than he had first thought or had he just assumed that she was young because her brother was only sixteen? She could be as much as two or three years older than Grace.

He picked up the history of the Romans he had selected. His taste in books seemed to be one thing he had in common with Father, who must have sat in this very chair. He tried to picture what life with his parents had been like before Mama died. All he could remember clearly was how happy they had all been. Then Mama was gone, leaving behind a new-born baby and an inconsolable young boy. He hardly saw Father after that. It had felt like he had lost both parents. In one sense he had, the laughing man he had once known had been replaced by a stranger. If he had children would he be as poor a father? Fiend seize it! It would be better if he never married.

He made a determined effort to read his book but eventually gave up and wandered down to the stable in search of Fletcher. He found him grooming the hired carriage horses.

"I've been down to the river with Spencer, my lord. He agrees with me that unless we have more rain, which he doesn't expect, we should be able to set off for London to-morrow." He patted the neck of the horse he was grooming, a sturdy looking bay. "Some good animals these. They should get us back to their home stable quickly after a rest today. If they give us some more speedy ones, I don't think we'll need to spend more than one night on the road."

"That's good news, Fletcher. My sister will be wondering where I've got to."

He strode back to the house and this time made some progress with the history of the Romans until Mrs Spencer came in with a tray of tea and some more of her delicious egg custard tarts.

"Dinner will be at six o'clock, my lord. I thought you might need something to sustain you until then."

Luke couldn't suppress a laugh. "Thank you, Mrs Spencer. You read my mind."

He poured himself a cup of tea and popped a tart into his mouth in one bite. "Mm these are delicious. Could you be ready for an early start in the morning?"

"Of course." She narrowed her eyes. "I remember your aunt a little. Is she as kind and generous as she seemed in her youth?"

Luke stiffened. Really his aunt's disposition was no business of Mrs Spencer. She rubbed her hands on her apron and gave a nervous cough.

He relaxed. "My Aunt Theo is a darling. I can assure you that she will take great care of Miss Davenport." Miss Davenport had no one else to take her part and Mrs Spencer had obviously taken on the role of her protector.

A slow smile spread across her face and she gave a shaky laugh. "Thank you, my lord. She's a lovely young woman but she never considers herself. She's always too busy worrying about that brother of hers. Before her Aunt died, she took great care of her."

"How long have you known Miss Davenport?"

"She has been living here for about three years."

Luke watched her face. "Did you not know the Davenports before that?"

"I remember her father coming here with his horses whenever the old viscount brought a hunting party. A pleasant gentleman he was and well liked. He never sold a horse that the purchaser wasn't happy with, so that made him quite a favourite."

She looked into the fire for a moment, appearing lost in thought. Luke waited patiently.

"He never gambled in those days. Later I heard talk that he couldn't get over losing his wife. They were such a devoted couple. He closed his stud and sold all his horses off. You never know what a man will do when he is knocked over by grief. Men keep it to themselves, see. Makes it harder to deal with. Now your father was the opposite. He buried himself in his work by all accounts. Anyways, I had best get on. Call me if you want anything else."

Luke nodded. Speech was beyond him. Had his father been knocked over by grief when Mama died? That was a possibility he had never considered. Father had kept his feelings so well hidden it would have been difficult to tell. It might go some way to explain his actions if he had. Most men he knew would have thrown themselves into whatever their business was to find their solace. Father had always seemed to be busy on estate business after her death.

Hadn't his only son been his business though? He had been a boy and seen things with the black and white clarity of a child. His father's withdrawal from him had left him feeling lost. The wound was still raw all these years later and now he would never have the opportunity to find out the truth. It was no good looking back but, if he had found out more about his father's life from him when he reached adulthood, he might have found it easier to come to terms with his childhood loss. It was a wound which had never truly healed.

Spencer came in with another mug of ale. "Here you are, my lord. I thought you might like this instead of tea."

"I rather like tea, but thank you I shall enjoy your ale even more."

Spencer grinned and went out.

Luke sipped at his drink. He had better stop thinking about it before he sent himself mad. He would never solve the riddle that was his father. It would be far more productive to turn his mind to the problem of Miss Davenport. He had no doubt that Aunt Theo would happily take her in, but he would have to tell her about the rumours of Miss Davenport having been Father's mistress. Rumours like that could be a problem. They would spread all around the district and people had relatives to spread them further, perhaps even as far as Town. If anyone could dampen them down it was Aunt Theo. If she managed to get Miss Davenport successfully married then he needn't feel guilty about forgetting to look into the family after he had encountered young Edward Davenport.

Luke finally managed to concentrate on his book. He read solidly until the tall, old grandfather clock at the other end of the library struck five. He put the book down on a side table and stretched his arms and shoulders. There was just time to find Fletcher for another report on the state of the roads before he dressed for dinner. He strode down to the stables and found Spencer and Fletcher in the tack room, deep in conversation. They seemed to be getting on really well.

"Any more news on our chance of leaving tomorrow?"

They both turned towards him and Fletcher answered. "Spencer thinks we will be safe to set off tomorrow. There is no sign of any more rain and when we had another walk down to the river crossing a while ago the water level has gone down quite a bit. We carried on and checked the first mile or so of the road where it's low lying and it was clear of flooding. I'm confident we'll have a clear run through."

"Excellent. We'll start as soon as the ladies are ready after breakfast. I'm sorry to be taking your wife away, Spencer, but Miss Davenport needs a maid on the journey. I considered taking you as well but that leaves the house unattended. As soon as Miss Davenport is settled with a lady's maid, I'll have Mrs Spencer escorted back here. Hopefully within a day or two."

"That's really good of you, my lord. I'm sure she wouldn't mind coming back on the stage."

"I think it best if I have Fletcher drive her all the way. I may send one or two more grooms with him. There is something which has only just occurred to me. Is there anyone you could get in to look after your horse?"

Spencer scratched his chin. "Not really, but I can manage on my own for a few nights."

"I'm sure you can but I'm worried that this Sir Walter Greenough might cause trouble for you after you saved Miss Davenport from his clutches. If there really is no one you can call on then stay close to the house and don't answer the door to anyone until Fletcher gets here, especially not the magistrate."

Spencer's mouth dropped open. "I hadn't thought of him laying charges against me. It was instinct to get him off the young miss. I'm sure it was him spread those nasty rumours to keep other men from showing an interest."

"I applaud your instincts. I don't think Sir Walter will lay charges. He will probably want to keep his actions private but I'll send my secretary with Fletcher just in case you have any problems in that direction. Sir Walter sounds a nasty character. Right. I had better change for dinner."

It was fortunate that he was used to dressing himself in the army more often than not. He hadn't left much time. With a bit of a scramble he managed to be ready, in reasonable order, just before the gong rang. He ran lightly down the stairs to find Miss Davenport waiting for him in the hall. She was wearing a black gown which did nothing for her. Her hair was piled up on top of her head with a few tendrils escaping. It was a fairly fashionable style but fastened a little too tightly. The effect was to make her expression seem strained. There again she was bound to have heard they were leaving tomorrow and was probably feeling nervous.

He gave her what he hoped was an encouraging smile and

held out an arm for her. She stayed where she was at first but then moved forward and placed her hand on the outstretched arm. He tucked it firmly into the crook of his elbow with his other hand. She had still said nothing. Heavens, she was the quietist female he had ever come across. He led her into the dining room and she dropped his arm as if it was a burning red coal as soon as she neared the table.

"Thank you, my lord. I understand from Mrs Spencer that we are travelling to London tomorrow."

She raised an eyebrow at him as she sat down. Ah, so she was angry with him for not telling her himself. For a provincial female she certainly had an air of command. She must be in her twenties to have developed such a manner.

"As long as Spencer's prediction of another dry day proves accurate, we are indeed." He couldn't resist teasing her a little. "I trust that meets with your approval."

"Of course, my lord. I am entirely at your disposal."

She lowered her eyes but not before he saw a flash of anger in them. He groaned inwardly. He shouldn't have done that. It was one thing to tease Grace, who knew she was his equal in his eyes, but quite another to banter with this young woman. She was very much in his power and obviously not comfortable with that. A flush heated his cheeks. She might think he was deliberately tormenting her.

Mrs Spencer came in with a meat soup and served them. He thanked her and selected a chunk of freshly baked bread from the platter already laid out on the table.

He smiled at Miss Davenport. "I'm sorry for rushing you away so abruptly but if that awful man comes back to badger you it won't help your situation. The sooner you are safely with my aunt the happier I will be." He groaned aloud. "I didn't

47

mean to imply that I wasn't enjoying your company."

To his relief she burst out laughing. "Don't worry I know what you mean. I too am happy to escape the attentions of Sir Walter." Her expression darkened. "It's just that I'm used to looking after other people, not the one being looked after. I don't want to be a burden to anyone. It's making me feel nervous."

Luke squeezed her hand and drew his own back quickly when the door opened. Spencer put a frothy tankard in front of him and a glass of what looked like lemonade down for Miss Davenport and withdrew.

"My aunt is a sociable sort and she will be happy to entertain you. My sister will be overjoyed. Her best friend in London has just married my best friend from the army and gone off on a bridal trip. The other good friend she has made since her come out is about to marry next week. She is sorely in need of a new companion. You will be helping Aunt Theo out by entertaining Grace."

"It's kind of you to say that, my lord. I will try not to be too much trouble. I shouldn't need to stay there very long."

He was about to ask why not when Mrs Spencer came in with a pie followed by Spencer with a dish of carrots. Silence reigned whilst they ate. He wanted to know more about this young woman before he handed her over to Aunt Theo, but it wasn't proving easy to draw her out. Something prompted him to ask her if she played cards. A shadow crossed over her face but she answered calmly enough.

"We played cards a lot at home, but rarely for money."

"Which game do you prefer?"

She wrinkled up her nose in concentration. "I think probably piquet. It has so much skill attached. It was my father's favourite."

"Would you agree to play a hand or two with me after dinner?"

"Why not. Most of my things are packed and it will be something to do."

She certainly didn't waste any time flattering a man but then she seemed on edge. She only had his word for it that she would be welcomed in London. It was natural for her to be apprehensive. He ought to be grateful that she was the sort who was quiet when worried and not one who would gabble on to soothe their nerves.

Once the meal was over, he opted to have his port in the drawing room. Miss Davenport sent Spencer to fetch a card table and once that was done, he set the port decanter and glasses down on a side table. Mrs Spencer followed with a tea tray.

"If I offer to share the port with you, would you consent to pouring me a cup of tea?"

"Of course, my lord."

She set about the task efficiently and handed him a steaming cup. He sipped it and watched her over the rim. She seemed composed enough but her mind was clearly elsewhere and still she made no attempt at conversation. She must have seen him watching her. She put down her cup.

"I'm sorry if I'm not very good company tonight. It will be a wrench to leave my home county behind tomorrow. Memories of childhood keep distracting me."

"Was it a happy childhood?"

She smiled. "Very happy until Mama died when I was fifteen. Edward was only seven. Father never really recovered from losing her. Being eight years older it fell to me to look after him. Once I was eighteen, Aunt Lucy wanted to bring me out in London but I couldn't leave them to manage on their own. What about you?"

"We have a lot in common. Like you I had an idyllically happy childhood until my mother died."

"How old were you?"

Luke tensed, that was a question he didn't want to answer. "I was eight."

"Not much older than Edward."

She waited for a moment and when he didn't reply went over to a cupboard and found some cards. It was as if she had sensed he didn't want to talk about it. Either that or her lack of conversation was her normal state. She held up a wooden box.

"Shall we use counters instead of coins? I never play for money, even when I had some to play with."

"What a good idea. I'm not a deep player myself. I only stake the minimum to be sociable as a rule."

So much for letting her win so she had some pin money when she got to London. He didn't think she would accept money from him and of course it would be most improper. He would have to instruct his secretary to arrange an allowance through the estate. If necessary, it could be passed on through Aunt Theo. Miss Davenport was in a difficult position. He suspected she would have done anything to avoid accepting his charity if it hadn't been for her brother. He got up and moved the side table closer to them. Miss Davenport accepted a glass of port and quaffed half of it before setting it down. Good lord, did she regularly drink a lot? She had downed at least two glasses the night before.

He smiled at her. "Would you like to deal first?"

Luke considered himself a good card player but it didn't take him long to realise that he had met his match. She matched him trick for trick. Even when he had the run of the cards for several hands she limited her losses. The luck turned and he found himself going down heavily to her. His half of the counters exhausted he held up his hands with a grin.

"I surrender. Where on earth did you learn to play piquet like that?"

She gave him a shy smile and he found himself warming to her. "From my father. He was the best player in the area by a long distance."

Luke frowned. "I thought he didn't play cards very much?"

"No, he didn't, except at home with me for counters. He said it wasn't fair to take people's money off them simply because they couldn't match his skill. He was the most honest man I have ever known."

Luke couldn't stop the question tumbling out. "So how did he manage to lose your family's fortune?" He frowned.

She closed her eyes for a moment. "That's what I would like to know. They were playing piquet. He swore to me that he had only had two small drinks and yet I can think of nothing else, other than being foxed, that could cause him to lose." She sighed and then continued in a voice so soft he had to strain to hear it. "Aunt Lucy and I always suspected foul play but we had no idea how to prove it."

Chapter Five

Kitty climbed the last stair and turned into the corridor which housed her room. Perhaps Lord Enstone wasn't as arrogant as she had first thought? He had looked surprised when she beat him so easily but not particularly put out. On the odd occasion when she had played in public most men had looked seriously upset when they lost, to the point when she had often considered deliberately losing. She was glad she had decided against hiding her skill tonight. At least playing cards had meant she could stop worrying about what to say to him. What could you say to a man who was keeping you every bit as much as he kept any mistress? Did he have a mistress?

Why on earth had that thought come to her? Perhaps because he was handsome, at least when he smiled, had a figure any tailor would enjoy clothing and an elegance that set him apart from the men she had previously encountered, in her admittedly limited experience. The lowering truth was that as soon as he had delivered her to his aunt he would have no further interest in her. She would do better to contemplate her future than worry about whether she had bored him to tears.

She was simply too unsettled to think of anything but herself, and proper conversation had been beyond her. Selfish no doubt but there it was. The future loomed before her, an unknown chasm of pitfalls. Maryanne, the vicar's daughter, was having an awful time as companion to a dowager countess. Becoming a governess might be more enjoyable but at least as a companion there was the possibility of glossing over her being in paid employment, so many rich older ladies took on impoverished relatives. It would look better for Edward. If she was a governess her status would be obvious.

She slipped into her room and looked around. It was cosy by candlelight. The thin patches in the red damask drapes didn't show and the fire gave out a warm glow. Would she be afforded the luxury of a fire when she was working? She probably wouldn't if Maryanne's letters were anything to go by. For all His Lordship's confidence in his aunt, there was no guarantee she would have a fire in her bedroom when she was staying with her. She stood looking into the flames. She would enjoy it whilst she could. It wasn't like her to be maudlin. That was His Lordship's fault too. His attitude towards her was a reminder that her chance of marrying well, if at all, was now very slim.

Early the following morning Kitty sat in the dining room forcing down a slice of toast and a few mouthfuls of coffee. The rain she had half prayed for, to give her a reprieve, had refused to show up. She was glad now. The sooner she got to London the sooner she would know her fate. There was no sign of Lord Enstone apart from an empty plate next to her. The gaps in the food laid out on the sideboard suggested he had consumed a hearty breakfast. Nella bustled in, throwing last minute instructions to her husband over her shoulder.

"Everything is set, Miss Davenport. Our bags are loaded and His Lordship sent me to tell you we'll be ready to leave in a quarter of an hour."

Exactly fifteen minutes later Kitty followed Nella out of the front door, stopping long enough to throw her arms around a startled Spencer to give him a hug. He might be a servant but he had been like family to her for three years.

"Thank you so much for all you have done for us. I hope I see you again one day."

Spencer touched his forelock to her and she gave him a watery smile before walking towards a comfortable looking coach. The paintwork gleamed and a coat of arms was emblazoned on the door. Lord Enstone himself opened the door for her. She raised her hand, expecting him to help her climb in. He ignored it and surprised her by putting his hands at her waist and lifting her in as if she weighed no more than a small child. A surge of awareness shot through her and she kept her eyes lowered as she took her seat with a murmured word of thanks. He handed Nella in behind her and jumped up to take the seat with his back to the horses.

Nella stared at him. "I ought to take that seat, my lord."

Lord Enstone shook his head and banged on the roof of the coach. She was sure it wasn't the behaviour expected of a proper young lady but Kitty leaned forward and waved to Spencer as they drove away from the house. She fished a handkerchief out of her reticule and tried to dry her eyes so Lord Enstone wouldn't see. She saw him turn away from her. He must have noticed but was pretending he hadn't. For a gentleman of the ton he could be surprisingly kind to a nobody. Perhaps he had decided the simplest thing to do was to treat her as he did his sister. Whatever his reason, she was grateful for his tact.

They crossed the bridge over a full but not overflowing river.

The churned-up water reflected the state of her insides. A few minutes later they turned onto the main road and the sun peeped out from behind the clouds. Perhaps that was a good omen. She took a deep breath and sought for topics of conversation.

"Do you live in London, my lord?"

"I'm not really sure." He laughed. "That must seem like a strange answer. It's less than a year since I sold out of the army. I haven't decided where my main residence will be yet. I will have to spend at least part of the year at my country seat, but at the moment I am living at my London house. I will probably stay there as long as Grace is in town."

"What's your sister like?" Perhaps she shouldn't have asked that but he didn't seem to mind.

"She's fairly tall for a woman and dark haired like my father. I've got my mother's colouring although I'm told her hair was lighter than mine and without the red tinge."

"It's strange isn't it how siblings can differ so much. I'm dark like my mother but my father had light brown, almost blonde hair when he was younger. Edward takes after him." She tried to smile but her lips trembled. She really must pull herself together.

"I liked your brother. There seemed to be an instant connection between us and he is certainly enterprising. It's interesting that we both lost our mothers at a similar age."

She smiled then. "As if the experience had branded you in some way? Perhaps it had."

"Perhaps. Aunt Theo was so kind to me. I'm sure you will like her."

Lord Enstone closed his eyes and seemed to doze off. Was she glad or sorry? It was a relief in one way as she didn't know what to say to him. On the other hand, it gave her thoughts the opportunity to crash in on her. He had said his aunt was lovely. Would she be the same to people outside her family? The movement of the coach soon lulled her into sleep after such a restless night. She awoke with a start when the coach came to a halt in the yard of a busy coaching inn. Lord Enstone jumped down and she heard him talking to Fletcher. He reached a hand inside and offered to help her down.

"Fletcher is going to see if he can engage a private room for us. I'm sure a walk will do you good."

She jumped down and he threaded her hand through his arm. They weren't the only customers and she was glad that Nella had persuaded her to wear her best lavender gown. The occupants of one carriage had elected to stay where they were and a very superior looking lady was staring at them with the intensity that only the aristocracy could manage. The yard was full of yelling ostlers taking horses away to the stables behind and bringing out fresh teams. The viscount guided her around the edges of the melee and into the back entrance to the inn. Fletcher caught up with them, escorting Nella.

"I've settled the reckoning with the tip you suggested and I've been promised their best team. The landlady should be here in a moment to show the ladies to a private parlour."

"Thank you, Fletcher. Efficient as always. I forgot to tell you that you have passed your trial period with room to spare. My secretary will negotiate a salary with you when we are back but be warned, I intend to offer you the post of major-domo. Your skills of organisation would be wasted as a groom, although I expect I will take you on my travels in that role sometimes."

Kitty couldn't help but smile at the delight on Fletcher's face. It seemed that Lord Enstone was a good employer.

"Thank you, my lord. I'll go and make sure they keep their word on the team."

"Have some refreshment first, man. We don't want the horses put to for half an hour or so."

Fletcher saluted and disappeared towards the back of the inn. A plump, jolly looking woman arrived and she and Nella followed her to a pleasant parlour. There was a merry looking fire and a padded sofa as well as a table and chairs at one end of the room.

"Here you are ladies. The necessary house is down the end of the corridor if you want it. My maid will bring coffee and cakes."

Kitty smiled at her. "Thank you, Mrs.?

"Mrs James, my lady."

She bustled out before Kitty could correct her mistake. What would it be like to be married to a man like Lord Enstone? A maid followed and laid the table. The food was excellent. He certainly liked to travel in style. It was good of him to have them so well looked after but she couldn't suppress a wave of disappointment when it became obvious that he didn't intend to join them. They had finished eating and she was staring out of the window when he finally appeared. Even after hours of travelling he looked as immaculate as ever.

"The coach will soon be ready to start if you have finished, ladies."

Kitty hoped she wasn't blushing at the sight of him. "We have, my lord. Thank you."

He held out his arm and she tucked her hand through it. They reached the coach and she caught her breath. This time he assisted her into it very properly by supporting one hand as she climbed onto the step. She could feel the warmth of his hand through her glove. Heavens she was obsessed with the man after he had lifted her up in the morning. Perhaps her reaction was inevitable given her lack of experience with eligible gentlemen. This was going to be a long journey.

* * *

Luke climbed into the coach and banged on the roof for Fletcher to start off. What bacon-brained impulse had made him lift Miss Davenport bodily into the coach when they left the house? He could swear she was disappointed when he hadn't done it again, in the yard of a busy inn, although he could be mistaken. Wouldn't a respectable young female react with shock or anger at such improper behaviour as lifting her into a coach? Perhaps even be afraid that he was intending to offer her a carte blanche? Was she trying to trick him into marriage after all?

To be fair, even if she had shown signs of reacting to his nearness it didn't prove that she was a woman of easy virtue. He closed his eyes and tried to think. Her being Father's mistress simply didn't seem feasible but could he be sure that there wasn't some truth in the rumours but with a different man? The way she had clammed up when she realised that he hadn't heard the rumours about her had bothered him at the time. What if Sir Walter wasn't such a villain as she portrayed him to be? He could have heard the rumours and offered her his protection after receiving some encouragement. She might have been angling for marriage and sent him off when she realised that wasn't what Sir Walter was offering.

His face grew hot. He was going to have to tell Aunt Theo of his suspicions without admitting that his own behaviour had stoked them. He would be the perfect gentleman for the rest of the journey and forget how good it felt to have her in his hands. He must have absentmindedly treated her like he had treated Grace when she was younger. In some ways she didn't seem as old as Grace. She certainly lacked Grace's phenomenal ability to make conversation. Had she had much to do with company living so quietly in the country? There was so much he didn't know about her.

Perhaps it was the close proximity of the carriage but she seemed more appealing as the journey went on. He tried to keep as far away from her as he could but every time they rounded a bend and their thighs touched, however briefly, warmth flooded through him. He took care to avoid her company as much as possible at their next stop to change horses. At their final stop of the day he left her to dine in a private parlour with Mrs Spencer and took his meal in the coffee room with Fletcher. Afterwards they found a quiet corner and he had the landlord bring them a large jug of the ale they had sampled with their food.

"This is very good. Some more, Fletcher?"

"Yes please, my lord."

Luke glanced around the coffee room as he poured the ale. No one was close enough to have heard Fletcher but the room was filling up.

"No need to call me my lord here. Let's see if we can sit quietly without attracting any attention."

Fletcher grinned at him and nodded. "We've made good time. I think we should be in London by mid-afternoon tomorrow."

"That would be good. I want to hand over our guests to my aunt in person. Since she's not expecting us, she may well be out if we're any later."

They sipped at their ale. It was some of the best Luke had tasted.

"I missed English ale when we were abroad." He laughed. "Spencer kept plying me with tankards of his irresistible home brew."

"I had plenty of that. Mrs Spencer fed us well too. They think the world of Miss Davenport, I expect they were determined to keep you in a good mood."

The noise level increased and they fell into a companionable silence. He had been lucky to hear that Fletcher had left the army and needed a job. Surviving a few battles and other difficult situations together taught you more about a man than any amount of polite conversation and Fletcher was both intelligent and trustworthy. A group of men took seats behind them and he caught snatches of conversation. He tried to ignore it until he heard his own name mentioned.

"I saw the new Viscount Enstone handing a young lady into his carriage at the Black Horse in Bitterley this morning. My wife pointed him out. I didn't know he was in the way of becoming leg-shackled."

"Neither did I! Are you sure it wasn't just a lady friend?"

There was a burst of ribald laughter that had Luke bunching his hands into fists under the table. Fletcher raised his eyebrows but said nothing.

"No, she looked a lady. She had a dragon of a maid with her. Perhaps it was his sister."

"That will be it."

They turned to other subjects. Luke and Fletcher finished off the last of the ale and quietly slipped out of a back door. Luke beckoned to Fletcher who followed him into a quiet corner.

"I expect the landlord knows who I am."

"I gave your name as Mr Bamford being as you're travelling on a family matter so to speak. I've arranged for the private parlour again in the morning for breakfast. If we make an early start, we should be able to get you all out and avoid those men. From the looks of them they'll be drinking for hours yet anyways."

"Thank you. I'll say goodnight then."

Luke waited until Fletcher was out of sight then walked around to the back entrance of the inn. A quick glance into the parlour confirmed that Miss Davenport and Mrs Spencer had gone. The table had been cleared so they had probably left some time before. He could only hope that no one had seen them on the way to their room. He made his way upstairs, keeping to the shadows. He passed one gentleman in the corridor leading to his room but he showed no sign of even noticing him, let alone recognising him.

He closed the bedroom door behind him and turned the key in the lock. Thank goodness for Fletcher's caution. He was slipping. Why hadn't he considered the possibility of being recognised? He had enjoyed the anonymity of the army. The lack of privacy was the worst thing about his new position and something he still wasn't used to it seemed. Lord, the last thing he wanted was gossip about his relationship with Miss Davenport before he had even got her to London.

He sat down on the bed with a thump and shuddered as he remembered how close he had come to lifting her into the coach the second time, the very moment when they had been seen. That would have been a disaster. He would have felt compelled to marry her if that had come out. She would have been irretrievably ruined otherwise. Tomorrow he would have

61

to eat breakfast with her despite his resolution to avoid her company as much as possible.

Chapter Six

Kitty surprised herself by sleeping really well. The worries that had beset her were overlain with excitement at the prospect of her first sighting of London. She led Nella down to breakfast. Fletcher had managed to wake them by scratching at their door at such an early hour that Nella had grumbled about being dragged out of bed before the servants were up. There was a group of people in the coffee room as they passed it. This was a busy posting house so it was probably a stagecoach stop. Fletcher appeared from nowhere and opened the door of their private parlour.

The weather had improved but a small fire burning in the grate cast a rosy glow over the room. The oak table that dominated the centre was polished to a high sheen and gave off a comforting smell of beeswax. The heavy oak door closed behind them and drowned out the sound of the coffee room party. Kitty hesitated at the edge of the room, aware that they were not alone.

Lord Enstone rose to greet them. "I hope you don't mind starting out at such an ungodly hour but I want to arrive in London as early in the afternoon as possible."

Kitty smiled at the expressions flowing across Nella's face.

The scold which she had promised to unleash on Fletcher when she saw him again, melted away at the sight of His Lordship.

Kitty accepted the chair he pulled out for her. "For my part I don't mind at all. I've never been to London and I'm looking forward to seeing it."

Fletcher whispered something to Lord Enstone and then left them to their meal. A maid entered with plates of eggs and toast and set them on the table. How thoughtful of Lord Enstone to remember her favourite breakfast. The maid was followed by another one with a fresh coffee pot. The smell of it reminded Kitty how hungry she was and she settled down to enjoy her food.

"This is lovely, thank you."

"I'm glad to see you have recovered your appetite."

"I'm still nervous about the future but now we are on our way it doesn't seem quite so bad. We lived very quietly in the country and I haven't seen many places at all. My mother lost several babies and it took a toll on her health. We lived a quiet life although my father did go away delivering horses from time to time."

"I suppose you needed the income."

"I'm not sure that we did. I remember Mama saying that the income from her funds was enough for us but Papa needed some company from time to time. He loved his horses though and he did make some quite large profits." She sighed and hoped she didn't look too forlorn. "There should have been a good sum put by for Edward but no one could trace anything after Papa's death. He must have lost that as well."

Lord Enstone glanced across at Nella who was staring out of the window.

He laid a hand over hers. "I'm sorry things worked out so

badly for you" he said softly.

Kitty stiffened and he snatched his hand back. Had he felt the tension in her or was he worried that Nella would see? Whenever he touched her, even in passing, it did strange things to her insides. Her parents had been so happy together, despite their problems, she longed to find someone to cherish her as her mother had been cherished. Perhaps, if she was lucky in her employer, she might have opportunities to meet a suitable gentleman. It would be wonderful to be loved by a man like Lord Enstone but surely there would be joy to be found with other men of good character who wouldn't see her as beneath them.

As soon as he had finished eating, Lord Enstone stood up. "If you will excuse me, I'll go and find the carriage." He smiled at Kitty and her heartbeat quickened.

"Fletcher said he would pull up as close as possible to the back door at the end of this corridor. Your bags are loaded so come out as soon as you're ready."

He rolled his shoulders as if to loosen them and strode out at a stiff legged trot. Why did he seem so tense, worried even? Some of her fears resurfaced. Was he afraid his aunt would be angry at his presumption now they were close to London? She knew a moment of dread but shrugged it off. She was young and she was on her way to London. She would make something of her life somehow and the future looked bright for Edward.

Lord Enstone closed his eyes as soon as the coach moved off. He had insisted on sitting with his back to the horses as he had the day before. When Nella also slipped into slumber Kitty took the opportunity to study him. His tightly fitting buckskin breeches revealed powerful thighs. His clothes were of the first quality even to her provincial eyes. His cravat was

65

knotted in a very simple style for a gentleman of his status but then he was without his valet. Despite his elegance he had the look of a natural athlete. Right from her first meeting with him she had sensed a restless energy that suggested he was finding it hard to settle down to civilian life.

Fletcher helped them down at their first stop and escorted them to a private parlour. Lord Enstone joined them a few moments later. Kitty was struck by the contrast to the inns they had stopped at the day before. This one was smaller and quieter and a slightly unkempt look suggested that it was a lot less successful. He wasn't running out of money was he after the unexpected extra charges for the carriage horses he had arrived with? She had assumed he was rich but not all noblemen were.

Some families had gamesters amongst them who squandered the family resources but hadn't the old viscount been something of a recluse in his later years? The current Lord Enstone hadn't shown any sign of being a gamester but he hadn't really had the opportunity to and he had asked her to play cards with him to pass the time. She had beaten him quite easily too. Even in the army it must be possible to lose money at cards.

They stopped for lunch at a similar establishment. Kitty glanced around the shabby entrance hall Lord Enstone escorted her through. She narrowed her eyes and studied him. He had noticed her looking. Was that a blush staining his cheeks? Her insides contracted. What if he was short of money, would he be able to honour his promise to assist Edward into a good career? She lifted her head. He might have simply miscalculated how much money to carry with him. It was too soon to panic.

She had been doing far too much of that in recent months, what with the uncertainty caused by having no reply to her letters and Sir Walter beating a regular path to her door. She shivered. It was best not to think about Sir Walter. He was old enough to be her father and had become besotted with a young face and figure. Not that she had any great claims to beauty. She knew that. There wasn't much chance of her attracting a rich husband.

They set out on the final stage of their journey. Before too long the villages became closer together until eventually it seemed as if every piece of land was taken by a building of some description. Kitty stared out of the window of the chaise, transfixed by the sights and sounds of London. She was fascinated by the cries of street sellers advertising their wares. She couldn't resist opening her window to lean out. The smell that hit her was a pungent mix of horse manure, rotten vegetables and something worse.

Lord Enstone laughed. "I would close that, if I were you, until we come to the more salubrious parts of London."

Kitty did as she was bid. Within minutes the coach slowed as they reached a corner. It turned into a street of far more prosperous looking houses. Kitty stared open mouthed.

"Have you ever been to London before, Nella? I can't believe how many people there are and carts and horses and buildings."

Nella laughed. "I went to London with the family a few times when I was a young maid. I had forgotten how noisy it was. Now His Lordship has inherited perhaps we'll have a few more visitors to Shepley." She looked at Lord Enstone. "It will be a mite too quiet without you and Sir Edward there."

"I'm taking time to assess all my properties, Mrs Spencer. I told your husband that whatever I decide to with Shepley Hall you will both have secure employment with me."

"Thank you, my lord." Nella gave Kitty a sidelong glance before turning back to Lord Enstone. "It could be a lovely dwelling with a bit spent on it. It would be a shame to let it go. Your father had some wonderful house parties there."

Kitty watched as Lord Enstone's face assumed a wooden expression. Why did he always poker up when his father was mentioned? Had there been some sort of rift between them? It was time to change the subject. She gave a small shake of her head for Nella's benefit.

"How old did you say your sister was, my lord?" Kitty smiled at Lord Enstone.

"She's just had her twentieth birthday. Her come out was postponed. Firstly because of my father's illness and then of course we were in mourning. I can't say I'm sorry about the postponement. I don't like the thought of young women being pushed into marriage at seventeen or eighteen before they know anything of the world. There are plenty of bad marriages around and I would hate my sister to become trapped in one."

Kitty nodded. It must be wonderful to have an older brother to be so concerned with your welfare. Edward cared, of course, but he was too young to be of much help. They turned onto a wider road, lined with large houses that could only be described as mansions. The coach picked up speed and bowled along. They must be getting close. Kitty took deep steadying breaths. What would his sister think of her and even more to the point what would Lady Grant think of her?

The coach pulled up in front of a handsome mansion. The huge front door had sconces on either side. It must look magnificent when those were lit. The door opened and a very proper footman, in an impressive livery, helped her to alight. Nella followed and then Lord Enstone. He threaded her hand through his outstretched arm. Surely this was a dream and she would wake up soon? There was something comforting about the warmth of his arm and the solid bulk of him next to her. He addressed the footman.

"Is Lady Grant at home this afternoon?"

"Yes, my lord."

"Excellent. Be so good as to inform Her Ladyship that I have arrived with Miss Davenport, a friend of the family."

"Yes, my lord." The footman scurried off.

"It seems we are lucky enough to find my aunt at home." Lord Enstone patted the hand resting on his arm. "There is no need to look so worried, she won't bite."

Kitty hid a grimace. She wouldn't see Lady Grant's true reaction to her nephew's news now she had been forewarned. Luke led her up a set of marble stairs into the house. A soberly dressed gentleman was waiting for them in the hallway. He must be the butler. He called a footman forward to take their outer clothes. Lord Enstone helped her out of her pelisse and handed it to the footman before allowing the butler to remove his greatcoat.

"Thank you, Harvey."

The butler's name was Harvey. Kitty tried to commit it to memory.

Harvey opened a pair of double doors and ushered them into a stylish drawing room. Kitty clung to Lord Enstone's arm as he led her across a huge expanse of brightly coloured carpet. She concentrated on breathing steadily to stave off the dizziness that threatened to overwhelm her. Their progress slowed and she dragged her eyes upwards to meet the calm gaze of a fashionable lady of middle years. They drew to a halt.

"Aunt Theo, allow me to present Miss Kitty Davenport."

Kitty dropped into a deep curtsy.

"I'm delighted to meet you, Miss Davenport." Lady Grant patted the empty place on the blue and gold patterned sofa she was sitting on. "Come and sit down."

She smiled at Kitty, a friendly smile that crinkled the corners of her eyes. Kitty let out a pent-up breath.

"Thank you, my lady."

"So, you're Henry Davenport's daughter."

Kitty dropped down onto the sofa in a daze. She glanced up at Lord Enstone as he sat on a chair nearby, all his concentration on his aunt. He looked stunned by her comment.

"You knew my father, Lady Grant?"

"I knew both your parents. We were all young people together." She glanced at Lord Enstone. "Luke, is Miss Davenport staying with me?"

"Yes, if you don't mind."

Lady Grant smiled at Kitty again. "Mind? I'm delighted. Why don't you leave us for now and come back before dinner? Grace is engaged with friends today and will have dinner out. We will have plenty of time to talk then."

Luke nodded to his aunt. "Thank you, Aunt Theo. May I join you about an hour beforehand?"

"I will look forward to it. I wondered what sort of adventure you had gone off on. I never dreamed that you would come back with the daughter of one of my old school friends."

Lord Enstone hesitated and looked as if he wanted to say more but had thought better of it. He bowed to both of them.

"Until later then." He smiled at Kitty. "I'll leave you in my aunt's capable hands."

Once he was gone, Lady Grant took her hand. "Now my dear, I don't like to pry but I would like to hear your version of how my nephew came to escort you to me." Her smile was friendly but intelligent hazel eyes studied Kitty intently.

Kitty took a deep breath and plunged into her story. "My father died a few days after Aunt Lucy took us in. He had gambled away our home and income. I think he died of shame." Kitty shut her eyes but it wasn't enough to keep away the tears.

Lady Grant squeezed her hand. "You have had a bad time. I remember Lucy. She married Lord Rupert Swift, didn't she?"

"Yes. Uncle Rupert had died unexpectedly a year before. His heir was a distant cousin and threw Aunt Lucy out with only the jointure that was hers legally. It would have been generous if she had been living rent free in the Dower House, but renting a small cottage on the estate left her with little to spare. Aunt Lucy wrote to the then Lord Enstone asking for help. She said he was a very dear old friend and he might let us rent a cottage somewhere on one of his estates cheaply. Then, if we were frugal, we would just about afford Edward's school fees."

"Did he let your aunt rent a cottage?"

"He did much more than that. We lived at Shepley Hall rent free and he paid Edward's school fees. He also had a small allowance sent to Aunt Lucy's solicitors. I wrote to Lord Enstone to inform him of her death and received no reply but the allowance continued to be paid. I had nowhere else to go and my brother to think of so I waited to see what would happen. Lord Enstone had visited Aunt Lucy a few times and seemed a pleasant enough gentleman. I assumed he was busy and would come to see me when he could."

"My brother-in-law was ill for some months before he died. He probably never read your letter."

71

Kitty nodded. "Eventually the current Lord Enstone found out about us and came to Shepley Hall." She decided not to mention her brother's part in bringing them to his attention.

"That's quite a tale. There is one thing I don't understand."

"I haven't been out in the world. I didn't realise...," Kitty stuttered to a halt."

"Not about you, but your father. The Henry Davenport I knew would never have gambled away his home. He loved that place."

"My aunt and I could never understand that either. He was hopeless with money but he was never much of a gambler. Sir Peter Sewell, the man he lost it to, had only just moved into the area. We didn't trust him but there was nothing we could do. Father came home foxed, which again wasn't like him. He accepted what Sir Peter and the other men there said about him staking his home and investments." Kitty sighed. "He didn't live for very long after that."

Lady Grant patted her hand. "I'm sorry to hear that, Kitty. I hope you don't mind me calling you Kitty?"

"I'm honoured, Lady Grant."

"Good. Why not call me Aunt Theo. I played with you when you were tiny and your mother was one of my best friends. It feels like I've found a long-lost niece."

Kitty blinked hard. It was hard to believe someone like Lady Grant would take an interest in her, but then she had never been to school and made close friends. "Thank you."

Lady Grant smiled. "My brother-in-law never mentioned your circumstances to me or I would have invited you to London before now. Let us talk of something more pleasant. Let me think. You must be twenty three or four, since you were about three or four the year Luke's mother died."

"Yes. I will be twenty four later in the summer."

"Luke's sister, Grace, is twenty but a serious sort of girl under her light chatter. I have a feeling you and she will get on splendidly. You'll meet her in the morning. I intend to take you both on a shopping spree."

Kitty tried to protest but Lady Grant laughed off her disinclination to accept clothes from her. "Nonsense. Had the circumstances been reversed I know that your parents would have looked after my children. I will enjoy dressing you so please indulge me."

Kitty was carried along on her enthusiasm and allowed her scruples to be overborne. "Well perhaps just a few things so I don't let you down whilst I'm here."

"Good. That's settled then. You must be tired after your journey and what am I thinking in not offering you tea. I'll have a maid take you up to a guest room and arrange for a tray to be sent up to you."

Lady Grant rang the bell and Harvey appeared almost immediately.

"Miss Davenport will be staying with us for a while, Harvey."

"I anticipated as much, my lady. I've had the housekeeper prepare a bedchamber. A maid is waiting to show Miss Davenport up."

"Thank you. Ask the housekeeper to send a tray of tea and cakes for her if you will." She turned towards Kitty. "I'll see you at dinner my dear."

Harvey escorted her out and a young maid was waiting for them in the hall.

"Annie will look after you, Miss Davenport. She will help you to dress for dinner when you have rested."

The butler bowed and left her with Annie.

Annie bobbed a curtsey. "Follow me, Miss. I'm so glad you've come. Miss Grace's maid has been giving me some training as a lady's maid and now I can try it out on you." She blushed and looked around. "No sign of Harvey. He would be cross if he heard me admitting this was the first time I've looked after a lady of my own, if you see what I mean."

Kitty smiled; Annie didn't look seriously worried. Harvey was wonderfully efficient but it seemed a happy household. Her spirits rose. Why not accept Lady Grant's hospitality for a while and enjoy herself? It was true that her parents would have wanted to look after a friend's child left in difficulties. She followed Annie up the broad staircase, barely registering the quiet opulence of her surroundings. It was strange to feel looked after when she had been the nurturing one in her family for so long. Even Aunt Lucy had needed cossetting as her health failed.

Nella was sitting in a chair looking out of the window as Annie ushered Kitty into the largest bedchamber she had ever seen. Kitty's smile deepened. She ran across to her.

"Oh Nella, you were right. Lady Grant is lovely. I'm sure she will help me find the position I need."

Nella gave her a crooked smile. "I hope she will but it may not be what you think."

"What do you mean?"

Nella shook her head. "That's not for me to say, Miss Davenport. Now don't get trying to rush into anything. Be guided by Lady Grant. Fletcher says we will be off early in the morning so I've been allowed to come up to say goodbye."

"Oh Nella, I'm going to miss you."

Kitty forgot about Annie and threw her arms around Nella. When she stood back Nella's eyes were as damp as her own.

"We'll miss you too. Come and see us when you can. I'd better be off now. I've shown Annie your jewellery box. I only remembered it at the last minute. Lady Swift left it with me for safekeeping. Your mother's pearls are in it."

Kitty's mouth dropped open. "But didn't those have to go with everything else?"

"Your aunt said they had already been given to you so she didn't see why they should. She told me to pass them on to you when the time was right, which it is now."

Nella gave her another quick hug and walked out.

Kitty opened the blue velvet box and pulled out her mother's pearls. They were exquisite and must be worth a considerable amount. If she had known they still had these she would have sold them to pay for Edward's schooling. Perhaps that was why Nella had kept them hidden. She didn't believe for a moment that she had forgotten them. She handed the box back to Annie.

"The pearls are beautiful, Miss. Have you brought many evening gowns with you?"

"I haven't brought many gowns at all. We're only recently out of mourning." She glanced down at her lavender gown. "I'm wearing my best one."

There was a knock at the door and Annie opened it to a maid carrying a tea tray. She took it off her and set it down on a small table near to the window.

"Here you are. This will brighten you up, you look tired. I'll see what I can find amongst your gowns and then I'll have a hot bath brought up for you."

A soak in a bath scented with one of the lavender sachets she had brought with her did much to restore her spirits. Annie came back in time to help her dry her hair.

"I'm looking forward to dressing your hair, Miss Davenport.

It's so thick and glossy. I'm glad powder has gone out of fashion it would be a waste to cover it up. I've had your grey evening gown pressed and with the pearls it will be perfect. I've found a string of little seed pearls that I can thread through your hair to match the necklace. It will show up well against such shiny hair."

Annie clapped her hands together. "You will look so beautiful."

Kitty smiled at her. "I'm not sure about that but I will be content if I look respectable enough for Lady Grant's dining room."

It was a novelty to have a maid to dress her but even one as enthusiastic as Annie was never going to make her beautiful. It would be wonderful if she could make her attractive enough for people to notice her properly. Especially so if a man like Lord Enstone noticed her.

Chapter Seven

L uke walked out of his aunt's drawing room and let out a deep breath. Aunt Theo would never let him down but even so that had gone much better than he had expected. He allowed Harvey to help him into his greatcoat.

"Your carriage carried onto your stables, my lord. I can have one of Her Ladyship's sent for to convey you home."

"Thank you but that won't be necessary." Luke laughed. "After two days of sitting in a coach my legs will appreciate a good walk."

He set off at a furious pace. He was an idiot. Why hadn't he asked Aunt Theo if she knew the Davenports when he had been called to Edward's school? Perhaps because he had been so amazed at his father's philanthropy? One thing was for sure. His father might have been a cold and even rather strange man but he knew what was due to his name. There was no possibility that he would have made the daughter of old friends his mistress. He blushed at the memory of his early suspicions.

Despite her reserve he was confident that Miss Davenport had a great deal of intelligence. She had been aware that he didn't trust her. That had been largely Mrs Spencer's fault though looking back. The way she had acted he could be forgiven for thinking there was a plot to force him into offering for Miss Davenport. Of course, if the Davenports had indeed been as close friends as Aunt Theo had suggested then she would be an eligible match for him. Mrs Spencer might well have seen that as a way out of Miss Davenport's difficulties.

The rumours spread about her were a worry. If they got out it would be a slur on his family's honour as well as hers. Now he was in town he could go round to his clubs and see if any of his army friends were in town. There might be some who were hanging out for a wife. Miss Davenport was a sensible young woman who coped well under pressure and didn't go off into hysterics at the drop of a hat. The perfect wife for an army man. If she was safely married the rumours might die down. He would feel awful if they didn't.

When he arrived home, he found his valet in his dressing room tutting over the clothes he had taken into Leicestershire.

"You were right, Garner. I did regret not taking you with me. The Spencers look after Shepley Hall. They asked to be remembered to you."

"Robert and Nella, do you mean?"

"Yes, that's them."

"I remember Nella on her first day as a kitchen maid. She was so nervous but she soon got into it and rose to assistant housekeeper surprisingly quickly. I knew she and Robert had secured positions on one of the smaller estates. So that's where they ended up."

"Humour me. I know I can trust your discretion. What else do you know about them?"

Garner put down the jacket he was brushing and studied him for a moment. "Not a great deal. I'm surprised Nella didn't get something bigger but then I expect it suited her when they had the children. I didn't know Robert all that well. I wasn't interested in horses and he was a groom but I do know he was well liked."

"Yes, he was an affable sort. Did you ever go to Shepley Hall with my father for one of his house parties?"

"I did once as it happens. I was a young man and working as a footman. My father had started training me as a valet when we could find time. He asked your father if he could bring me in case any of the guests had come without a valet. He said I was ready to get some practice." Garner laughed.

Luke damped down his impatience and waited for Garner to tell him more.

"Canny one my father was. There was a young man who came with his father and was sharing his valet. I worked for young Mr Montague for a few years until my father was ready to retire and I came back to take up the position with the old lord."

"I've been told that my parents met when Father was staying at Shepley Hall."

Garner cupped a hand around his chin. "I remember now. It was when I was there. The Montagues arrived early. They had arranged to ride over to a stud farm, somewhere within a day's ride there and back, to view some horses. Lord Enstone rode over with them. I believe your mother was staying there with her sister."

"Do you remember the name of the family who owned the stud?"

"The Davenports you mean?"

Luke closed his eyes and took a steadying breath. "Ah so it was them. Your account tallies with what Spencer told me. Did you meet my mother then?"

"No, it was a bachelor party but I remember Sir Henry

79

Davenport. He came to stay for a while with some more of his horses. I went with the Montagues afterwards but I think Father went with the old lord to stay with the Davenports after the party broke up."

Luke nodded. It seemed there was nothing Garner could add. "When I have time, I'll explain why I'm so interested. For now, I need to dress for dinner as soon as you can manage it."

"Where are you dining, my lord?"

"With my aunt, so something smart but it doesn't need to be too elaborate." He sighed. "I wish Nat was still here. He always gives good advice."

"Major Overton is going to be away for quite a while. Bright's back and he said they will probably move to Overton Grange. They'll come and see you first and reclaim Bright."

"Bright's back. Why didn't you say so? Is he staying here with Nat's horses?" He reached for the cravat he had just discarded. "I want to talk to him."

"He said staying here would be easiest if you don't mind, my lord. Why don't we have him brought up to your room to save time?"

"Of course, my wits have gone begging." He grinned. "Since Nat doesn't need him at the moment, I have a job for him to do."

* * *

Luke arrived a good few minutes before the time Aunt Theo had suggested but she was dressed for dinner and waiting for him in the family drawing room. He loved this room where he had spent so much of his childhood with his cousins. Less formal than the blue drawing room, the furniture was old and comfortable and the walls were decorated in rich shades of red. Red upholstered chairs and sofas rubbed shoulders with leather armchairs. The armchairs still bore the scuff marks of their childhood play. Aunt Theo rose to greet him and grasped both of his hands.

"Luke, you look worried. What is it?" She led him to a sofa.

Luke sat back and laughed. "I don't know where to start. I hope I haven't brought you too much trouble."

Aunt Theo frowned. "Amelia Davenport's daughter could never be too much trouble. I wish your father had confided the full extent of their difficulties to me so I could have helped them too."

"What I don't understand is why Father agreed to help the family at all." Luke's hands tightened into fists. "He was a hard man. I find it difficult to believe he would do such a thing without getting something in return."

Aunt Theo laid a hand on his forearm. "Oh Luke, you never really knew your father." She shook her head. "I told him he should be more open with you. He never recovered after losing your mother. We all hoped he would meet someone else but it wasn't to be. I know exactly why he agreed to help the family, indeed was eager to do so."

He stared at his Aunt. "How much of the family's story did you know?"

"All he told me was that he had heard of Henry Davenport's death from Lucy Swift. He mentioned paying Edward's school fees to help them out but nothing more. He was repaying a debt. It was Henry Davenport who kept him sane in the months after your mother died."

"Has Miss Davenport told you the full extent of her difficulties after Father died?"

"Probably not. I felt there was more for her to tell but she looked tired. I sent her up to rest."

Luke ran a hand through his hair. "This is so difficult."

Aunt Theo stared at him. "In what way?"

"She was left without a chaperone for months after her aunt died. A local man started pestering her and there are rumours that she was Father's mistress flying around." Luke leaned forward and put his head in his hands for a moment. "I have to say that at one stage I seriously wondered if the rumours might be true." He grimaced.

"Heavens above, Luke, you have got a strange view of your father. He was a man of honour. He most certainly wouldn't have made Kitty Davenport, the daughter of a friend, his mistress. I can't believe he would have made any girl of her age his mistress either." Aunt Theo sighed. "I can't be entirely sure, but I don't think your father ever kept a mistress."

Luke stared at the floor. "Are you absolutely sure? In my wilder moments I've even wondered if Kitty might be my half-sister who he placed with the Davenports. Kitty mentioned her mother had lost several babies."

Aunt Theo spluttered. "Luke how could you think such a thing?"

Luke sighed. "He wouldn't be the first rich man to do that."

Aunt Theo stared at him. "I suppose you have a point. He was a very private man. I've always kept a journal, I'll read through the ones before and around Kitty's birth to see if I can put your mind at rest."

"Thank you, although, now my anger with him has cooled down, I don't think it likely. I can see now that I did him a grave disservice in believing the story of Miss Davenport being his mistress might be true. I questioned Spencer and he told me that Father visited quite often to talk to Lady Swift. Those visits must have been noticed."

"Gossip has been known to spread for less cause."

"I know and I feel dreadful that I didn't go to Shepley sooner." Luke swallowed and ran a finger inside his cravat. "Miss Davenport referred to the rumours herself when I first arrived but clammed up when I asked her to explain. That made me wonder if there was any truth in them when I uncovered what was being said."

"Oh, poor Kitty. I expect she was too mortified to say anything. I thought I had brought you up better than to embarrass a lady." Aunt Theo scowled at him.

Luke winced. "There's worse. I'm convinced that Mrs Spencer was trying to manoeuvre me into offering Miss Davenport the protection of my name. At one stage I even wondered if Miss Davenport might be a party to the endeavour."

Aunt Theo studied him, with her head tilted to one side. "Hmm. From what I've seen of her and what I know of her parents, I don't believe she would entertain something like that for a moment. She appears to be an intelligent girl. I hope she didn't sense hostility from you?"

"I hope she didn't." Luke looked at the floor as heat flooded his face. It was far more likely that she was afraid he had dishonourable intentions towards her after the way she had flinched when he caught her hand in sympathy at breakfast.

"There is the added complication of Sir Walter Greenough. He has been bothering Miss Davenport for weeks. Spencer had to pull him off when he forced a kiss on her. I've sent Bright down tonight and Fletcher and Wallace, my new secretary, will follow tomorrow. I'm afraid Spencer might have problems with Sir Walter as a result of his rescue."

"Good gracious. Kitty has been having a time of it." Aunt Theo sounded shocked. She paused for a moment deep in thought. "The lack of a chaperone for months is a worry."

"They were in mourning and Mrs Spencer was there with her. Won't that suffice?"

"For a week or two perhaps but I can understand why there was talk with it being months. I'll do my best to squash any gossip that follows Kitty to Town. Your Father's reputation as a man of honour should help with that. This unwanted suitor could be a problem but nothing that a marriage to a man from a good family wouldn't override."

"I was hoping you would say that. I'll stand the nonsense of course but it will have to appear to come from you. Some fashionable clothes and a bit of Town bronze and you should be able to find her a decent match. She's the daughter of a baronet and with your sponsorship it might be possible to bring a country squire or a military man from a genteel rather than an aristocratic background up to scratch."

Luke petered out. He had never seen Aunt Theo look so stern. "I'm sorry if I've presumed too much. If you feel that it's an imposition I'll think of another solution."

"You will do nothing of the kind. Kitty is the daughter of a dear friend of mine. Amelia was at school with me and your mother. Now I know of Kitty's situation I will take her under my wing both for her own sake and for her mother's. She's an intelligent young woman who misses nothing and it sounds to me that the nervousness I sense in her has a lot to do with you. She's a person not a problem to be shuffled off at the first available opportunity."

"I can assure you I was always polite."

"Pressing her to elaborate on the rumours circulating about

her was hardly polite. I expect she was well aware of your mistrust..." Aunt Theo's reply was cut off by Harvey opening the door and announcing Miss Davenport.

She smiled at Aunt Theo and then she saw him. The smile faded and she halted briefly before walking towards them with faltering steps. Good Lord. Perhaps Aunt Theo was right and he had upset her. His suspicions had been aimed at his father more than her but she wasn't to know that. He jumped to his feet and bowed to hide the warmth invading his cheeks.

"Good evening, Miss Davenport. I hope you are not too jarred up from our long journey."

She curtsied. "Your carriage was very comfortable, my lord."

Aunt Theo patted the seat next to her. "Come and sit by me, Kitty. We have so much to catch up on."

Luke moved away from the sofa to make room for her. She looked a lot more striking after the ministrations of a lady's maid. The light grey gown she was wearing showed off her glossy, brown hair. He took the armchair opposite to them. The maid had dressed her hair in a much softer style, with little seed pearls showing through the curls arranged on top of her head. His eyes were drawn to the exquisite string of pearls around her creamy throat.

* * *

Kitty sat by Lady Grant but she couldn't take her eyes off Lord Enstone. He was even more magnificent in full evening wear than she could have guessed. His dark evening coat set off his burnished locks and accentuated his broad shoulders. It was his stern expression that caught her attention. His glance dropped to her pearls and she felt the heat rise in her cheeks.

85

Kitty's hand sought out the pearls and stroked them. "These were my mother's. Nella gave them to me this evening. I didn't know we still had them. I assumed they had gone with everything else. If I had known I could have sold them to fund Edward's education and not troubled you, Lord Enstone. I'm sorry."

His Lordship glanced at Lady Grant and, for a brief moment, he almost looked sheepish.

"Miss Davenport, there is absolutely no need for you to sell your pearls. My aunt tells me that your mother was a great friend of hers. My father's health was failing for a long time before his death. I suspect he meant to place you with Lady Grant once your aunt died but it slipped his mind."

Kitty lifted her head high. "He was everything that was kind when I met him but I would hate to take advantage of good nature."

Lady Grant shook her head at Lord Enstone and took her hand. "Kitty, what my nephew is saying is that I am delighted to welcome you to my home. We want no other reward than to see you and your brother happily settled. Your father was a good friend to the late Lord Enstone when he was widowed and we are both happy to find a practical way to repay that debt."

Harvey opened the door to announce dinner and Lady Grant accepted an arm from Lord Enstone. Kitty went to follow on behind but he held out his other arm to her. She tucked her hand around his elbow and tried to ignore the rush of heat that shot through her at his touch. He looked uncomfortable but she had walked in on a disagreement between him and his aunt for sure. She couldn't blame him for being cautious about helping her. It seemed unfair if that had been the cause of the

86

disharmony between them. At the same time the realisation that Lady Grant was truly pleased to welcome her gave her a warm glow.

She sat down with a gentle sigh. It was such a relief to have some respite from constant worry. She looked around with interest. This must be a family dining room. It was too small to be the main one for a house of this size. Even so the table was polished to such a high gloss that the light of the candelabra suspended above them bounced off its surface. Lord Enstone seemed quite subdued but Lady Grant smiled at her.

"Have you been to London before, Kitty?"

"No, I haven't, through one cause and another. It's an amazing place. I wouldn't have thought such noise and bustle was possible."

Lady Grant laughed. "You will soon get used to it. Grace will be so pleased to meet you tomorrow. She was afraid that things would be sadly flat with both of her friends marrying and leaving London."

A footman arrived with a tureen of soup. Kitty allowed her dish to be filled. She took a tentative taste. It was a creamy soup with some sort of vegetable.

"This is tasty but I can't recognise the vegetable in it."

"It's asparagus. The season for it has just started and it's a favourite of Luke's."

"Yes indeed. It's delicious and not something that army kitchens ran to."

Lord Enstone seemed determined to please and kept up a steady flow of conversation, for his aunt's benefit no doubt. Every other dish was just as good. It was a long time since she had sampled such a feast.

"You have an excellent cook, Lady Grant."

Lord Enstone nodded in agreement.

Lady Grant laughed. "I hope so. I certainly pay him enough. We'll leave you to your port, Luke."

Lord Enstone seemed about to protest but Lady Grant rose and put a hand on his shoulder.

"I don't expect you will be long. We'll wait for you before we order the tea tray."

"Thank you. Tea was something else that we missed out on most of the time in the army and I find I enjoy it now much more than I did as a boy."

Kitty followed Lady Grant but not before she caught him studying her. She turned away quickly. Was he admiring her or was that wishful thinking? He was more likely wondering if she had deliberately kept the pearls hidden. Not that she wanted his admiration. He was far too arrogant, although he hadn't been too haughty to break her fall from the library steps. Even if it had been his fault she had fallen. So why was the feel of his solid body gathering her to him something she wouldn't forget? Even through his greatcoat the strength of him had been obvious and yet she hadn't been afraid as she had been whenever Sir Walter got anywhere near her.

Lady Grant led her to the same sofa in the drawing room as before. "Kitty I must apologise for my nephew. I suspect he wasn't as kind to you as he ought to have been when he arrived at Shepley Hall. He had a rather troubled relationship with his father. I believe he was angry with him over the way he had left things. Indeed, I'm angry myself. If Luke's father had told me the whole story I would have written to Lucy and kept in touch with you all. Once Lucy died, I would have had you brought to me straight away. I trust your months with no official chaperone won't hamper your chances.

Did Lady Grant mean to try and marry her off? She forced a deep breath into her lungs and fingered her mother's pearls.

"Lady Grant, I don't expect you to do any more for me than help me find suitable employment. I have no wish to impose on you."

"My dear, I couldn't reconcile it with my conscience to do any less for you than I know Amelia would have done for my daughters." She grasped Kitty's free hand. "You will wear those lovely pearls away. I thought we had agreed on this?"

Kitty let go of the necklace. "I agreed to let you replenish my wardrobe but it wouldn't be fair to ask any more of you."

Kitty groaned when she noticed Lord Enstone approach them. She didn't want him to think that she was pestering his aunt for help. From the smile playing about Lady Grant's mouth she had heard her groan. Well if Lord Enstone had heard too she didn't care. He took the seat opposite to them and surprised Kitty with a smile that appeared perfectly genuine.

"You won't escape from my aunt's clutches that easily Miss Davenport. She will dress you and parade you in front of the ton and find a nice tame duke to marry you before she will countenance letting you go."

Lady Grant laughed. "Don't listen to him, Kitty. My daughter, Laura, married a duke but he was entirely of her own choosing. In any case, I'm sure there are no dukes looking for a wife this season."

A maid appeared with a tea tray and put it down on a side table.

"Harvey has anticipated again, Lady Grant. You have excellent servants."

"I do indeed. Do you both want tea?" Lady Grant walked over to the tea tray.

89

"Yes please," they said together.

Lord Enstone sat on the sofa by her. "I'm truly sorry I never thought to talk to my aunt after I met your brother. She would have sent for you immediately and saved you at least some of the unpleasantness with Sir Walter."

"You weren't to know. It's only been a few weeks since Sir Walter Greenough started bothering me. I'm glad you came when you did though. I would have been confined to the house in an attempt to avoid him after the incident where Robert had to pull him off me."

"I've sent a reliable man to Shepley Hall tonight. Fletcher and Mr Wallace, my secretary, will escort Mrs Spencer home tomorrow and stay a few days." He put a hand on her arm. "I'm a little worried that Sir Walter might lay charges against Spencer out of spite."

A hand flew to Kitty's mouth. "That never occurred to me."

"Don't worry. I've told them all to stay down there until they are sure that Spencer is safe from him. Mr Wallace will take an inventory of everything that needs doing whilst he is there."

Lord Enstone jumped up to collect teacups from Lady Grant before Kitty could reply. He stayed chatting for some time. He was much more relaxed in his aunt's house and the flashes of arrogance she had seen at Shepley Hall failed to resurface. It seemed she didn't really know him.

Chapter Eight

Luke noticed Miss Davenport's eyes drooping. He looked away and stared down at his feet. She looked so defenceless and it was largely his fault. It was time he took his leave. The poor girl must be exhausted after all the worry he had put her through, followed by two days of travelling. He said his goodbyes and left them. Harvey sprang forward to help him into his coat. He stepped out in to the street, deep in thought.

Aunt Theo was right. He had taken out his anger and frustration at his father on Miss Davenport. He should have seen straight away that she was an innocent young lady. Her natural quiet air of command had confused him but it was no excuse. Perhaps Bright would turn something up about Sir Peter Sewell. Something felt very wrong about the way her father had lost everything to the man. If he could find out what and perhaps restore Davenport Court to young Edward that would go a long way to making it up to her.

If only Nat had still been in Town to discuss it with. There was no one else he could trust with something so delicate. What to do with himself? It wasn't even ten o'clock and he didn't feel like going home. Perhaps he ought to give Brooks a try now that he was a member there. It was a bit of a walk but it was a pleasant evening and the exercise would help clear his head. He reached the corner of St James and studied the yellow brick and Portland stone façade of Brooks. He wandered in and looked around for any acquaintances. Luck was on his side when he was hailed by the Duke of Cathlay, Nat's new brother-in-law.

"Good to see you Enstone. Are you going to take up your seat in the Lords?" Cathlay gave him a hopeful look. "There are some important bills coming up."

"I will do so if estate matters permit."

Luke allowed himself to be drawn into the Duke's circle and accepted an invitation to play a few hands of cards with them. He followed him up to the card room on the first floor, illuminated by an enormous chandelier hanging over the middle of the room. They settled down at a free table and passed a pleasurable couple of hours with Luke finishing slightly up. He smiled to himself. Kitty would have beaten them all. The Duke invited him to share a brandy with him afterwards.

"Let's go downstairs and find a private table, Enstone. You seem rather subdued if I may say so. Is it anything I can help you with?"

Why not talk to the Duke? His discretion could be relied upon. "Have you ever heard of someone called Sir Peter Sewell?"

The Duke shook his head. "I don't think so. Is it important?" He raised his eyebrows.

"I don't know, it may be." Luke hesitated. They were on their own, he may as well tell Cathlay more about it. "I've recently escorted the impoverished daughter of old family friends, Miss Kitty Davenport, to stay with Aunt Theo. Sewell's the man who won their home and more off Miss Davenport's late father. She's not convinced he won it honestly. I suppose she might be inclined to think that but she seems sensible and rather intelligent. Probably nothing in it but I would like to be sure." The truth was he wanted it to be true for Kitty's sake and he wanted to put it right for her.

"I'll see if I can find anything out about him, without alerting anyone. If casual enquiries turn nothing up, I can put you on to a good man with the Bow Street Runners."

"Thank you. Bright was there when I arrived home and heartily glad of something more to do than look after Nat's horses until he is back. I've sent him to the area of Davenport Court to investigate. If he doesn't find anything out then I'll have that name off you."

A smile played around the Duke's mouth. "Bright is better than anyone. I won't tease you for the details but I'm intrigued. It goes without saying that I will keep my own enquiries discreet. With your permission, I'll ask my wife to see if she can find anything out. Again, she is completely trustworthy."

"Of course, Your Grace. I'm hoping that Her Grace will help Aunt Theo launch Miss Davenport into society. She lived quietly with her widowed father and then nursed her aunt before her death. She has never had a season."

"I'm sure Augusta will be delighted to assist. How old is Miss Davenport?"

"I believe she is about twenty three. She has a much younger brother who is still at school."

"She is not too old to launch successfully. I've always thought it a mistake to marry a girl off too young before she has had time to mature." The Duke smiled as he studied him. "I shall watch with interest."

Luke tried to ignore the heat stinging his cheeks at the

Duke's scrutiny. "Aunt Theo is determined to help her as much as she can. She was at school with Miss Davenport's mother."

They were joined by a group of the Duke's friends and the talk turned to politics. It was another hour before Luke made his way home, deep in thought. The Duke had a point about the fashion of marrying girls off at a young age. Many men might be interested in a slightly older girl who had a strong sense of family duty. Miss Davenport certainly had that. If he discreetly provided a respectable dowry, Aunt Theo should be able to marry her off successfully. The sponsorship of the Cathlays would help enormously.

He shrugged his shoulders and his hands formed into fists. He should have acted much more quickly. If her time alone became common knowledge it would be a problem. Perhaps he could find an old army friend on the lookout for a wife who would have the sense to disregard that? The Duke's train of thought had been all too obvious but he wasn't ready for marriage and perhaps never would be. The idea of loving someone and risking rejection was terrifying. He had always managed to steer clear of the few marriageable females he had come across during his time in the army.

* * *

Kitty woke to the sound of a maid bringing her a cup of hot chocolate. The bedchamber was cosily warm, the fire must have been lit for some time. She couldn't help being excited by the prospect of some new clothes. The only pretty things she had ever had were bought for her by Aunt Lucy before Uncle Rupert died. She sat up in bed and accepted the tray with a smile. There was toast as well. The luxury of breakfast in bed was something she had only ever had when she was ill.

"Thank you. That looks appetising. What's your name?"

"Betty, Miss. Is there anything else I can get you?"

"No, thank you."

"Just ring the bell if you want anything. Annie will be along in a while to help you dress." Betty bobbed a curtsy and slipped out of the room.

It was a beautiful room with cream and gold wallpaper complemented by ruby red drapes with golden trimmings. Colourful oriental rugs of a quality she had never seen before were dotted around the floor. With breakfast in bed, a fire in her room, maids to do her bidding, she was living in the height of luxury. Annie arrived, with the lavender gown over her arm, before she had finished her breakfast.

"I've had this washed and pressed it myself. It should be suitable for day wear. I'm going to enjoy looking after all your new things. I expect you'll buy lots today and order some gowns." Annie's eyes glowed with excitement.

The gown looked as good as new. Annie shone with pride and Kitty hadn't the heart to tell her that she intended to leave as soon as she could find suitable employment. Her main worry for now was how Lord Enstone's sister reacted to her. What would she be like? Annie must have read her mind.

"You will love Miss Bamford. Such a sunny-natured young lady she is and has a smile for everyone."

* * *

Kitty braced her shoulders and walked into the parlour to find Lady Grant and Miss Bamford waiting for her. Miss Bamford ran forward and caught her hands. Her hair was much darker than her brother's but she had his hazel eyes.

"I'm Grace Bamford. I can't tell you how excited I am to meet you." Grace gave her a warm smile before she dropped her hands.

Kitty smiled back. "Please call me Kitty."

Lady Grant walked across to a writing desk and extracted pen and paper. "Grace, help me to make up a list of shopping targets. This late in the season we should be able to clothe Kitty quite quickly."

Grace named so many shops that Kitty started to feel dizzy.

"Oh please, Lady Grant. I don't need more than a few items."

"Kitty, I am so looking forward to clothing you." Lady Grant smiled. "You are not going to deny me that pleasure are you?"

"I don't know what to say. I would hate to take advantage of you."

"You won't be. You will be indulging me."

What could she say? It seemed churlish to keep refusing. "Thank you."

"Good, that's settled then. Off you go and get ready. The coach will be at the door in half an hour."

Grace took her hand and led her upstairs. "This will be so much fun. Aunt Theo is a wonderful shopper. I don't want you to think that I'm an empty-headed moppet though. The things I most enjoy about London are the museums and galleries and theatres and so on. I'll be happy to show you the sights. Now Luke's back he can escort us."

Grace left Kitty at her door and carried on to her own room. Kitty wandered across to the bedroom window, which overlooked the street. The sights and sounds of London were fascinating. She would dearly love to explore with Grace but did she want to spend time with Lord Enstone? The answer that sprang into her mind surprised her. The last thing she wanted was to fall for a supercilious nobleman who was far above her touch but she did want to spend time with him. Merely thinking about him made her feel breathless, but then she had never come across anyone as fashionable as him.

Lady Grant's prophecy proved accurate. After a frantic couple of hours that left her head spinning, they had left orders in several shops to be delivered within a few days. A footman followed them carrying various packages containing smaller items such as gloves and underwear. They climbed into the coach and Kitty sank back onto the cream coloured, silk squabs with relief.

"I don't know why it is but I can walk miles in the country and not feel tired but shopping is very hard work."

Lady Grant laughed. "I know what you mean. We haven't quite finished, there two more shops we need to visit."

To Kitty's surprise the coach pulled up at tailor's shop. She looked at Lady Grant in bewilderment. "Why are we stopping here? Oh, perhaps there is a shop further along you want us to visit."

"No, this is our next destination. Surely you ride, Kitty? I don't believe your father would have neglected to have you on a pony as soon as you could stand."

Kitty felt the blood rush to her face. Of course, the material of the riding habit her father had found for her to ride out in company had felt more like a man's coat. When they had the stud, she had spent most of her time riding astride in breeches. It would have been impossible to break in the young horses any other way but it was something best not talked about.

"Oh yes he did. He bought my riding habit for me and a local seamstress adjusted it to fit."

Lady Grant sighed. "I do wish he had contacted me. I would have loved to have arranged your come out if no one in your family could."

"My Aunt Lucy wanted to when my uncle was still alive but I couldn't leave Father on his own and he said he couldn't face London."

"Have you asked Luke to arrange for your horse to be brought to Town for you?"

Kitty wiped away a tear and hoped the other two didn't notice. It was a long time since she had been forced to sell Star but how she missed her. Such a sweet natured horse and they had been inseparable since Star was a few days old.

"My mare had to be sold when Father lost Davenport Court."

"My dear, I'm so sorry. Had you had her long?"

"Ever since she was born. She was only five when we sold her."

Lady Grant patted her hand. "Between us, Grace and I have several horses that would suit you. You must miss riding."

Kitty was fitted for a riding habit in a warm russet colour with a rather military cut. The quality was far superior to her old habit. Heavens, how would she ever repay Lady Grant? She ought to refuse, not that Lady Grant would listen. She was engrossed in every detail of their shopping spree and seemed to be enjoying herself hugely from her delight every time they found something she declared to be perfect. The prospect of riding again was wonderful, in any event. They climbed back in the waiting carriage.

Lady Grant sat back with a satisfied sigh. "I've asked the coachman to take us to a dressmaker who my friend uses. The poor woman had a large order from a family with three girls. They disappeared without paying for the ones they had received and now she is left with a lot of other items to try and sell. There might be something suitable for Kitty that could be altered quickly."

Kitty tried not to stare at her. "Surely I won't need any more clothes?"

"You will be surprised at how many clothes a fashionable lady needs." Lady Grant laughed. "Ask Grace to show you her cupboards if you don't believe me. Besides, I hate to see someone cheated like that. We may be able to help her out."

The dressmaker's shop was in a slightly less prosperous area than the one Lady Grant patronised but the window display was enticing. Smart walking gowns in shades of green, brown and blue gave way to elegant day gowns in paler colours. A beautiful, dusky pink evening gown, with a silver gauze overdress, at the centre of the display, caught Kitty's eye. She had never seen anything so fine.

"I like the style of some of these," Grace said. "I might see if they have anything to suit me."

Madame herself greeted them. She was a tiny lady and her sing song voice, with the merest hint of a French accent, added to Kitty's impression of a birdlike creature.

Lady Grant indicated Kitty's lavender gown. "As you see, my niece's friend is recently out of mourning. We want to show her around London. Have you any gowns which could be ready quickly so we don't waste any time?"

"We do have a few already made that could be altered to fit, I think."

Madame's assistant brought out an array of gowns to show them. Some were too long for Kitty.

Grace's eyes lit up. "I'll try on the ones that are too long for you."

They found several gowns apiece that would need very little alteration. Madame disappeared to find an evening gown she had remembered. Kitty moved to Lady Grant's side.

"I don't feel I ought to buy too many things. Lord Enstone will be sure I'm taking advantage of you."

Lady Grant took her hand. "There is no need to worry about what Luke might think. He will expect to you to be dressed fashionably and trusts me to help you find what is needed." She stroked a soft green walking gown. "These are of excellent quality and the designs suit you."

Grace nodded in agreement. "I was only thinking the other day I needed to replenish my wardrobe. The quality and style are excellent. I can't resist some of these, they are the right length and the bodices fit quite well."

Madame returned with a beautiful, white satin evening gown. It was embroidered with gold thread and with gold lace trims at the neck and hem. It fitted Kitty well, apart from being too long.

"What a pretty gown. It suits you." Lady Grant turned to Madame. "How quickly could this one be altered?

Madame smiled. "We can have it delivered later today."

"Thank you. That would be most helpful."

An assistant followed with a simpler gown of blue silk.

"Kitty tried it on. It was a perfect fit."

"That looks lovely my dear." Lady Grant turned to Madame. "Perhaps we could take that one with us today?"

"Of course, my lady."

"Girls, would you go out to the carriage and send the footman in for the parcels we are taking with us today."

They agreed and Kitty followed Grace out after they had thanked Madame. She overheard Lady Grant offer to take everything that would fit her and Grace. The figure Madame named before the door closed behind them was astronomical. Grace asked the footman to help them into the coach and then sent him off for the parcels. She sat next to Kitty.

"What's the matter? You look quite stricken."

Kitty's put her hands over her hot cheeks. "What on earth will your brother think of me allowing your aunt to spend so much?"

"What should he think other than you have replenished your wardrobe? Besides, from the sum Madame suggested to Aunt Theo as we went out, the gowns are a bargain."

Kitty's eyes opened wide. Grace seemed perfectly serious. "Really?"

Lady Grant joined them.

"Well that was a most successful afternoon, girls."

Kitty made conversation as best she could on the way back. How would she ever repay such a vast sum of money? The coach dropped them at the door and Kitty allowed a footman to hand her down from the carriage in the wake of Lady Grant and Grace. Kitty couldn't stop her mind wandering to the times Lord Enstone had helped her into and out of carriages. She had assumed that the fluttery reaction she had to his touch was the strangeness of being close to an attractive young man but she had felt nothing when taking the hand of Lady Grant's handsome young footman. Did that mean she was developing warmer feelings for Lord Enstone? She shivered as she heard Harvey tell Lady Grant that Lord Enstone was waiting for them in the family drawing room.

"There is also a visitor for Miss Davenport, an old neighbour." Harvey threw back his shoulders and sniffed. "I told him you were out but he insisted on awaiting your return."

Him! A finger of dread touched Kitty. It couldn't be could it?

"I've taken the liberty of putting him in the blue drawing room to avoid an unpleasant scene, my lady. A Sir Walter Greenough."

Kitty collapsed onto a convenient hall chair. Lady Grant ran to her and chafed her hand.

"Kitty, what is it? You've gone chalk white."

A spurt of anger restored her strength and she jumped up. "That man has been chasing me for weeks. He has no right."

She handed her pelisse to the waiting Harvey. "Which is the blue drawing room?"

Harvey passed her coat to a footman. "This way Miss Davenport."

She marched to the door that Harvey indicated, barely aware of being followed. Harvey threw it open and announced her.

Sir Walter Greenough jumped to his feet and strode towards her with a smile that didn't reach his eyes. "My dear, I have missed you so much."

How dare he talk to her in that honeysweet tone as if he owned her? She backed away from him but he was too quick for her. He grabbed her by the shoulders and pulled her towards him. The familiar smell of snuff and stale wine assailed her before his lips fastened on hers with a sickening thud. Kitty drew back her right hand and thumped him so hard on the side of his face that he staggered. Kitty stepped out of his reach before he could right himself.

"How dare you follow me here? I made it plain I wanted nothing to do with you."

Greenough leered at her. "You will soon be begging me to marry you, my fine lady. The tales I can tell will have you thrown out of this house immediately. Why don't you explain to your society friends here what you have been doing since your aunt died?"

Kitty had herself well in hand but a cold fury gripped her. "How dare you. I have spent the last few months avoiding you to the point of having my servant throw you out. I see you still bear the bruises where he hit you."

"Don't think I have forgotten that. A lover's disagreement, nothing more." His nostrils flared and his hands balled into fists. "Spencer will suffer for it when I get back."

Kitty felt a dark-clad shape brushing past her. Greenough was lifted off his feet and carried by his lapels to the wall adjacent to the door. Lord Enstone held him against the wall, his feet still dangling.

"You are the one who will suffer for that. He was protecting his employer's betrothed. Now get your snivelling hide out of my sight before I forget there are ladies present."

He let go so that a trembling Greenough slid down the wall. Greenough got to his feet and threw a look of such venom at Lord Enstone that Kitty gasped.

"You will regret this, my lord. I will make sure that every gossip in Town knows that she was alone at Shepley Hall for months and worked her way through the local men."

"Why would anyone take your word against that of Viscountess Enstone? Harvey, throw him out before I kill him."

Sir Walter Greenough was ushered out, breathing heavily. He glared at Kitty as he passed her. "You haven't heard the last of me."

Kitty's legs started trembling again. It had nothing to do with Sir Walter. Lord Enstone had said she was his betrothed and referred to her as Viscountess Enstone.

Chapter Nine

L uke brushed his hands together as he watched Harvey escort Greenough out. Miss Davenport was white-faced. Was that from the shock of seeing Greenough or his comments suggesting they were about to marry? He moved towards her but Aunt Theo put a hand on his arm.

"Grace, take Kitty up to her room if you would. She needs to recover from that intrusion. I'll have refreshments served in my sitting room in half an hour or so."

Miss Davenport glanced up at him. She looked as if she might say something but changed her mind and allowed Grace to take her arm. He watched them leave the room.

"Luke, are you resolved on offering for Kitty or was that a spur of the moment thing to distract that awful man?"

Aunt Theo was frowning at him, but he had to marry sometime and Kitty was a capable sort of girl. She seemed a nurturing sort from the way she cared for her brother and had nursed her aunt. The sort of girl to make a good mother to any children they had. As the daughter of a baron she was a reasonable match for him. No one outside the family needed to know about her lack of fortune. It was the best solution for all of them.

Luke smiled at himself. "I'm not ready for marriage and I

don't think I ever will be but my duty is clear. I will have to marry someone and the family honour is at stake here."

Aunt Theo put her hand through his arm. "Come into my sitting room."

A cold sensation settled into his stomach. Was Aunt Theo about to tell him that Miss Davenport could possibly be his half-sister? That would leave them in a terrible coil and yet it wasn't that which bothered him. He didn't want to let Miss Davenport down. Harvey was hovering in the hall. Aunt Theo paused by him.

"Arrange for tea and light refreshments in my sitting room in half an hour please. In the meantime, we'll have the brandy decanter."

"Yes, my lady."

"Oh and, Harvey, bring the decanter yourself."

Harvey bowed and went on his way.

Aunt Theo led him to a sofa in front of the fire. "That's better. I wonder when we are going to get some warmer weather. Are you sure about this, Luke?"

"Why? Did your diaries turn up any indication that Miss Davenport is anything to do with father?"

"No, I can put your mind at rest on that one. Kitty's birthday is in the middle of September. You and both your parents stayed with us for several weeks over the preceding Christmas. It seemed wildly unlikely to me anyway but we can be quite sure she is no relation of yours."

"That's a relief. Miss Davenport has been without a companion for nearly a year and her reputation is ruined unless someone marries her now Sir Walter intends to bandy that information around. The only other option is to pay him off but that would lay us open to blackmail. Any lingering scandal from gossip spread by him would soon be scotched if she marries me."

"I'm sure you are right. We could even pretend there had been a long-standing engagement between the two of you since your fathers were friends. All in all, it could have been an awful lot worse. But are you sure you are happy about such a marriage?"

Luke jumped up and stood with his back to the fire, his hands underneath his coat tails. "My father took on the responsibility for the family and the task became mine. I failed to do my duty. I heard about the family a while ago and waited until now to do anything. Miss Davenport shouldn't suffer for my sins."

Aunt Theo sighed. "All very noble but shall you suit? I like what I've seen of Kitty and I want her to be happy for her own sake as well as her mother's. I want you to be happy too."

"I think I could be as happy with Miss Davenport as I could with anyone. She has a strong sense of family duty and is an improvement on so many of the young girls one sees in ballrooms. She is rather quiet but in many ways she's a restful companion. She's not afraid to speak up sometimes but not in a strident way. I think she could become a good Viscountess with you to guide her."

Aunt Theo clasped her hands together and grimaced. "Luke, she is all of those things and much more besides. I'm asking you if you are attracted to her as a woman because if you are not then I can't see a marriage between you working."

Luke felt the heat rush to his cheeks. "I thought her quite plain at first but on the journey to London she seemed quite a taking little thing." So much so that he had avoided her company as much as he could but that he was keeping to himself.

"We can find another solution if you're not sure, Luke."

"No, my mind is made up. I will marry her."

"You can't say that without asking her."

Luke resumed his place on the sofa. "Are you saying you don't think she will have me?"

"I think it a distinct possibility."

"What? Does she find me repellent?"

The door opened to admit Harvey. He placed a tray with decanter and glasses on a side table.

"Thank you, Harvey. Leave it a while longer before sending the tea tray in if you would."

Aunt Theo waited for the door to close behind him before continuing. "I've seen her look at you when she thinks herself unobserved. She likes you very well which is why I think she may refuse you."

Luke threw up his arms. "What kind of logic is that?"

"Think about it, Luke. What could be worse than marrying a bad man? Marrying a man who you come to love but is indifferent to you."

"I'm sure I could feel strong affection for her. Isn't that enough?"

He had seen Nat in the throes of unrequited love before he persuaded Eliza to marry him, surely a marriage of convenience would be much more comfortable than a love match? Love terrified him but he couldn't admit that to Aunt Theo. He had loved his father so very much but all his youthful overtures, seeking love and reassurance after his mother had died, had been met with stern rebuffs. The last thing he wanted was to fall in love with his wife and risk that sort of pain again.

* * *

Kitty allowed Annie to help her out of her gown. She lay down on the bed and closed her eyes. She tried to relax every part of her body in an effort to calm down. Sir Walter showing up and pretending to be her betrothed was bad enough but when Lord Enstone had claimed her as his she had been ready to sink through the floor. He could look much higher for a bride and she didn't want to feel that he had been forced into offering for her and yet it seemed like that was what was going to happen.

Annie bounced back into the room carrying a bandbox. "Oh, Miss Davenport, the dressmaker has sent round one of your evening gowns. I've already unpacked the gown you brought back with you."

Kitty felt obliged to sit up and watch as Annie lifted the gown out of the box. The combination of white satin and gold embroidery looked even more stunning in the light from the large window in her room than it had in the shop. Annie gasped.

"It is beautiful is it not? I don't feel deserving of all this finery."

"Why ever not? The blue gown should be ready for you to wear now it's had a chance to hang. I'll tidy up your hair as well."

Annie had her ready in a matter of minutes. She stood back to admire her handiwork.

"You look so beautiful." Annie clapped her hands together. "I never imagined I would have the chance to look after such a lovely lady. I'm sure Lady Grant would let me go if you was to offer me the job permanently." She raised beseeching eyes to Kitty.

Kitty couldn't help but smile. "If I should ever be able to take on a lady's maid it will be you, Annie."

A grin transformed Annie's face. She went to the door to answer a knock. Betty came into the room.

"Lady Grant asks if you will join her in the family drawing room as soon as you are ready, Miss."

Kitty gulped down a deep breath. "I'm as ready as I will ever be."

She followed Betty downstairs. What was she to do? If only Aunt Lucy was here now she would help her decide. A chuckle escaped her. If Aunt Lucy had been alive the situation wouldn't have arisen. Marrying Lord Enstone would secure Edward's future. It would give her stability and he was an attractive man. Too attractive to have chosen her if he hadn't felt obliged to. It was no good thinking about that. She wouldn't have been summoned if he wasn't serious in his intention to marry her and surely the advantages of a match with him outweighed the disadvantages? So why not surrender to the inevitable and accept the situation? Why was she so reluctant? She closed her eyes. Because she loved him.

How would she cope in the fairly likely event of him taking a mistress? He could already have one for all she knew. She must stamp on the fantasy of a love match which had disturbed her ever since she had travelled to London with him. He had done nothing to encourage her to hope and yet a part of her couldn't help it. If she married him it would be a marriage of convenience and nothing more. As long as he was kind to her she would work hard to make him a good wife. She would learn to accept that she had no say over the rest of his behaviour. Dreams were for children. Perhaps he would come to care for her in time. Even if he didn't there might be the compensation of children. She shivered at the thought of what that might entail.

Harvey came forward to open the doors to the drawing room and announce her. She walked in as calmly as she could. Her eyes were drawn to Lord Enstone. He rose and gave her a deep bow but when he stood up his face looked stern.

Lady Grant smiled at her. "Kitty, Lord Enstone desires a few moments of private speech with you." She too rose and took Kitty's hands. "Are you happy for me to leave you together?"

Kitty felt like saying no but common sense dictated that she might as well get this interview over with. "Yes, my lady."

Lady Grant squeezed her hands gently before letting them go. "I shall come back in a quarter of an hour."

Kitty stood, uncertain of what to do. The door closed and she tried to smile but her mouth felt stiff.

"Won't you sit down, my lord?"

His face broke into a sudden smile. "I believe it would be more appropriate to go down on one knee."

Kitty stifled a laugh. "Oh no please don't. I wouldn't want you to get your clothes dirty."

Lord Enstone gave her a quizzical look. "Well in that case as soon as you sit down I will too."

He took her hand and escorted her to the sofa. He must think her stupid for leaving him standing like that. They sat down and Kitty realised he was still holding her hand. He was near enough for her to catch the scent of him she had come to know. Spices and citrus mingled with a hint of clean male. Her heart raced. The effect he had on her when they were close was getting stronger. He cleared his throat and she looked up at him.

"That's better. I can't say I'm comfortable with proposing to the top of your head. Miss Davenport, will you do me the honour of accepting my offer of marriage?"

Kitty tried to speak but her mouth was too dry. She swallowed and tried again. "I am fully aware of the honour that you do me, my lord. Are you quite sure that you are happy to go through with this? It's not your fault that Sir Walter Greenough is such a bounder, as my father would have said."

"The honour would be mine." He smiled at her. "Apart from my duty to the honour of both our families I have been dreading finding a bride in the glare of society. So you see you would be helping me out."

"But what about love, my lord?" Kitty gasped. Had she really just said that?

"We haven't known each other long enough for that but I assure you that I have a great regard for you. Of course, if you have taken me in aversion nothing more needs to be said."

He was watching her intently. Kitty felt heat flood through her from head to toe. She could only hope he would assume it was from the embarrassment of the situation.

"My lord, of course I haven't."

His expression relaxed. "Well then, surely mutual liking and respect should be enough to base a good marriage on?"

She closed her eyes for a moment. His breathing sounded louder. She would be safe with Lord Enstone. Edward's future would be secure and she wanted what was best for him. Could she be sure that Lord Enstone was free of doubts himself?

"My lord, are you certain this is what you want?"

He ran a hand through his hair. A habit she was becoming rather fond of.

"I would be lying if I said I was certain but we live in an uncertain world and a union between us would be sensible. I am confident that we can make it work." He leaned towards her and smiled. "Come, what do you say?" His voice was gentle.

Well that was honest. He was a decent man. She would be mad to turn him down. She closed her eyes again.

"I accept your offer, my lord." She opened her eyes with a start when he placed a kiss on her cheek.

"Thank you. I will do my best to make you happy. You would make me happy by calling me Luke."

"I will, as long as you call me Kitty."

He stood and pulled on her arm gently. His other hand rested lightly at the small of her back, drawing her close. Kitty smiled up at him, her pulse racing. Their eyes met and it was a few moments before Luke looked away and broke the spell.

"Let's find Aunt Theo and tell her the good news."

They had barely reached the door when there was a knock and Luke opened it to admit his Aunt Theo. Heavens, she would be her Aunt Theo too once they were married.

"You are to wish me happy, Aunt Theo." Luke said. "Shall we send for Grace now?"

If his family were unhappy about the match there was time to back out. Kitty watched Lady Grant's face. She seemed content enough and she broke into a smile when she noticed Kitty watching her.

"Let me wish you happy, my dear. I'm sad your mother isn't with us to see this moment. I think a lot of my rascal of a nephew. I am sure he will be kind to you."

Luke laughed. "You are putting me to the blush, Aunt Theo."

Kitty smiled. "Thank you, Lady Grant." She glanced at Luke. His cheeks did look rather red.

"I'll leave you two for a moment, Kitty, so Aunt Theo can tell you all the other things about me she doesn't want to say with me here. I'll send for Grace."

Lady Grant laughed at his retreating back. "Come let's move closer to the fire. You're shivering." They sat on the sofa that Kitty had shared with Luke.

"Luke is a good man but he was very affected by his mother's death. His father was too devastated to help him. Don't worry if it takes a while before he lets you into his life fully. I think you will suit very well. Indeed, as soon as I saw you, I was hoping Luke would take to you. He has been in the army for seven years and the young women he has met so far have been little more than children. He needs someone like you with some depth to their character."

"You paint a rosy picture of me. I hope I can live up to it."

Lady Grant kissed her on the cheek. "I'm sure you will."

Kitty blinked away a tear. Lady Grant couldn't have been more welcoming of her joining the family. If Grace accepted her as readily there was no reason for her not to go through with the marriage. She sensed that honour was important to Luke and he seemed genuine in his determination to do his duty by her. It was a long way from her childhood dreams of romance, coloured by her parents' happy marriage. He was as handsome as the man of her dreams but she had imagined love and passion and excitement. Duty and respect seemed a poor substitute. She had her own duty to follow but she could hope that affection would blossom between her and Luke. It still felt strange to call him Luke.

Grace bounced into the room. "I'm so happy to congratulate you, dear friend. I heard a group of old tabbies discussing who might win Luke the other evening. Lord, there wasn't one of the girls they suggested who wouldn't have had me running away from home if I'd been a man destined to marry them. I'm so glad he's going to marry someone sensible like you."

Kitty was touched by the warmth and excitement in Grace's voice. She laughed at her. "You hardly know me. I'm shockingly expensive you know."

Grace wrinkled her nose up. "What a bouncer. You were fretting yourself to flinders every time Aunt Theo bought you a handkerchief."

Kitty exchanged a glance with a smiling Lady Grant. There could be no doubt of Grace's approval. Grace bent to kiss her before taking a nearby chair.

"Luke is so reserved I thought he would never marry." Grace blushed deep red. "Oh, I'm so sorry. I shouldn't have said that to you."

"Luke has offered for me because he feels he should. I don't wish to pretend anything else." Kitty held her head high.

"I know, but how could he fail to fall in love with you after such a romantic start?"

Lady Grant saved Kitty from having to reply. "Grace, you have surprised me. I never thought of you as having a romantic turn of mind."

Grace smiled at Kitty. "I think it's Luke who is the secret romantic. I love him dearly but it's rare he shows any emotion. I expect it comes of spending so much time in the army. All those perilous situations must take it out of a man. It's time he had some fun in his life."

Kitty forced a smile. She should be happy that Grace approved of her, so why did Grace's comments on Luke's lack of emotion make her feel miserable? She was the hidden romantic, harbouring dreams of marital bliss. Heavens, she was old enough to know that it was silly to expect too much of people. She ought to be grateful to him for offering her a secure future.

She turned to Lady Grant. "Luke, Lord Enstone, insisted it was his duty to offer to marry me. Was he right? It doesn't seem very fair to him."

Lady Grant regarded her steadily. "Yes, he was right to do so. It seems to me that he has been fortunate. He is waiting in the library. Shall we send for him now?"

"Yes, of course." It seemed strange to be deferred to in connection with Luke.

Lady Grant rang the bell. Harvey himself arrived almost immediately.

"We are ready for the tea tray now, Harvey. Perhaps you would be so kind as to tell Lord Enstone that tea is about to be served."

Harvey bowed low. "Of course, my lady."

He smiled as he went out. It seemed even the servants approved. Annie would be excited. Should she check with Luke before offering her the position of lady's maid? Lady Grant patted her hand and moved to a chair next to Grace. A wide grin spread across Grace's face. She jumped to her feet with sparkling eyes and ran across the room. Luke engulfed her in a hug. Kitty's heart beat faster as she imagined him doing that to her.

Luke held Grace away from him and laughed. "I think I can take it that you approve of my choice."

"Of course I do. I hope Kitty and I are friends already and she's a huge improvement on the silly ninnies whose names I've heard linked with yours recently."

"What! I'm glad I wasn't aware of this speculation about me. Tell me Grace is making it up, Aunt Theo."

"I'm sure she is not. A new viscount at the age to be looking around him is bound to arouse speculation."

He sat down next to Kitty. "It seems you have saved me from a terrible fate, my dear. I can't think of anything worse than facing a battalion of matchmaking mamas. I had rather face a cavalry charge with us outnumbered two to one. I would have more chance of coming out alive."

Kitty laughed with the rest of them. Was he trying to make her feel better about his being forced to offer for her? If so, it was well done of him. She glanced up at him and their eyes met. He smiled down at her and her heart skipped a beat. He was so much more relaxed than he had been when they first met and it suited him. He couldn't be too unhappy about having his hand forced. If she hadn't already lost her heart to him, and she rather thought she had, how would she be able to keep it safe when he smiled at her like that?

A footman entered with the tea tray and a maid followed with plates of delicate pastries. Lady Grant poured the tea and Luke handed out cups to Kitty and then Grace. He placed one of the plates on a side table by him and Kitty.

"You must try some of these Shrewsbury cakes. They're my favourites."

There was something surprisingly intimate about sampling his favourite cakes with him. She must make sure to ask Lady Grant's cook for the recipe before the wedding. A shiver ran through her. She was going to be married. Nella would be pleased. She had a strong suspicion that Nella had been trying to push Luke to offer for her at Shepley Hall. He was too intelligent not to have realised, which may have accounted for his coldness to her to begin with.

There was a knock at the door and Harvey entered bearing a note on a silver salver.

"A note has been delivered by the Duchess of Cathlay's

footman, my lady."

Lady Grant scanned the note. "The Cathlays find themselves with a free night. We are invited to dinner tomorrow evening. Augusta apologises for the late invitation but now Cathlay has told her of Kitty's arrival she is longing to meet her."

"Am I invited too?" Luke asked.

"Yes you are. I happened to mention to Augusta the last time I saw her that we were unusually quiet for the first part of this week. She says if you were planning to dine with us to bring you too."

"I am certainly free tomorrow. I had a vague plan of dining at my club but I made no arrangements with anyone. How do you feel about going, Kitty? The Cathlays are good friends and it would be an opportunity to meet them in private."

Kitty bit back a refusal. She owed it to Luke to do her best to make him a good wife. A man in his position would be expected to give and take hospitality. She may as well get used to it.

"Of course we must go. As you say it will be a good opportunity to meet them privately."

"I'll ring for you when I've written an acceptance note, Harvey."

Lady Grant moved across to her writing desk and Grace followed.

The door closed behind Harvey. Luke captured Kitty's hand and a shiver of heat shot through her.

"You hesitated there. It's not too late to change your mind if you would rather have a few quiet days to become used to our betrothal." He raised his eyebrows in enquiry.

Kitty smiled. "How thoughtful of you but it's not just men who must do their duty."

His expression seemed to harden.

Kitty pressed her free hand to a suddenly hot face. "I don't want you to think I'm making sure of you before you have had time to consider."

"There is nothing to consider unless you are having doubts?"

"I want what is best for you. If you are happy to go ahead then I am."

He nodded and let go of her hand. There were spots of colour high on his cheeks. Was he having doubts or was it the result of Grace's return? She had looked away but she had almost certainly seen their linked hands.

Lady Grant finished her note. "Before I ring for Harvey, will you be having dinner here with us tonight, Luke?"

"Yes please." He smiled at Kitty and cleared his throat. "That is if you are not too tired for more of my company?"

Kitty caught her breath. "Of course I'm not too tired to spend time with you, Luke."

Lady Grant laughed. "That settles it then."

She rang for Harvey and ordered an extra place to be set for dinner before handing him the reply to be delivered to the Duchess. Once they had all finished their tea Lady Grant ushered Grace out.

"I think you two need a few minutes to talk privately."

The door closed softly behind them. Luke moved closer to her so that their thighs were touching. The heat from him made her leg tingle. He really was the most attractive man.

"I haven't changed my mind, Kitty. Will you allow me to prove it to you?"

She nodded, mesmerised by the heat in his eyes. She dropped her gaze to the floor. He lifted her head with a finger under her chin until their eyes locked. Then he allowed his glance to travel to her lips.

"Are you sure?" His words were a whisper against her ear.

"Yes please." Heavens had she really just said that?

He lowered his lips to hers and an explosion of heat shot through her. She pressed closer to him. He put his hand behind her head and pulled her closer. She gasped as his tongue played with her lips. His tongue accepted the invitation of her open mouth and started work on the inside of her lips. New sensations shot through her and settled deep in her abdomen. She tentatively tried to copy him. His response was to pull her closer still until she was almost lying on her side.

He pulled out of the kiss leaving her feeling bereft. One arm went around her back and the other one threaded its way under her knees. He picked her up as if she weighed no more than a feather and placed her across his lap with his right arm supporting her shoulders.

"Are you comfortable?"

"Yes. Would you kiss me again?"

He grinned at her and lowered his lips to hers. She responded and gave herself up to the sensations running through her as the kiss deepened. Joy ran through her. He must desire her to kiss her like this. His left hand settled on her waist and his thumb caressed her side. Slowly his thumb moved upwards until it found the sensitive flesh of her breast. A moan escaped her. She wriggled closer to him and he jerked away from her.

"We have to stop there, sweetheart."

His expression was wooden. Had she displeased him in some way? Her breath hitched. "I don't understand. Did I do something wrong?"

He gave a shout of laughter, quickly suppressed. "You did everything far too right. That's the problem. If we don't stop now ...." His face went red. "That is something I will explain to you once we are married. Aunt Theo will be back in a moment. We had better make sure we are presentable. He set her on her feet. "If Aunt Theo asks you what we talked about, you will have to make something up."

This time they both laughed. It was good to know that he had a ready sense of humour. Perhaps this marriage would work out better than she could have hoped.

Chapter Ten

L uke strode out of his aunt's drawing room. Any doubts about marrying Kitty had been put to flight by her response to their kisses. She was clearly untutored in the art of lovemaking but her innocent enthusiasm had nearly been his undoing. The frisson of excitement he had felt every time he helped her into or out of the coach on the journey to London was nothing to the sensation that had assailed him when she had started fidgeting on his lap. Simply remembering it was enough to make him want to run back into the drawing room and carry her upstairs to her bedroom.

He allowed a footman to help him into his coat and open the door for him. He ran lightly down the steps and set off for home, keeping his head down as he strode along. He wasn't in the mood to talk to any acquaintances he might pass. It was a shock to his system to go to one of his estates to decide what to do with his father's pensioner and become betrothed to her within days of returning to London. He needed time to himself to reflect on his changed status.

Now that he knew her better, he was sure that Kitty hadn't set out to trap him into marriage. Her anger and bewilderment to find that Sir Walter Greenough had followed her to London had been genuine. She was a quiet little thing and her determination to please him was almost irritating. She hadn't wanted to go to the Cathlays for dinner but felt it her duty. To be fair to her she must be feeling a little unsure of herself surrounded by people she didn't know. She had been magnificent in her anger at Sir Walter, which suggested strength of character hidden under her quiet demeanour. There had been nothing quiet in her response to him. He broke into a grin. The sooner they were married the better he would like it.

His idea of remaining unwed had never been realistic. Not least because he had never been keen on brief liaisons and the thought of taking a mistress horrified him. Reducing human lovemaking to a financial transaction seemed so sordid. There had been a few adventures as a young man but there hadn't been a woman in his life for a long time. His reaction to an innocent kiss had proved that the life of a monk would not suit him. Grace was right that Kitty had far more substance than most of the young damsels paraded on the marriage mart by fond mamas. Not that he really knew Kitty yet. There were hidden depths to her for sure and it was going to be interesting getting to know her.

She was a respectable rather than good match for him. Not that he cared for that sort of nonsense. He had more than enough money for both of them and a whole bevy of children if they were blessed with them. No one needed to know that she had no dowry. Both Aunt Theo and Grace seemed pleased with his betrothal to her. He was pleased himself now that he had adjusted to the idea. It would be good to be settled and not always looking over his shoulder for some trap to ensnare him. He wouldn't want to join old Richard Naismith, inveigled into a miserable marriage straight after leaving the army. The poor man eked out his existence between his club and the latest gambling house as much as he could. It would be interesting to find out if he had succeeded in getting back into the army to get away from the wife who he called The Witch.

There was no danger of him feeling like that about Kitty. He had been too quick to suspect her when they first met, perhaps influenced by Richard's experience as well as his amazement at Father helping the family so generously. Kitty would want to contact her brother of course. It was a pity he had dispatched Fletcher and Bright into Leicestershire together with Mr Wallace. He could have sent one of them to collect Edward from school for the wedding. Marriage by licence would be best and quicker too. He smiled to himself. He would have to apply for that in person.

It was probably too soon for Cathlay to uncover anything about Sir Peter Sewell. Without more information there was nothing he could do about satisfying his curiosity on what had really happened with Kitty's father. Her family hadn't had much luck. The new Lord Swift's dealings with Kitty's aunt sounded decidedly suspect. Bright might be back soon if he could find nothing out. If not, he could always send Garner with the family coach to fetch Edward. Would that serve or would it be better to fetch Edward himself? The school was far more likely to agree to Edward starting his summer holidays early if he went in person. He could apply for a special licence before he went. There would be no need to worry about Sir Walter Greenough spreading gossip once he and Kitty were married.

Luke turned into his street and strode along with his head down. He cannoned into a gentleman who appeared to be studying his front door. They staggered backwards with smothered exclamations.

"Bamf, it's you. Is this a new London fashion to look anywhere but the direction you're walking in?"

"Ram! What are you doing here?" Luke grinned. "You weren't exactly looking out for pedestrians yourself."

They shook hands and the other man slapped Luke on the back.

"Good to see you, I've got a week's leave in London and I thought I'd come and look you up but I wasn't sure of your house number. All the houses in this row look so similar. It seems I'd remembered correctly."

Luke glanced around to see a footman opening his door. "Come on in. I've a couple of hours before I need to dress for dinner." He hesitated for a moment. "I've got some important news I'll tell you if you promise to keep it quiet for a day or two."

Major Ramsay followed him into Enstone House. Once they were settled in the library, with glasses of brandy to hand, Ram leaned back in his chair and a grin spread across his face.

"Never say you're getting leg-shackled?"

Luke grinned back. "Yes. The lady has accepted me but we haven't announced the betrothal yet."

Major Ramsay leaned across and clapped a hand on Luke's shoulder. "That is good news, as long as she's a sensible girl. I bumped into Naismith last night. He's been accepted back in the army but his wife is going with him!"

Luke shook his head. "Poor fellow. He made a bad bargain but I've been much more fortunate."

"I'm relieved to hear it. Who is the lucky lady?"

"Miss Kitty Davenport."

"I can't place the name. Does she have any brothers in the army?"

"Her only brother is still at school." Luke laughed as Major Ramsay stiffened. "Kitty is eight years older than Edward. I haven't fallen for a raw debutante. She's lived quietly in the country because of family circumstances but her mother was a friend of my aunt, Lady Grant. Kitty is staying with her now she is out of mourning for her aunt."

"I've met Lady Grant, an excellent lady. Trust you to find someone without having to as much as run the gauntlet at Almack's I'll be bound."

"I've escorted my sister there a few times as it happens. Not a happy place for an unmarried gentleman."

They both laughed.

Major Ramsay wrinkled his brow. "Something's bothering you. I can tell from the way your face lights up when you talk about Miss Davenport, it's not her. What is it?"

That was just relief from having his future settled but best not to tell Ram that. Perhaps he might have some suggestions on how to unravel the mystery surrounding Kitty's father and his loss of their home.

Major Ramsay listened to Luke's account and accepted another glass of brandy. "You say this happened in Leicestershire. Do you know Captain Meredith?"

"I don't think I do."

"A good man, he served under me before he got his captaincy. I remember him telling us about an odd experience he had when he stayed with a cousin a few years ago. I think it was in that area. It may not be the same family but from what I can remember of his story it would fit your theory that Davenport was tricked if it is. I'm going to a regimental dinner tomorrow night. I could ask if anyone knows where he is at the moment. I probably would have done anyway in the hope he might be in

London."

"Yes please. I know I can trust your discretion."

"I should think so, old man. I won't mention your betrothal either."

"Thank you. It wouldn't be fair to broadcast it until Kitty's brother has been told. There is no one available to bring him to London and so I intend to post up to his school myself. I'll be able to seek his approval at the same time."

Major Ramsay gave a bark of laughter. "The approval of a school boy?"

Luke chuckled. "A rather scrubby schoolboy at that but he's Kitty's only living relative and I want to do this properly."

* * *

Annie helped Kitty out of her new gown and into a dressing gown. "There you are, miss. Why don't you have a lie down? I'll be back in an hour or so to dress you for dinner." She looked at Kitty and sighed. "You'll look lovely in that white and gold evening gown."

Kitty watched the door close behind her with relief. An hour of rest hardly seemed long enough to take in the enormity of what had happened. She walked across to the window and watched the comings and goings of carriages and people for a while but her concentration soon wandered. There was a fire burning in her room but she still felt cold. She wandered across to the bed and climbed under the covers. It seemed there would be excitement in their marriage if their lovemaking in the drawing room was anything to go by.

Kitty curled up into a ball and hugged her knees as she remembered the feel of Luke's kisses. He must at least care for her and it was wonderful to feel so safe with him to protect her from men like Sir Walter. He had been so angry at Sir Walter. A warm glow spread over her at the memory of Luke carrying him by his coat and slamming him against the wall. Did that mean he already had some feelings for her or was he just angry at the man's presumption?

She was already in love with Luke and it was no good trying to pretend otherwise. Her breathing quickened and tremors shook her. She had lived a life of worry and fear for so long, especially after Aunt Lucy had died, and it was hard to believe she was truly betrothed to him. Luke was a man of honour and he wouldn't change his mind now. Her breathing calmed. She had heard of arranged marriages that had turned into love matches. Everything would work out, she had to believe that.

She turned over in bed and tried to relax, only to be assailed by more doubts. Luke could have had his pick of the season's debutantes, was he disappointed to end up with her? It was no good thinking like that. She might not be beautiful, whatever Annie said, but she wasn't an antidote and they did seem to share a sense of humour. Aunt Lucy's marriage had been a happy one and their house had been filled with laughter. That was what she wanted from life.

Kitty was woken up by a gentle shake from Annie. "I'm sorry, Miss Davenport. I left you to sleep as long as possible but we have to make a start now or you won't be ready in time for dinner."

Kitty yawned and stretched before she sat up. "That's alright, Annie. Thank you for leaving it until the last minute. I feel better for the rest. It's been a busy day."

Annie grinned at her. "It certainly has, Miss."

She probably ought to be more dignified but Kitty grinned

back. Annie soon had her ready for her new evening gown. She lifted it over Kitty's head and straightened out the skirts as it fell into place.

Annie tied up the lacing at neck and waist. "You look lovely in this, Miss. I've found a shawl to match the gown."

She placed a golden silk shawl, another one of the purchases they had made only that morning although it seemed a lifetime ago, around Kitty's shoulders. Kitty had never owned anything so fine and couldn't resist stroking it. Annie was right about the colour. It matched the trims and embroidery on the gown perfectly. She went up on to her toes in front of the looking glass and twirled around. What would Luke think about her dressed like this?

Kitty was barely aware of descending the stairs. It was as if she was floating. The thought of seeing Luke again sent her pulses racing. Lady Grant and Grace were alone in the drawing room when she entered. Perhaps that was as well. It would give her time to regain her composure. After several minutes of chatting she was close to asking if Luke had cried off when she heard Harvey answer the door.

"The ladies are all in the drawing room, my lord."

"Thank you, Harvey."

Luke swept in and all her good work in calming herself went to nought. She glanced at the floor so he wouldn't see her expression, which was probably similar to that of Edward's dog when he called it for a walk. For someone who had disliked Luke at first the change in her feelings was unsettling. When she looked up Luke was bowing to them all. He walked across the room and took the chair next to hers.

Grace jumped up. "Why don't you two share this sofa?"

Lady Grant shook her head at her. "Grace, behave. In any

case it's time we went into dinner."

Luke laughed. "I'm grateful that Grace approves of my choice in any event."

He stood and held out his arm for his aunt. She hesitated but placed her hand on it and allowed him to lead her into the family dining room. Kitty and Grace followed them, arm in arm. Kitty was disappointed when a footman pulled back her own chair before Luke had settled his aunt. She stroked the string of pearls that had belonged to her mother and looked up at Luke as he took the seat next to her. If he was thinking about their encounter of the afternoon, he was doing a better job of hiding it than she was.

Grace kept up a string of chatter and Kitty was able to relax and enjoy her meal. They were a delightful family and the light-hearted banter between Luke and Grace had her longing to see Edward. He would be delighted at her betrothal. His letter home after his meeting with Luke had been full of praises for him. Edward had been too long without the guiding hand of an older male. It would be a relief to hand over responsibility for his future to a man like Luke.

Lady Grant touched her hand. "It's time for us to leave Luke to his port, Kitty."

"Oh, have you been waiting for me. I'm so sorry. I was in a daydream."

Grace came around the table and took her arm. "We could see that. You looked so happy we left you to it for a while."

Kitty nearly swooned with embarrassment. She glanced at Luke but he was concentrating on the port decanter Harvey placed on the table in front of him. She allowed Grace to lead her to the drawing room and place her on a sofa.

Lady Grant smiled at Kitty when Grace found a chair at some

distance from her. "Grace is determined that you should have an opportunity to talk to Luke."

Kitty smiled back. Lady Grant was so kind and would help her to find her way as a Viscountess.

They all looked up when Luke entered. Kitty felt her cheeks heat up at the grin Grace gave her. Luke duly took the seat next to her on the sofa. Grace gave her a triumphant look and started up a conversation with her aunt.

Luke gave a soft laugh. "I see Grace is determined to throw us together. That girl is a minx. I despair of ever finding her a husband."

"Grace isn't ready to marry yet. When she does it will have to be someone with political ambitions."

Luke took her hand in his and held their linked hands close to him so his coat tails largely covered them. "I see you're clever as well as beautiful. You have summed up the situation perfectly after a mere few days of acquaintance with Grace."

Kitty smiled at the unexpected compliment. "Why thank you, kind sir."

Luke moved his hand and massaged her palm with his thumb. A shiver of delight ran through her.

"We haven't had much time to become used to each other, have we? My time at Shepley Hall with you can hardly be counted."

"Why ever not?"

"I was suspicious about the whole set up at Shepley and I apologise for my boorish behaviour."

Kitty stiffened. "I didn't imagine a certain amount of hostility towards me at first then?"

Luke drew his hand away from hers and looked at the floor before turning towards her and capturing her gaze. "If I had known you better I wouldn't have felt hostile. Please believe me when I say my feelings weren't directed towards you. My father was a cold, hard man. I found it difficult to believe that he would show compassion to an old friend. I was searching for an answer and you were the only lead I had."

Kitty drew her brows together. "I'm puzzled. I've heard Grace speak of her father with affection. It's as if you are talking about two different people."

"My mother died giving birth to Grace. She is eight years younger than me. Either my father mellowed, although I saw no sign of it, or he treated females differently." His expression hardened. He turned away and seemed to be staring at something she couldn't see.

"My father was never the same after my mother died. Grief can do strange things to people. Perhaps you didn't know your father as well as you thought?"

"Perhaps, but let's forget about him and talk about us. I have reams of urgent estate business to get through. I want to talk to my secretary about some of it before I fetch Edward. Would you mind if I spend tomorrow catching up and hoping for the return of Wallace?"

"Of course not."

"Thank you." He gave her a smile that made her catch her breath. "I think I could find time to show you my London house. My servants haven't been told of our betrothal yet, except for my valet, although some of them may have guessed. It will be easier for you to meet them before they know."

Kitty took a steadying breath. Meeting some of Luke's servants sounded a terrifying prospect but the sooner she adjusted to dealing with his households the better.

"That would be lovely."

They were interrupted by the arrival of the tea trolley. They accepted cups from Lady Grant. Luke put his down on a side table.

"I've invited Kitty to view my London house tomorrow, Aunt Theo. Are you and Grace free to accompany her?"

"What time, Luke?"

"I was thinking we could all have luncheon together and give you a tour of the house. You haven't seen all the improvements Wallace has arranged."

Lady Grant looked at Grace, who nodded. "Yes, we can manage that."

"Excellent. In the absence of Wallace, I'll send Garner out tomorrow to discreetly discover how I apply for a marriage licence of some sort. I'm rather hazy about the mechanics of getting wed. I sincerely hope that it won't take more than one day for me to obtain it, leaving me free to set off to fetch Edward the day after that. We can't make firm plans until we know if Edward will be allowed to miss the end of term."

Lady Grant laughed. "You're not my nephew if you can't talk a headmaster round."

Luke found Kitty's hand whilst they drank their tea. When his thumb found the inside of her wrist Kitty nearly dropped the cup she was holding in the other hand. His touch sent sparks of heat shooting up her arm. He gave her a smile which promised much before putting his cup down.

"I intend to get up early in the morning to work on urgent estate business. I'll bid you goodnight."

Grace immediately jumped up. "There is something I need to talk to you about aunt."

Lady Grant shook her head at her. "Grace what can I do with you? I suppose you are right. We should give the happy couple a few minutes to talk."

She gave Luke a mock glare which, to Kitty's amusement caused him to colour up.

"No more than five minutes, Luke. Kitty has had an exhausting day."

"As you wish."

The two of them left the room and Luke regained his seat on the sofa.

"I have a horrible feeling that Aunt Theo knows what we were up to this afternoon. I don't think we should let that stop us from trying another kiss."

In answer Kitty put a hand on his arm and leaned towards him. Would he think her too forward? He threw his arms around her and claimed her lips. It seemed he liked forward women. Kitty gave herself up to enjoyment of the kiss and sighed when he eventually pulled away.

"I'm sorry, Kitten. Do you mind if I call you that? You remind me of a kitten mesmerised by a ball of wool, with your hair rumpled and that dreamy expression on your face. We don't want to upset Aunt Theo and if we keep this up I'll be here much longer than five minutes." He gave her a wicked grin. "We might be able to engineer some time alone tomorrow when I show you my house."

He dropped a kiss on her forehead. "Goodnight."

Kitty watched him go. How could she have ever thought him forbidding. She laughed at the thought of her reaction if someone had told her then that she would marry him. It seemed incredible, almost too good to believe.

Chapter Eleven

The grandfather clock that dominated his hallway chimed twelve times, loudly enough for Luke to hear even with the library door firmly closed. Good Lord, noon already. He signed the document in front of him with a flourish and put down his quill. He leaned back in his chair and stretched. It did little to ease his aches and pains. He wasn't used to being hunched over a desk for hours at a time but he must remember to insist that Wallace took regular breaks. There was a satisfying pile of signed papers in front of him, but it was nothing to the tottering pile still to be attended to. Many of them made little sense and he needed Wallace to guide him. He would have to wait until Wallace was back before he collected Edward. Some of them looked like legal documents to do with property sales, leases and purchases and could be urgent.

Despite his assurances to Kitty there was no guarantee that he would be able to have Edward straight away. In his experience, headmasters could be supremely unpredictable. It was possible he could be left kicking his heels for days. He sprang out of his chair. That was a problem for another day and it was time to make sure everything was ready for his guests. How would Kitty take to his servants? It was important that she got off to a good start with them. She had seemed overawed when they first arrived at Aunt Theo's house but she should be used to grand mansions by now.

His housekeeper was waiting for him in the hall. A tall thin woman, she was even more impeccably turned out than normal. The hair that was visible beneath her lace edged cap was streaked with grey. Luke always found it hard not to think of her as the head of the nursery she had been when he was a boy.

"Three guests did you say, my lord?" Her voice sounded higher pitched than normal and there was curiosity in her eyes before she lowered her gaze.

Luke's lips twitched. Mrs Cater knew very well how many and must be impatient to know who the third guest was. His marriage to Kitty would save him from the inevitable speculation of his servants as well as of the Ton.

"Yes, Mrs Cater. My aunt and sister are bringing the family friend they have staying with them, Miss Davenport."

"I see. We've tried to provide a selection for luncheon that will appeal to ladies of all age groups."

Mrs Cater seemed to quiver, whether from dread or excitement he wasn't sure. It was rare that he entertained at home except for male friends so it was hardly surprising that she should wonder. It might be better to take her into his confidence.

"Come into the library for a moment, Mrs Cater."

He ushered her in and closed the door behind him. "I know this won't go beyond this room but as my housekeeper you ought to know. Miss Davenport has done me the honour of accepting my hand in marriage."

Mrs Cater smiled. "Let me wish you every happiness, my

lord."

"Thank you. We haven't announced our betrothal yet. I need to travel up north to speak to her brother first. I would be grateful if you would keep this news to yourself."

"Of course, my lord."

Luke smiled and shook his head as he watched her depart. He had no idea how long they could keep it secret. Indeed, Sir Walter Greenough might have spread the news already, although he doubted that. He ran lightly up the stairs to his dressing room to wash the ink off his hands and arrived back at the foot of the stairs at the same moment the butler opened the door to his visitors. He stayed back in the shadows for a moment, unable to take his eyes off Kitty. The soft green of her gown, with the darker green of the spencer jacket she wore over it, suited her to perfection. She looked fresh and natural as she greeted the housekeeper. Her smile seemed confident, but now he knew her better he could tell she was nervous from the hint of a frown that wrinkled her brow.

He stepped forwards as Mrs Cater rose from a deep curtsey, his gaze firmly fixed on Kitty. She looked up and smiled at him. He took a sharp breath. Why did her presence in a room set it aglow for him? He greeted his guests and led them into the breakfast room once the butler had taken their outdoor wear.

"I thought we would eat in here if you have no objection, Kitty. Enstone House only has one dining room and it's big enough to accommodate a state banquet." He pointed at the main window with a view over a small but pretty garden. "This is one of my favourite rooms, partly because of the view."

Kitty looked around the sun-filled room. "It's lovely, I'm perfectly happy to eat in here unless anyone else objects."

The other two shook their heads. Luke showed his aunt to

the chair on the right-hand side of his place at the head of the table. Grace took to the chair to her right. He placed his hand on Kitty's elbow and led her to the chair to his left. Touching her sent a jolt of energy through him and from the pretty blush colouring her cheeks she must have had a similar reaction.

Once they were all seated, Lady Grant studied the laden table. "You have very nearly managed a banquet in here, Luke."

Luke laughed out loud. "My servants are determined to make a good impression on you all it would seem."

Grace snorted. "For heaven's sake, Luke, they've met us before. This is all for Kitty's benefit."

He heard Kitty gasp and smiled at her. "I have a confession to make. I felt that Mrs Cater had guessed that you were a special visitor, Kitty. I decided it was best to take her into our confidence." A pang of anxiety hit him. "I hope you don't mind. I'm sure that she will keep it to herself until I announce our betrothal formally to the staff."

"I don't mind at all. That was well done of you, Luke. She has gone to so much trouble for a simple luncheon party that she must have at least suspected. It's important to be on good terms with your housekeeper."

After lunch Luke offered to take them on a tour of the house. Aunt Theo and Grace exchanged glances and Aunt Theo suggested that he take Kitty whilst they investigated his library.

"What do you say, Kitty?"

Kitty looked uncomfortable but took his arm readily enough. "That would be interesting."

Grace pushed him gently between the shoulder blades. "Off you go then before Mrs Cater comes in and offers to show Kitty around."

Luke laughed and shook his head at her but set off with Kitty on his arm.

"Let me show you the ballroom first. It hasn't been used for some time. We decided it would be easier to have Grace's come out ball at Aunt Theo's. I suppose we will have to hold a ball here once we're married."

He threw open the doors to a large room, with long windows down to the floor along two sides and a minstrel's gallery at the far end. All the sofas and chairs around the edges of the dance floor were shrouded in Holland covers.

"Do you like it?"

"It's a beautiful room. I like the two big chandeliers down the centre of the room. I can imagine this room looks spectacular when they're lit up. We must host a ball but could we leave it until I am used to running such a large household do you think?"

"I don't see why not. If we have a bridal trip it will take us nearly to the summer recess and I expect to retire to the country. A ball planned for the beginning of next year's season should suffice."

He led her onto the dance floor. "I've never thought to ask you how proficient you are at dancing."

Kitty's eyes lit up. "I love dancing. I shared a dancing master with some friends before we left Davenport Court. I'm out of practice but I know all the usual dances."

"We have some time. Why don't I take you through a few of my favourites?"

"Yes please. I should enjoy that." She licked her lips and smiled up at him.

Lord was she aware of the effect drawing attention to her lips had on him. He cursed the modern fashion for tight fitting pantaloons. There was only one thing for it. He led her into a cotillion sequence, where talking her through the positions the other three couples in a set would be was so complicated that he was forced to concentrate. Even then the constant joining of their hands proved a distraction. She was light on her feet and had a strong sense of rhythm. They stayed in time despite the lack of music. They danced until they were breathless and he called a halt.

"You are a beautiful dancer, Kitty."

"Thank you. I do enjoy it but I will need some practice before I dance in public."

He feathered a kiss on her forehead. "I'm sure I can arrange to find time to practice with you."

She dropped him a deep curtsy. "Thank you, my lord." Her eyes sparkled as she smiled up at him.

A shaft of sunlight highlighted her figure as she rose from the curtsey. He caught his breath and placed her hand on his arm. The desire to kiss her thoroughly was almost overwhelming.

"Let me show you around the rest of the ballroom. It takes up the entire end of this wing of the house, so there are gardens on each side. It was added as an afterthought. It's more usual to have the ballroom on the first floor, sometimes with steps down to the gardens if there are any."

Kitty gazed through the nearest window. "It's beautiful. I'm amazed to see how large an area the house and gardens cover."

"Enstone House is an old-fashioned mansion with plenty of space."

Kitty laughed. "Davenport Court is a good size but nothing like as large as this." A shadow crossed her face.

He rested a hand on her shoulder. "It's a shame Davenport

Court wasn't entailed."

"I know. That's unusual isn't it? Funnily enough, losing it doesn't bother Edward as much as it does me."

"It may bother him a lot. Men tend to hide their feelings." The hand on his arm tightened its grip.

"Is that what you do, hide your feelings? You seem to harbour considerable anger towards your father." She stroked his forearm.

Luke sighed. "He was a hard man but I am old enough not to let that bother me. Come, let's enjoy the present as well as we may. I wonder if we might arrange to buy Davenport Court back."

Kitty shook her head. "Edward won't want to be any more beholden to you than he has to be."

"I know. You have a very sound brother. Now that's enough about everyone else."

He turned and pulled her into a curtained alcove. "We had better join the others soon but I think we have time for a kiss. What do you say?"

Kitty nodded and pressed her body against his. He lowered his head and moulded his lips to hers. She opened her mouth to him and he lost himself in the kiss. She wound her arms around his neck and his hands caressed her back almost of their own volition. He let them slip lower until they cupped her buttocks and drew her closer still. His pulse pounded in his ears. This was madness. He had better stop soon.

He returned his hands to her back and gently slowed the kiss. It was a few moments until he found the strength to pull away. Kitty sighed and stepped back slightly. She licked her lips and gave him a tremulous smile. Her eyes held a faraway expression. She blinked a few times and pulled away further. He longed to have her back into his embrace but reason prevailed.

He gave a shaky laugh. "I hope Garner has managed to find out what I need to know to get us a marriage licence. The sooner I have you to myself the happier I shall be."

"So shall I. Now we have made the decision I want to get on with the work of adjusting to such a different life."

He studied her face intently. "I haven't frightened you with my ardour, have I?"

Kitty shook her head. "Of course not, I'm sure you will be kind to me. Aunt Lucy explained what I needed to know about marriage most carefully." She smiled. "What she didn't tell me was how exciting a kiss could be."

He laughed. She must have felt that pull of attraction between them too. "Did she explain what kisses might lead to, sweetheart?"

"Yes she did. Even if she hadn't, living and working on a horse breeding farm I could hardly fail to have a good idea of what's involved." She looked away from him, chin down.

Luke cringed. Of course she would know and she must have realised how aroused he was. He gave a mental shrug. His embarrassment didn't matter. Something was bothering her.

"If you aren't worried about the physical side of marriage, what is worrying you?"

She stared at the floor and hesitated for a moment. Then she raised her eyes to his and took a deep breath.

"This must sound feeble to you but I'm afraid I might not be able to run your household and perform all the other public duties you will need of me. At least not perform them to the standard you are entitled to expect."

He brushed a stray lock behind her ear and adjusted his

cravat. "Let's go back into the ballroom proper so we won't be found here."

He tucked her hand through his elbow and took her on a slow promenade around the room.

"Now tell me why you feel you aren't good enough to be my wife."

She was silent for a few moments. "I haven't been brought up to occupy a great position." She pointed her free arm around the room. "Even your London House is at least twice the size of Davenport Court. I dread to think how big your country home is."

"Ah. You have me there. My main residence is quite large. We don't have to live there. I have several smaller residences, including Shepley Hall. I spent most of my childhood as part of Aunt Theo's household. Enstone Court has never been home to me."

She stroked his arm. A comforting, consoling caress of the sort Aunt Theo had ministered his younger self with, when he had let her. Kitty was such a caring woman and would make a wonderful mother. Luke's chest tightened and he struggled to breathe for a moment. He might have children of his own. How did he feel about that? He shook his head in an effort to shut out the powerful emotions the thought roused in him. He loved children but what sort of a father would he make if he took after his own father.

Kitty's voice made him jump. "Was your childhood so very bad?" she asked, softly.

"No of course not. I was very lucky to be part of a loving family. I simply meant to reassure you that you don't need to live anywhere that makes you uncomfortable."

"I don't expect to be uncomfortable, exactly. I'm worried

that I won't make a very good Viscountess."

"I'm sure you'll find that you go on very well once you have found your feet. You have the knack of earning the loyalty of your staff."

He kissed her briefly on the lips. "We had better join the others. You can practice your skills on Mrs Cater. I'm sure she is itching to show you around the bedrooms."

Kitty laughed. "It might be better if she shows me that part of the house."

"Infinitely better."

* * *

As Luke had predicted, Mrs Cater was hovering in the hallway, with a worried frown, when they left the ballroom. She looked more nervous than Kitty felt and her ready sympathy was quickly engaged. The arrival of a new mistress must be a worry for the servants.

Luke drew them to a halt. "Ah, Mrs Cater. I've been neglecting my other guests. I would be obliged if you would show Miss Davenport around the other floors so I can attend them."

"Certainly, my lord."

"Thank you. We will be in the red drawing room when you have finished."

Luke's departure left Kitty feeling bereft. His kisses had left her wanting so much more. She forced a smile for Mrs Cater.

"Where would you like to start, Miss Davenport?"

"Perhaps with the reception rooms on the next floor? I gather the layout of Enstone House is rather unusual, with the ballroom on the ground floor."

Her ploy worked. Mrs Cater launched into a history of the house and started to look a lot more relaxed. Every room they looked at was spotlessly clean with not a speck of dust in sight. Whatever problems Luke's father had experienced with his agent and secretary didn't extend to his housekeeper.

Oh heavens. Mrs Cater probably knew all about the family being supported by Luke's father. She pressed her lips together as heat swamped her cheeks. There was no point being embarrassed by it. If she didn't mention it then the housekeeper wouldn't. The Spencers had accepted her authority perfectly readily. She ignored a little voice pointing out that they were in imminent dread of being turned off when the Davenport family arrived. They would have been glad to welcome any family.

They reached the red drawing room. Kitty gasped at the beauty of it. Heavy damask curtains, in a deeper shade of red, complemented the flocked wallpaper. It was an attractive room but the addition of dark, solid looking furniture resulted in a rather masculine effect.

"This looks as if it has been redecorated quite recently, Mrs Cater."

"It hasn't long been finished. Lord Enstone chose the decoration. Let me show you the blue drawing room. That hasn't been touched since Lord Enstone's mother died."

Kitty followed Mrs Cater to the next room. Kitty wandered around trying to imagine Luke's mother sitting in there playing with a golden-haired little boy. All the furniture was distinctly feminine down to the exquisite little writing desk.

"Oh. This is so lovely."

"I'm afraid it's rather faded, but the late lord didn't want anything changed."

"That's the problem with blue isn't it? It does fade very easily. This must have been glorious."

"It was beautiful and such a happy room."

Mrs Cater lowered her eyes but not before Kitty saw a gleam of speculation in them. To live here successfully she would have to make this room her own at some point. She would have to tread carefully.

"It's sounds as if you have worked here for a long time, Mrs Cater."

"I joined the staff at Enstone Court when I was fourteen, Miss Davenport. I moved here as a senior maid a few years later. I was promoted to housekeeper shortly afterwards."

Kitty smiled. "I can see why from the standard of care you have given this house. I managed my father's property after my mother died when I was sixteen but it was nowhere as near big as this. I'm grateful to find I shall have someone so expert to guide me."

"It's good of you to say so, Miss."

"Not at all. Thank you for entertaining me. I am impressed with the cook too. It must have been quite a task to produce such a banquet for lunch at very short notice."

Mrs Cater beamed at her. "Thank you. I'll pass your compliment to cook."

"Have you ever wanted to go back to Enstone Court?"

"The old lord rarely went there after his wife died. This was his main residence and there has only been a small staff at the court ever since."

Mrs Cater pushed an invisible stray hair back into her cap. She appeared calm but her clenched fists, half hidden behind her starched, white apron gave her away. This must be really difficult for her.

"I see. I'm not sure where we will spend our time but I promise to make sure Lord Enstone consults you before we make any decisions that might affect the staff. We wouldn't want to lose your expertise and loyalty."

They heard voices and Kitty looked up to see Luke approaching with a lady on each arm.

"Thank you, Miss Davenport. I'll leave you to your guests." Mrs Cater bobbed a curtsey and scurried away.

Luke ushered the other two into the red drawing room. "Come and see what you think of my refurbishment."

He left them to it and caught Kitty's hands before she could enter the room. "Thank you, Kitty. It seems you have managed to put Mrs Cater's mind at rest when I could not. What did you say to her? She looked worried when I told her of your visit."

"I asked about your main residence and realised she was worried what would happen to her if we spent a lot of time there. I promised to make sure you would consult her about any decisions."

"I said as much but it made no difference. She must have taken to you. She was extremely kind to me as a boy and I didn't like to see her so worried."

"I also told her we wouldn't want to lose her expertise."

Luke frowned. "She could never have thought that I would turn her off could she?"

"I'm ashamed to say that I was so embarrassed by the thought of her knowing about my family's dependence on your father that it didn't occur to me at first. Servants can easily find themselves in a precarious position when a master takes a new wife."

Luke put an arm around her waist and drew her close. Her pulse raced as his breath skittered over the sensitive skin of her neck.

"There, you see, you understand people. You will be a great mistress of our households, Kitty. I told you not to worry."

* * *

It was nearly time to leave for Cathlay House. Kitty walked slowly down the stairs to join Lady Grant and Grace, fingering her mother's pearls to calm herself. Wearing a new evening gown of blush pink silk that had arrived just in time, she was as ready as she would ever be to meet the Duke and Duchess of Cathlay. Luke was a viscount and he needed a wife who could hold her own in company. She mustn't let him down but she was ill-equipped for society gatherings. Supper at the vicarage wasn't much of a preparation. The room moved around her for a second. What was she thinking? She had been raised as a lady. All she had to do was be polite and attentive.

Kitty walked into the drawing room to find Lady Grant and Grace the only occupants. She had barely joined Grace on a sofa when Harvey announced Luke. She blinked as he entered the room. He was magnificent from his shiny boots to the intricate neck cloth at his throat and yet everything about him was quiet elegance. He swept them all a deep bow and walked across to her. His warm smile as he looked down at her sent a rush of heat flooding through her body. For a moment they seemed alone in the room apart from the louder than normal ticking of the grandfather clock. Grace jumped up to give him a hug and the spell was broken.

Luke held Grace away from him and laughed. "Steady on, Grace. You'll ruin my cravat. Garner said it's the best result I've managed."

Grace stood back and swept a glance brim-full of mischief towards Kitty. "I recognise that style. Now let me think. Ah, I remember, it's called Trone d'Amour. How fitting, Luke."

A deep red blush spread across Luke's face and Kitty felt her own cheeks heat up at this mention of love.

Lady Grant rose and tapped Grace on the arm with her fan. "Grace, you are incorrigible. Let's go and ask Harvey to send for the carriage and give your brother some peace." She swept out of the room with Grace on her arm.

Kitty rose, keeping her eyes lowered. She gasped for breath as a strong arm encircled her and she was pulled against Luke's chest.

Luke studied her face, his eyes dancing. "Now that my sister has ruined my cravat there is nothing to stop us enjoying a little dalliance."

Kitty's lips parted of their own accord and she went on tip toe to reach up to him. Luke's lips found hers and Kitty gave herself up to a rush of emotion. Her body tingled and she pressed against him, as he deepened the kiss. He jumped back quickly but not before she was aware of parts of him a young lady was not supposed to know about. He was definitely aroused by her. Aunt Lucy's explanation of what to expect when she married came to mind. She had a good idea of what happened physically. Luke broke away from the kiss and she gasped. Of course, that must have been why he had stopped so abruptly when she had been on his lap earlier. There was so much she didn't know. Aunt Lucy had forgotten to mention the feeling of restless excitement simply being near someone could create.

"Kitty, I think it might be best if I procure a special licence if I can. Garner tells me it gives us more choice of wedding venues than a bishop's licence. What do you think?"

"Whatever you think is best, as long as we don't have banns. Sir Walter might hear of it and make trouble if we do." She smiled at him. "Does a special licence mean we can be married quickly?"

He laughed. "Yes, it does, but I'm sure you will still want me to go and fetch Edward from school so he can be there for our wedding."

"Oh, yes please. I hope we don't have to wait for the summer holidays."

"I've made a call on my bank. I'll get him off school early even if I have to promise to fund a new roof or whatever." He gave her a wicked smile that left her breathless. "Once we are married, we can forget about Sir Walter."

They heard footsteps in the hall and jumped apart. Harvey reached the doorway.

"The coach has arrived, my lord."

"Thank you, Harvey." Luke held her back with a hand on her arm. When Harvey was out of sight he bent down and his breath tickled her ear. "But that's not the only reason we should marry quickly."

Kitty went out to the carriage on Luke's arm consumed by a dream of a blissful marriage. Luke's interest in her was real and vital and exciting. Surely he would fall in love with her with that between them? He handed her up into the carriage and his touch sent a thrill through her. The feel of his thigh pressed against hers as he jumped in and took the seat beside her caused her heart to skip a beat. She sat back and closed her eyes. Grace started a conversation about the Duchess of Cathlay and Kitty's happy mood evaporated. How was she going to cope with such exalted company?

Her first view of Cathlay House did nothing to reassure her. It was a mansion of enormous proportions, the largest she had seen since her arrival in London. Their carriage drew up before an imposing door, flanked by two liveried footmen. Kitty stared up at the handsome building in awe as Luke handed Lady Grant and Grace down from the carriage. When it was her turn, Luke lifted her down as he had that first day on their journey to London. He tucked her arm through his and led her up the steps to the door behind the others. His solid presence at her side was reassuring.

Her breathing slowed down but her relief was short-lived when they were shown into a handsome red drawing room of regal proportions. A tall man, with an upright bearing, rose to greet them. He had to be the Duke. Without the grey at his temples he could have been mistaken for a much younger man. The Duchess rose too and walked towards them. She was dark haired and had the deepest blue eyes Kitty had ever seen. Both were smiling and the tightness at the back of Kitty's neck eased. She copied Lady Grant and Grace in curtseying to the pair. She rose and forced a smile for the Duchess, who placed a hand on each of her shoulders.

"My word, I would have known you for the daughter of Henry and Amelia anywhere. You have such a look of your mother."

"You knew my mother well?"

The Duchess led her to a sofa. "Yes. We were all three at school together, your mother, Lady Grant and I. It's delightful to meet you." She looked across at Lady Grant. "We must find a good match for Amelia's daughter."

Luke was talking to the Duke and Kitty couldn't stop herself from looking at him. He smiled at her before bowing before the Duchess of Cathlay. He glanced at his aunt, who nodded.

"It seems you have either guessed our secret or are just about to. Miss Davenport has done me the honour of accepting a marriage proposal from me. We don't intend to announce our betrothal until I have posted up north to see her brother."

The Duchess shook her head at him. "Such topsy-turvy manners you young people have. Would it not have been better to ask his permission first?"

Kitty tried and failed to smother a laugh at the thought of Edward being responsible for her. What would the Duchess think of her? "Edward is eight years younger than me and I am his guardian, rather than the other way around."

Luke bowed again. "I intend to visit him at his school and ask for his approval of the match."

"Ah, I see. That should be sufficient in the circumstances. My memory must be failing for I was sure that Amelia had a son first but it was years ago."

"I did have an older brother but he only lived a few months. After me, there wasn't a live child until Edward was born."

"I am sorry. If dear Cathlay hadn't been Scottish, with his main residence in the highlands, I daresay I would have kept in touch better."

A dark-clad butler entered and announced dinner. Luke offered his arm to the duchess who waved him away.

"Let's not stand on ceremony tonight, Lord Enstone. You should take your betrothed into dinner."

"Thank you, Your Grace."

Fortunately, Luke waited for the others to leave the room before tucking her arm through his. Now that she had calmed down after the Duchess's friendly welcome, she was acutely aware of him. She caught her breath at the feel of his body pressed against hers from shoulder to hip. Why hadn't she thought to provide herself with a fan? Her cheeks were on fire. She risked a glance at Luke and he smiled at her. His eyes sparkled as he captured her gaze but he looked away quickly and briefly patted the hand that rested on his arm. He leaned towards her and his lovely scent of spice and citrus seemed stronger than ever. There was a new edge to it, a hint of warm male. His free hand pulled at his neck cloth, until she longed to smooth it down. She studied his face. His cheeks seemed redder than normal. He drew in a shuddering breath.

"We had better join the others. I hope you're not feeling too overwhelmed."

Kitty laughed aloud. "The Duke and Duchess are quite intimidating and yet I sense they are good people."

"You're braver than me. They terrified me when we first met, but yes they are very good people."

He dropped a kiss on her forehead and Kitty's cheeks felt ready to combust as she saw the butler enter and back his way out of the room. Luke turned towards the door in time to see him disappear.

Kitty laughed up at him. "We really do need to join the others."

Her feet seemed to be floating as they made their way to the dining room. Could it be that Luke had formed a tendresse for her already? It seemed unlikely but oh how happy she would be if he had. It had taken her time to realise it, but she had fallen for his charm on their journey to London. It wouldn't do to get too excited. She didn't deserve to be that lucky and yet how else could she interpret his actions? The glowing eyes, fidgeting and high colour reminded her forcibly of their first footman at Davenport Court, when he was in the presence of her mother's lady's maid before they married.

Their heated exchanges were probably the result of nothing more than desire. Did their tender kisses mean anything more? It was too soon to know. She must be the best wife she could be and hope that the regard he had shown did indeed deepen into love. The Duchess of Cathlay had been taken up with learning about her family's history and seemed disposed to think well of her, despite her inappropriate laughter. All eyes turned towards them as they entered the dining room and Kitty regretted the lack of a fan for her heated cheeks once again.

The room was much smaller than Kitty had expected, presumably a family dining room. The Cathlays didn't stand on ceremony and they ignored the ends of the table, three places had been set on either side.

"I hope you will forgive us using this room, Miss Davenport," the Duchess said. "As we are a small party, almost family, it is so much cosier. We usually converse across both sides of the table when we dine amongst family and friends in here."

Kitty was seated next to the Duchess of Cathlay with Luke on her other side. Opposite her was the Duke with Lady Grant on one side and Grace on the other, opposite to the Duchess. Grace slipped into a deep conversation with the Duke of Cathlay as soon as they were seated. If only she had Grace's poise. Luke must have felt her discomfiture. He gave her hand a squeeze, under cover of the table, before engaging his aunt in conversation.

Kitty turned towards the Duchess. Her bearing and firm voice suggested a formidable woman. Kitty smiled at her and received a smile in return.

"Do you live mainly in Scotland, Your Grace?"

"We spend the summer months at Cathlay Castle and often have Christmas there. I would say we are in London for at least half the year. My husband is very much involved in politics."

Kitty couldn't remember any mentions of the Duke of Cathlay on the government benches, despite reading the squire's newspapers regularly when they had lived at Davenport Court. Could she risk assuming he was a member of the opposition? Luke answered for her.

"The Duke of Cathlay is a leading opposition politician, Kitty. He is determined to have me on the Whig benches as soon as may be."

Kitty gave a shaky laugh. "I should think so too, my lord. My mother would have approved."

The Duchess laughed. "She would have indeed. I remember your grandfather. He and Cathlay would have got on well. Cathlay mentioned that you have no relatives except for your brother. That must be difficult for you. Are there no cousins alive on your mother's side?"

"I don't think so. My mother inherited from a family trust set up by my grandfather. I don't know to any living relatives of his, but my father had no contact with my mother's family so I can't be sure."

Oh heavens, why had she said that? The Duchess would think she was an heiress unless she told her about her father losing everything they owned. The soup arrived and provided relief in the form of a pause in the conversation.

The Duchess lowered her soup spoon. "As a member of a large family, with several children of my own, I find it hard to imagine having no relatives. What about the other side of your mother's family?"

"My aunt's man of business did make enquiries to see if there were any cousins on my maternal grandmother's side but he couldn't find any."

The Duchess waited until a footman had removed their dishes and patted her hand.

"At least you will be able to share Luke's family."

The rest of the meal passed smoothly. There was so much she didn't know that was important to Luke. She must learn as much as she could from Lady Grant and Grace. It seemed the Duchess of Cathlay was disposed to like her, for her mother's sake, but other society ladies might not be so forgiving if she got things wrong.

Chapter Twelve

The ladies left them to their port and Luke obeyed an invitation from the Duke to move to the seat next to him. Kitty had been a little overawed to start with but she had acquitted herself well. With Aunt Theo to guide her she would do very well in society. He accepted a glass of port and held it up to the light from the chandelier suspended above the table.

"There's a lovely colour to this." He took a sip. "Yes, an excellent port."

The Duke laughed. "I expect you've got some in your cellar. It's from one of the batches Nat had delivered for us. He and Eliza are so happy we couldn't have wished for a better brother-in-law. I'm pleased to see you and Miss Davenport have the same aura about you. I'm glad that you have found a love match."

Luke was stunned into silence for a moment. "You mistake the matter. This is a marriage of convenience although I hope my betrothed is as fond of me as I am of her."

The Duke's mouth dropped open and he rubbed at his bottom lip. "Apologies. I was certain it was a love match after seeing you together."

Luke found himself explaining the circumstances of their

betrothal. His anger revived at the memory of seeing Sir Walter Greenough forcing his attentions on Kitty.

The Duke gave a shout of laughter. "From your fierce expression I suspect you ejected the man quite forcibly?"

Luke grinned. "I picked him up by his coat and slammed him against the nearest wall. He looked as shocked as I felt."

"How could any young lady fail to fall in love with you after you championed her like that? I wonder how long Greenough has lived near to Shepley Hall."

"I'm not sure. Kitty said he had been making a nuisance of himself for weeks but he could have moved in months before that."

The Duke stroked his chin. "There was another reason we invited you tonight. Augusta remembers that Amelia's family were ambitious for her. They thought she could have made a better match. She received an allowance from the family estate after marriage but of nothing like the amount it could have been."

Luke stiffened. It felt wrong to be discussing Kitty's finances without her permission but the Duke looked like he had more to tell. "Kitty told me that they were not particularly well off."

The Duke nodded. "The thing is after our conversation the other night I consulted my man of business. His discretion is absolute. A friend of his has been looking for Miss Davenport ever since the family disappeared from Davenport Court. She is the sole beneficiary of her mother's family trust."

"Kitty mentioned the allowance but her father lost it as well as Davenport Court in that card game with Lord Sewell."

The Duke poured him another glass of port. "Legally, it wasn't Sir Henry Davenport's to lose. The terms of the trust were that Kitty should carry on receiving the allowance after her mother's death until whichever event comes first, her marriage or her twenty fifth birthday. At that point she, or her husband, becomes the owner of all the assets."

Luke shook his head. "Why didn't my father sort this out for them? I believe he visited Kitty's aunt, Lady Swift, several times before her death."

"I didn't know your father well. He was something of a recluse in his later years. Lady Grant might be able to answer that question better than me."

Luke blinked and studied his glass. What was he doing voicing such private thoughts? "You're right, of course. Thank you for the information about Kitty."

"Think nothing of it. Here's a card for my man of business." The Duke reached into his waistcoat pocket. "He won't pass any information about Miss Davenport on to his friend until he hears from you."

"I'll talk to Kitty about it first." Luke studied the card. "This reminds me of something else I have been meaning to do. Would your man take me on as a client?"

"He is very busy but I'm sure he will be able to accommodate a friend of mine." He stroked his chin. "You may have to make do with his son, which would be no hardship as he is showing great promise."

"I'm sure he will be excellent if you recommend him."

"I'll send word to him."

"Thank you again." Luke smiled. "When it's agreed and my very efficient secretary is back I'll have them draw up the marriage settlements for my approval."

The Duke laughed. "I see no problem. I'll have a message sent round with his details."

"I am so much in your debt I really must find time to take

my seat in the Lords to repay you. I have a lot to do getting my affairs in order but I will rely on you to tell me which debates I should make sure I attend."

"I will certainly do that but I imagine your wedding will take up your time for the moment." He rubbed his chin. "Nothing has come to light on Lord Sewell by the way, but I have a vague memory of hearing some unsavoury stories about the new Lord Swift."

"That's interesting. He didn't treat Kitty's aunt very well. I believe he is a distant relative. I'm hoping Bright has turned something up on Lord Sewell and I may have a possible lead amongst my army friends on him."

They sat quietly savouring their port. The Duke must have mistaken his relief at avoiding the marriage market as something stronger. He hadn't known Kitty long enough to be in love with her after all. For now, he was safe. His longing to be with Kitty was natural in a young man about to marry who had been celibate for a long while. Just thinking about her sitting on his lap made his pulses race. She was adorable and he would be kind to her but he must keep his distance mentally. Loving someone laid you open to rejection. He had enough of that at his father's hands. Strong emotional ties were best avoided. Even with his aunt and uncle he had shared their attention with his cousins and it hadn't seemed so risky loving them.

He didn't doubt that Kitty would have got a job as a governess or some such rather than ask him for help for herself. She adored her brother and had thought only of him. If she had children she would want them to be safe from the sort of childhood he had endured. That wasn't fair to his aunt and uncle and his cousins. They had loved him unconditionally and helped him to grow up to be a decent man but it had never been enough to make up for the endless rejections from his father. He closed his eyes for a moment in a vain effort to block out the memories of his father's searing words every time he had tried to spend time with him. He emptied his glass at the same time as the Duke.

"Perhaps we should join the ladies now?"

The Duke smiled at him. "We should. I'm sure the ladies are eagerly awaiting our presence."

Luke smiled back and hoped his colour wasn't too high. Would Kitty be eagerly awaiting him? He almost groaned out loud. Why had he let himself get so carried away? It was going to be difficult giving Kitty enough attention to keep her happy without raising too many expectations in her and he hadn't made a good start. The Duke rose and he followed. With luck they would have children quickly and all her attention would be taken with them. He would take up his seat in the Lords and work diligently. That would keep him from home a good portion of the time. Away from Kitty as much as possible he wouldn't have too much opportunity to fall in love with her. Although any children she had would be adorable and he must make sure to spend some time with them. He wanted to be able to support them if anything happened to Kitty. Not like his father, who had been so lost without his love that his son had been a nuisance to him.

Kitty only had eyes for him when they entered the drawing room. Oh Lord, she wasn't falling in love with him, was she? That would make things complicated. The Duke of Cathlay had said any young woman would fall in love with a man who had championed her against Sir Walter in the way he had. His stomach felt empty despite the meal he had consumed. He made a point of speaking with Aunt Theo first of all. Eventually, he felt obliged to join Kitty. She smiled up at him with a dreamy expression. Her smile faded to be replaced with a pinched look.

He must be giving her the severe expression that had served him well in keeping discipline in the army. He forced his features into a smile. His family honour was at stake as well as Kitty's reputation and the last thing he wanted to do was frighten her off. She patted the sofa next to her. All eyes were on them and he sat down but was careful to leave a few inches between them. Even so he could smell her floral perfume. Delicate and yet summery it suited her well. Perhaps he should overcome his scruples and change his mind about taking a mistress. He almost laughed out loud. What was the matter with him? He could have a happy marriage without falling hopelessly in love with his wife like his father had.

Kitty seemed to relax. He deepened his smile. The embroidery on her gown caught his eye.

"You look lovely in that pretty gown. I forgot to ask you how the shopping expedition went."

Kitty stroked the skirt of the pink gown. "It's beautiful isn't it? Lady Grant found a modiste with some gowns already made up. This one needed a little adjustment but they sent it round in time for this evening, which was most obliging of them."

Luke hid a smile. A protégé of Aunt Theo, especially one who needed a whole new wardrobe, was bound to get excellent service.

"That was good, although you looked lovely in the cream and gold gown you wore last night. A girl as pretty as you would look good wearing anything."

He sat back stunned at himself. She was pretty, beautiful even. Her face was pink, presumably from gratification and

161

she seemed at a loss for words. He must have been in a foul mood when he arrived at Shepley Hall to think her plain. He hadn't treated her very well.

"Did you find everything you wanted?"

Kitty blushed even deeper. "To be frank with you, I'm rather concerned at how much I bought. Lady Grant said it was all essential but I feel rather guilty at being so extravagant."

Luke smiled. "Whatever you've bought I'm sure it's not as much as Grace generally spends on a shopping trip."

"Grace bought a lot less than me. I..." She started to say more but stopped when Luke burst out laughing. "If you mean to tease me, I will say no more except to assure you that I wouldn't have bought the half of it if left to myself."

"If Aunt Theo says you need it then you need it. Grace's bills at the start of the season were huge. Have you had a riding habit delivered yet?"

"No, that had to be ordered from a gentlemen's tailors and it will be some days before it's ready."

"What a shame. I was hoping we could ride together in Hyde Park tomorrow. Would you like me to take you for a drive in my curricle instead?"

Kitty's eyes shone. "Yes please. That would be wonderful."

"That's settled then." He felt uneasy at her enthusiasm but everyone would expect them to spend some time together. Things would be easier once they were married.

"What time should I be ready?" Kitty licked at her bottom lip, only briefly but it was enough to send the blood to his loins. She was simply anticipating the treat of driving with him. He must remember that she was an innocent, albeit an enthusiastic one.

"That's a good question. I have no idea how long I will be at

162

Doctors Commons in pursuit of our marriage licence. I'll have a groom bring a note around to let you know."

"Thank you. What colour are your horses?"

In anyone else that would have been a strange question but it seemed she had her father's interest in horses.

"The pair I have with me in London are greys. Did you help your father with his horses?"

Her face assumed the most animated expression he had seen. She seemed more interested in horses than she had been in his proposal. He squashed the thought immediately. Their betrothal was probably as much of a shock to her as it had been to him.

"Yes. I spent a lot of time with the horses. Father let me study their breeding lines and decide on mating schedules too."

Her face turned scarlet when she realised what she had said. He couldn't suppress a grin. Since he didn't want her to be too dependent on him, why not establish a horse breeding operation for her at Shepley as a wedding present? That would give her something to occupy herself with. Although he was all in favour of Kitty studying mating schedules with him.

"Perhaps we ought to set up a stud farm or would that be something Edward would want to do?"

Kitty held her head on one side. "That's was father's plan for him but I'm not sure it's what Edward wants. He likes horses well enough but I don't think he was ever as interested as me. He was quite young when father lost the estate so I don't know for sure."

"We can discuss it with him. It would be something to do with Shepley Hall."

Kitty beamed at him and held her hands to her cheeks. "That

would be wonderful. Thank you so much for thinking of it, Luke. Even if Edward wants to do the same eventually, it will be some time until he has the opportunity."

"If that's what you want, I'll arrange it as a wedding present."

Kitty's eyes glowed and she beamed at him. "Thank you again. You are so good to me and Robert Spencer will be ecstatic to have some proper horses to look after."

Good Lord, for someone who was trying to establish a little distance he was making a mull of this. Still he had treated her shabbily when he arrived at Shepley Hall and she deserved to have some fun. He couldn't believe how suspicious he had been of her. It seemed father hadn't been quite as cold hearted as he had always thought. The Duchess engaged Kitty in conversation. Kitty seemed quite comfortable with her for such a short acquaintance. If she could cope with one of the most formidable matrons in the Ton then he had no need to worry about how she would settle down in society. Quick-witted as well as decorative, she would make him an excellent wife.

* * *

The following morning Luke had just sat down to break-fast when his butler ushered in Major Ramsay and another, younger man. Luke stood up to greet them.

"This is a pleasant surprise, Ram. What gets you out so early?"

"I've found Captain Meredith and I'm sure you'll be inter-ested to hear what he has to say. Apologies for disturbing your breakfast but we have been summoned to a meeting later this morning and may not have another chance to visit you."

Luke shook hands with Captain Meredith, a tall young man who looked as if he hadn't quite finished filling out his frame.

"I'm happy to meet you and I'm always glad to see Ram whatever the time of day. Why don't we talk over breakfast?"

Captain Meredith looked delighted. "Thank you, yes please. I'm not sure when we will have time for another meal today." He glanced across at Ram. "I wasn't expecting my new orders so soon but I'm more than happy to find I'm back under Major Ramsay's command."

Luke rang for the butler and ordered fresh coffee and more food. A footman arrived with a coffee pot and set two more places within minutes. Luke poured coffee for his guests as they filled their plates at the breakfast buffet. The butler came in with dishes of freshly cooked eggs and cold beef and ham.

"Thank you. I'll ring if we need anything more."

The butler nodded. "Yes, my lord."

Luke waited until the door closed behind him. "Eat up. Help yourselves to whatever you want. We can talk afterwards."

Luke hid his impatience to hear what Captain Meredith had to say. He was contemplating calling for more food when the young man set down his cup and looked directly at him.

"I don't think I can manage another thing but that was excellent. I shall remember this breakfast when we're making do with army rations." His expression became animated. "Major Ramsay says you would like to hear about that damned strange business with Sir Henry Davenport."

Luke leaned forward. "Were you there when he lost Davenport Court?"

"Yes. I was staying with a cousin of mine. I had recovered from a nasty sword wound and had a couple of weeks spare before I could re-join my regiment. Someone invited us to a card game at a local inn." He paused for a moment. "I don't think my cousin really knew the host. Can't think of his name, it sounded a bit like jewel but that wasn't it."

Luke felt suddenly breathless. "Could it have been Sewell?"

Captain Meredith slapped his thigh. "That was it, Sir Peter Sewell. He was staying with friends in the area."

"What exactly was strange?"

"Well, to start with, Davenport had to be persuaded to sit down with the party. He played a few hands and was winning. A damned fine card player I would say. He got up to go and Sewell insisted he have a drink before he went. If I was a betting man, I would say alcohol wasn't the only thing in that wine glass. The man was stone cold sober before he drank it, I swear. Afterwards he was slurring his words. He tried to leave but they pushed him back into his seat. He started losing heavily."

Luke pulled in a deep breath. "Did no one try and put a stop to it?"

"That was the strangest thing. My cousin had gone outside with his pipe and missed it. I protested and told them to leave the man alone. A glass was pressed into my hand and the contents tipped down my throat. The next thing I knew it was much later. I woke up, slumped in an armchair, with my cousin slapping my face to wake me up. All the card players had disappeared."

"Did your cousin see what happened later?"

"No, he wasn't much of a card player. He got into conversation with some friends and stayed outside chatting until he saw Sewell and his friends leave. He thought I had drunk too much and imagined having a drink forced down my throat out of guilt. It was all a bit hazy for a while. I decided he must be right but something felt wrong. Then someone new joined the regiment and mentioned what had happened to Davenport and the memories started coming back. I wrote to my cousin but he'd inherited an estate in Scotland and moved a short while after I stayed with him. He didn't know anything about it."

"Good Lord. Kitty's instincts that he had been cheated were right."

"Kitty?"

"I am betrothed to Miss Kitty Davenport, Sir Henry's daughter. We won't be able to announce it until I have been to see her brother up north, so please say nothing as yet."

Captain Meredith leaned back in his chair. "I see. I am as certain as I can be that Davenport was cheated out of his estate." He pulled out a pocket watch. "We will have to go in a minute but if I remember anything else I could write to you."

"Thank you very much. Could I trouble you to write down what you have said before you leave?"

Captain Meredith looked uncertain but Ram answered for him. "We'll make time. Don't worry, Merry, I'll square it with the colonel if we're late. Luke was a favourite of his."

"Thank you. I'll take my town carriage out and drop you off. I have an errand at Doctors Commons this morning." Luke ignored a grin from Ram. "Let's go into the library."

Luke sent the footman who was by the door to order the carriage. He showed Captain Meredith to a desk with paper, ink and quills set out on it. Ram tapped his shoulder and led him away to stand by the window.

"You're off to procure a special licence then?"

"Yes. If I obtain it today, I intend to set off for Kitty's brother's school tomorrow. With luck they will let him finish the term early so I can bring him back to London with me."

Ram beamed at him. "I can't tell you how pleased I am to see you so happy. If this is what being in love does for a man I might start looking around me for a bride of my own."

Captain Meredith called out to say that he was finished and held out the sheet of paper. "There you are. Is this detailed enough?"

Luke went over to him, as much to avoid replying to Ram's comments as to check the document. It was clearly and succinctly written, confirming Luke's impression that Captain Meredith was a highly intelligent young man.

"Thank you. This is exactly what I wanted." He handed it back.

Captain Meredith signed his account of the evening with Sir Henry Davenport with a flourish. "We have no idea where we are being sent yet, but if I'm in England I will be happy to testify if you want to bring the matter to court."

Luke thanked him warmly. "I don't think it will come to that, but I may be able to use your statement as a bargaining tool to try and get the estate back for Sir Edward Davenport, Kitty's brother."

Chapter Thirteen

Kitty awoke to bright sunlight streaming around the edges of the curtains. A maid must have pulled the drapes around the bed back. There was a knock at the door and Betty entered carrying a cup of hot chocolate on a tray.

"Here you are, miss. This will help you wake up." Betty set the tray on a small table and pulled it close to the bed. Kitty sat up and yawned. "Thank you, Betty. What time is it?"

"Nearly eleven o'clock."

"Good heavens. I must have slept deeply. Would you send Annie up to help me dress? Lady Grant will think me so rude."

"Lady Grant said to let you sleep in after such a busy day yesterday." Betty turned shining eyes on her. "Ooh Miss. Viscount Enstone is so handsome."

Annie came into the room. "Betty, you mustn't talk about him like that." She smiled. "Not that I don't agree with you. There is no need for you to rush, Miss Davenport. Her Ladyship said she would have a luncheon set out in the family dining room to make up for you missing breakfast." She threw a severe look at Betty. "That will be all, Betty."

Kitty hid a smile. Annie could be no more than a couple of years older than Betty. She sobered up quickly. Of course,

Annie was anticipating her elevation to the superior position of lady's maid to a viscountess. With so little experience of the aristocracy how on earth would she cope with being Luke's wife? The evening with the Cathlays had been a lot easier than she had expected but then they were close friends of Luke and his family.

The Vicar of Shepley's favourite sermon came back to her. Everything in life had a price. She would have to work hard to be the wife that a man like Luke would expect, in exchange for a good future for Edward and her own security. She had no right to expect anything more but she could hope that love would blossom between them.

"Don't let your chocolate go cold, Miss Davenport."

Kitty came out of her reverie with a start and dutifully sipped at her hot chocolate. Would Luke come to love her? How would she bear it if he didn't? Oh for heaven's sake. He had been so attentive she was worrying about nothing. She shivered in anticipation of the drive around Hyde Park that he had promised her for this afternoon. Would he have the special licence for their wedding that he was hoping to obtain today? Things were moving on so quickly it was difficult to take it all in.

At least she would have a few quiet days whilst Luke went to fetch Edward for the wedding. Luke would surely prevail in persuading the school to release him early. Edward would be happy to miss a few days of school. She drank the last of her chocolate and declared herself ready to get dressed. After luncheon, with an equally sleepy Grace and Lady Grant, Kitty followed the two ladies into the small family sitting room that caught the afternoon sun. Grace looked at her and laughed.

"Your first evening out in London and you look exhausted.

It's fortunate you won't have to run the gauntlet of the likes of Almacks."

Lady Grant laughed out loud. "Oh, Grace, it's not that bad."

Grace rolled her eyes at Kitty. "I tell you it's so deadly I'm hard put to stay awake past nine o'clock. Luke squired me there twice and declared that was enough to do his duty. I told him if I had to suffer he should as well."

"If it's so bad why do you put up with it?"

"That's easy, for Aunt Theo's sake. She meets all her friends there." She sighed. "Of course, it's the done thing to attend Almacks and if I had been denied vouchers I would have been devastated. Not that anyone sponsored by Aunt Theo is likely to be turned down. She knows everyone who matters in the fashionable world."

Lady Grant shook her head at Grace. "I don't believe that's your only reason for going. Admit that you enjoy watching all the manoeuvring by the matrons to find husbands for their charges."

"There is that I suppose. Oh, Kitty, I'm so glad Luke has settled for someone I can have a proper conversation with."

Kitty felt heat rush to her cheeks. Grace sounded so enthusiastic about her for such a short acquaintance. "I hope you won't end up disappointed in me."

Lady Grant moved across to sit by her and took her hand. "I'm sure that could never happen. Don't start worrying that Grace is one of those awful people who have enthusiasms and then drop friends as quickly as they made them. It's rare that she makes a friend but when she does she is steadfast."

"I didn't doubt it but this has all happened so quickly it seems unreal."

Lady Grant patted her hand. "I'm sure it does but everything will soon seem normal to you."

Kitty shook her head. "I don't think it will, but I'm grateful for your support."

Grace laughed. "I know what it is. You're having wedding nerves. It happened to a friend of mine. I'm sure we'll always be friends so don't worry about that."

Kitty smiled weakly. "Thank you, Grace."

They were so kind she felt like crying. She must stop feeling so undeserving and concentrate on the future. Harvey announced Lord Enstone. Luke entered and gave them all a bow. Kitty almost gasped aloud. He looked so handsome in his severe sort of way. He exchanged a few pleasantries before coming across to her.

"I'm a little later than I expected, but we now have a special licence." He patted a pocket in his waistcoat. "That means we can marry wherever we wish. Do you have any preference?"

"The place doesn't matter to me as long as Edward and your family are there."

"I will go and fetch Edward tomorrow. I'm sure Aunt Theo will be able to suggest a church. We had better be off for our drive."

Was it her imagination or was Luke a little aloof today? But then he was hardly likely to kiss her in front of his relatives. She must stop worrying.

"I'll go and fetch my pelisse. I won't keep you waiting long."

Kitty almost ran from the room and up the stairs. She returned to the sitting room in less than five minutes. Luke was seated next to his aunt, with one gleaming boot crossed over the other at the ankles. Kitty held her breath for an instant at the sight of him. He must have sensed her presence as he looked up in mid-sentence. A smile lit up his face and all her doubts vanished, to be replaced by the now familiar feeling of floating a little above the floor.

"My word that was quick. I do like a punctual female." He gave Grace a mock glare as he rose and she burst out laughing. He turned back to Kitty.

"I can see we're going to deal famously together."

Kitty felt flushed with pleasure. She smiled up at Luke and placed her hand through the arm he held out for her. A jolt of heat swept through her at his touch and she missed her step. He kept the arm she was holding steady and caught her free elbow with his other hand. Somehow, she stayed on her feet. He had of necessity turned towards her and she was reminded of his rescue in the library. This time he was wearing different cologne, the tang of citrus was replaced with a more floral scent. She heard his breath hitch but he recovered quickly and they were soon on the way outside. The touch of his hand on her arm sent shivers through her. She studied his horses to distract herself and her attention was caught by the truly splendid pair of matched greys. She was tempted to run her hands over their legs.

She looked up as Luke laughed. "My father would have approved of these. I'll warrant they're fast."

"I could tell you really liked them from your face." He handed her into the curricle. "I imagine your father must have taught you to drive. Would you be comfortable holding the reins whilst I replace my groom?"

Kitty heard a sharp intake of breath from the groom. She laughed. "I'm not sure your groom approves, but yes I'm quite capable of holding them."

The groom shook his head. "They're a bit lively, Miss."

Luke walked around so that he was standing next to the

groom. "Hand the reins to Miss Davenport, Ashton. When you're happy that she is in control of them jump down. I'll see you back at home."

Kitty accepted the reins but the groom's hands hovered nearby, as if he was expecting to have to seize them back. Her skill was tested immediately when the horses took exception to the shouts of a carter as he overtook them.

"Whoa boys." Kitty increased the pressure on the reins, talking to the horses as she did so.

She was gratified to see the groom drop his hands when she got the horses under control. They stood quietly for her as the cart disappeared from view.

"I ain't seen many women who could do that, Miss. Come to think on it, I ain't seen many men who could either." He jumped down, scratching his head.

Luke took his place. "I thought you would be able to drive well, but if I had seen that cart coming I would have waited. That was excellent driving."

He settled himself in the seat and took the reins from her. "We'll have to see about getting you your own carriage once we're married."

Kitty laughed up at him. "Does that mean that, despite my skill, you don't intend to let me drive your horses?"

Luke eased the curricle out into the road and didn't answer immediately. When the horses were settled into their stride he glanced across at Kitty.

"We've a lot to talk about today, but I promise to let you drive them when we have more time."

Kitty sighed. It would be wonderful to drive something more exciting than the old mare at Shepley Hall, but nothing would ever make up for losing Star. They turned into the park. Luke nodded to an acquaintance but made no attempt to stop. He sent his horses trotting down a quieter path.

"We're just before the main rush and it's a cold day, so hopefully it won't get too busy this afternoon." He studied her for a few seconds. "Why so sad at the prospect of finding your own carriage and horses?"

"I shall look forward to it."

"Then what made you look so sad when we were talking about horses?"

They were going to be married and they needed to be honest with each other. She ought to confide in him.

"The prospect reminded me of my riding horse, a mare called Star. She had to be sold with everything else, to cover father's gambling debts. I often think about her and hope she went to a good home."

Luke went past a stationary Landau at a smart trot. "Do you know who bought her? Perhaps we could buy her back."

Kitty leaned towards him and put a hand on his arm. "How I wish we could. I'm not sure who bought her. I couldn't bear to go to the sales. Edward went though, he might know."

"Talking about Edward, now I've got the marriage licence I'll drive up north to his school tomorrow. I shall be away at least a couple of nights but there is nothing else to be done. I was hoping Bright would be back to fetch him but there is no sign of him. In any case, I would like to tell Edward our news personally."

"Thank you. That would be best."

Kitty saw a turbaned matron, in an open carriage, staring openly at her. Heavens, she was still holding onto Luke's arm. She let go of him and moved across the seat a little.

"Oh dear. Did you see that lady staring at me? I hope I

haven't started a scandal hanging onto you like that."

Luke laughed out loud. "If hanging on to a man's arm caused a scandal then there would be hardly any ladies left untouched by it. There may be some rumours about us though. That was Mrs Pryce-Jones, one of the biggest gabsters in London. If you prefer, I can send a notice of our betrothal to the Gazette before I leave tomorrow."

Kitty shivered. "I'd rather you didn't. I don't trust Sir Walter not to try again. Could we simply place a notice after the ceremony?"

Luke took the reins in one hand and squeezed her hand gently with the other. "Of course, that's what I had meant to do. I'm so sorry you were left to deal with that awful man on your own at Shepley Hall. It can't have been easy for you."

Kitty shrugged. "I managed to avoid him mostly. The worst time was when he called when I was out. I arrived back after he had forced his way past Nella into the house. She ran out to warn me but he had the effrontery to pull me down from the gig and try to kiss me in front of her. He trapped my arm against my side so I couldn't even fend him off with my whip. Luckily Robert was near enough to hear the commotion. He came running and had to pull Sir Walter off me." She shuddered. "He really frightened me that day."

Luke put an arm around her shoulder. "What an awful experience for you."

She leaned into him. "Thank you."

"What for?"

"Caring about me."

Luke gave her a half smile. "Your family have had more than your share of bad luck and from what I can see of it you've spent most of your life caring for them. Now it's your turn."

A warm feeling swept over Kitty. It was wonderful to have someone taking such an interest in her. Perhaps this marriage would work out well. She sighed with pleasure and hid a sudden shyness with a smile. They reached the end of the path and Luke removed his hand to replace it on the reins. He steered the curricle on to the main path they had reached. There was more traffic here and Luke nodded to several acquaintances but made no attempt to engage any of them in conversation.

Kitty's eyes were drawn to his hands as he tooled the reins. Even the brown buckskin gloves he wore could not hide the strength in them. He was as skilful a driver as Kitty had seen. Father would certainly have approved of him. His rapport with his horses was obvious. He turned down a quieter path but seemed preoccupied. Kitty waited for him to speak. Eventually he cleared his throat and turned towards her. He opened his mouth but nothing came out. He shut it with a snap and frowned.

Kitty stiffened. Was he about to tell her he would take care of her but he would rather not marry her? His brow cleared and he smiled at her. Kitty let out a breath she hadn't realised she was holding in. How was it that in a few short hours the idea of marrying him had taken such a hold on her that the thought of him changing his mind was unbearable? If that wasn't the problem, he must be gathering his courage to say something romantic. She smiled back at him.

"I've just thought of something that had me wondering. The Duke of Cathlay said that he had heard some lurid tales about the new Lord Swift." Luke looked business-like rather than lover-like.

Kitty tried to blank out her disappointment. She shouldn't be upset that he was taking so much interest in her family's affairs. It showed that he really did care for her.

"I can't say I'm surprised by that. Aunt Lucy was so un-nerved by him she was too frightened to complain when he treated her shabbily. Uncle Rupert was such a sensible man that I couldn't understand how she could have been left so badly off. The new Lord Swift even charged her rent for the dower house. I don't think that's legal."

"You said your aunt used a lawyer. Didn't she ask him about it?"

Kitty twisted a stray strand of hair around her finger. "I'm not sure. I do know that she was overjoyed when she heard from your father, with the offer of Shepley Hall, but she told me to say nothing. We didn't move out until Lord Swift and his family went away."

"Perhaps she simply thought it would be easier that way?"

"I think it was more than that. She made sure that he couldn't trace us by taking a roundabout route so that if anyone saw us they would think we had gone to London. She didn't leave a forwarding address for us either."

"That suggests she felt he was a threat. I wonder if she thought he was a threat specifically to you."

Kitty stared at him. "Why would Lord Swift be a threat to me? She felt he had tricked her into paying rent on the dower house and was afraid he would try and find some way to get her jointure off her. That was all."

"Perhaps but, with your permission, I would like to have aunt's lawyer discreetly questioned. Can you tell me his name?"

"Mr Archibald of Archibald and Pinner. Their offices are in Dowling in Northamptonshire.

"There was something else the Duke of Cathlay told me to do

with your mother's trust fund. I'll tell you more when I return with Edward. The Duke of Cathlay is going to ask his man of business to take me on. I don't trust the one my father had. We can sort out the financial settlements once that's arranged."

Kitty wrinkled her nose. "There aren't any finances to settle."

"I'll settle some money on you whatever happens but we had better go back now. I've a lot to do before I travel tomorrow. I received a message this morning that my secretary is on his way back. He may well already be in London. There are bound to be things he will want me to deal with before I leave."

Luke drove his horses on to the avenue that led to the exit. There were more carriages around now and Luke's attention was taken with wending a passage through them. She would have to wait until they got back to the house to ask him what he meant. A thrill went through her at the prospect of even a few snatched moments between them. Within minutes they pulled up in front of Lady Grant's imposing front door. Luke signalled to the footman who had opened it.

"Help Miss Davenport down if you would." He tossed the young man a coin.

Kitty's spirits plummeted. He had sent his groom home, but why couldn't he at least get the footman to hold the horses so he could hand her down himself? She accepted the hand proffered by the footman and stepped onto the pavement. She glanced back in time to see Luke raise his whip in salute and drive off without looking at her. Why was he in so much of a hurry that he couldn't organise a few minutes with her for a proper farewell?

Her cheeks burned as she walked through the door held by the footman. It felt as if Luke had deliberately avoided being too intimate with her. Perhaps he was regretting his offer of marriage. She sighed and handed her pelisse and gloves to a hovering Harvey. Luke had been so caring when she recounted her ordeal with Sir Walter she ought to be grateful. Many women were forced into marriage with awful men and even if he didn't love her Luke was kind. He was a practical man too and he had been distracted by his secretary's return. He was a busy man, something else she would have to get used to. She ran lightly up the stairs, determined to make the best of things.

* * *

Luke drove home at a steady trot. There was a lot he needed to tell Kitty but it would have to wait until he was back. It was as well not to mention Meredith's account of her father's card game until he knew more. If it proved to be a young man's drunken remembrances, he would have got her hopes up for nothing. He arrived at his mews stable to find Fletcher waiting for him. Fletcher came forward to hold the horses and Luke jumped down.

"Good to see you again."

Fletcher looked gratified. "Thank you, my lord."

Luke signalled to a young groom to take charge of the horses. Once he and another groom had led them away Luke turned back to Fletcher.

"Come into the garden with me where we won't be over-heard."

They went through an iron gate and Luke checked for any servants but the garden was quiet.

"Bright didn't come back with you then?"

Fletcher shook his head. "No. He's staying with the Spencers for now. He followed Sir Walter Greenough all the way to Davenport Court from London. He and Lord Sewell seem to be good friends."

"Good Lord, that's interesting. I wonder."

"Lord Sewell has a terrible reputation in the district but he must know the right people. He's managed to get himself made up to a magistrate."

"Hm. The Duke of Cathlay seemed to think that Sewell was well connected. Did Bright say when he was coming back?"

"No, he's worried about Robert Spencer's position after the incident with Miss Davenport and Greenough with Sewell being a magistrate. He's found out the magistrate at Shepley is a retired military man and he intends to seek him out. If he's helpful and Bright feels it's safe to leave Spencer after talking to him he'll come back then."

Luke scratched his head. Had Sewell put Sir Walter up to pursuing Kitty? Was this all connected to the family trust which still belonged to her? It was good to know that Bright had Sewell in his sights.

"I can see why Bright's worried for Spencer after uncovering Sir Walter's link to Sewell, especially with him being a magistrate. Sir Walter was in London. I didn't know he'd left. I was hoping to see the situation with him resolved once Kitty and I wed. Now I'm not so sure."

Fletcher's eyes opened wide. "I wish you both happy, my lord."

"Ah. You won't have heard about our betrothal. I would appreciate it if you would say nothing about Sir Walter accosting Miss Davenport."

"I'm not one to gabble, my lord. You don't need to ask."

Fletcher's shoulders slumped.

Oh dear, Fletcher had taken offence. He had always been one to keep his own counsel. "I appreciate that, Fletcher."

"Thank you, my lord." Fletcher gave a curt nod. "Bright said to tell you that Mr Watkins, the new agent, has gone on to his next calls. Very impressed with him, Bright was. I liked him too."

"That's good news. I'm lucky to have such an excellent team around me." Luke glanced sideways at Fletcher.

"I'm going north to Northamptonshire tomorrow to fetch Sir Edward Davenport from school so he can attend the wedding. I'm glad you're back in time to come with me."

Fletcher seemed to unbend. "What do you need me to do?"

"First of all, go and get yourself a hot meal. I'm hoping to be back within two or three days but it may take longer. Make provision for at least a week."

"Yes, my lord."

Luke watched Fletcher disappear through the servant's door. He strode up the path that led from the mews to the house, with his thoughts swirling around in untidy groups until he let himself think about Kitty. He could swear that she had looked hurt when he asked the footman to help her down. She was from a family wedded to horses and must have realised he couldn't leave his curricle in the hands of a footman. Perhaps she hadn't heard him tell his groom to go home when he picked her up? That must be it but she knew he had to make an early start in the morning.

He was making excuses. They were betrothed and he couldn't blame her for wanting to spend time with him. His heart raced. As much as he longed to be with her he couldn't risk letting her think theirs would be a close marriage. If he fell in love with her and they had children he would likely react in the same way as his father if anything happened to her. He never wanted to be responsible for putting another human being through what Father had put him through. If he had understood Aunt Theo, grief had been the cause of his coldness to his son. He shook his head to try and forget the number of times he had asked Papa if he could spend at least part of the school holidays with him and been rejected.

One image haunted him. He had arrived back at Aunt Theo's after the summer term to find his father there. His delight had turned to despair when he realised Papa was only stopping one night on his way down to the family estates. He had begged Papa to take him with him only to be met with a curt refusal that had reduced him to tears in front of his cousins. No one teased him about his tears, which only added to the humiliation his twelve year old self had felt. He had never asked his father for anything again.

Luke left his driving coat and gloves with the butler and made for the sanctuary of his library. From the books in the library at Shepley Hall, he and Father had shared a taste in literature. There was so much he didn't know about him and it was too late to put that right. He paced about the room. He was unsettled because marriage was such a big step. That was why he felt so strange. There was a knock at the door and his secretary entered.

"Good to see you, Wallace. Thank you for sending a groom on ahead. How did you leave things at Shepley?"

Luke ushered him to a sofa in front of the fire. "You look as if you have come straight here. Come and get warm."

A deep red blush coloured Duncan Wallace's cheeks. "I'm sorry, my lord. I felt that I should see you before I changed out of my travelling clothes."

"You did right. I have some news for you." Luke went over to a sideboard and poured two brandies. Wallace glanced at him in surprise as he accepted a glass.

Luke grinned. "I suspect you've earned this. I don't suppose you expected to be sent half way around the country, on such strange missions as protecting a servant, when you accepted the job with me."

Wallace grinned back at him. "I was hoping that working for a military man might be a bit more interesting than the usual secretary's job." He paused. "I didn't mean it to sound as if I'm not happy with being a secretary." The ready blush that came with his red hair stained his cheeks again.

Luke laughed out loud. "Don't look so worried. I am very pleased with your work and delighted that you didn't argue when I sent you off to Shepley. I'm sure we will deal well together. I hope so, as I am about to make you very busy."

"You are?"

Luke nodded. "I have become betrothed to Miss Davenport. I'm setting off at first light tomorrow to fetch her brother from school for the wedding."

"Please accept my felicitations, my lord."

"Thank you. I've dealt with a lot of the papers you left for me but there are some I need you to explain to me later. I may be away for three or four days or longer, so best get them out of the way before I go."

Wallace sipped at his brandy. "I've brought back some more papers for you to sign on matters Mr Watkins has dealt with. I have most of them prepared."

Luke bit back a sigh. He needed to get on top of estate matters.

"Excellent. The Duke of Cathlay is arranging for his man of business, or his son, to take over my affairs. They will contact you whilst I'm away. I would like marriage settlements drawn up. I'll give you the details later."

"Yes, my lord." Wallace tossed back the rest of his drink.

"I'll be on my way then. There is a lot for me to do to have everything ready for you." He stuttered to a halt. "That is with your permission, my lord."

"You have it. I like a man with a sense of urgency. Off you go, but make sure you have a meal before you do anything else."

Wallace bowed his way out. Luke watched him go. He had come well recommended but he knew very little about him, apart from his efficiency. Getting to know Wallace better was something else to put on his long list of things to do. He had always made a point of getting to know his men well. Running a noble household was very much like being back in the army, except that he had been promoted to colonel at the very least. He would become accustomed to it all in time.

He found Garner in his room and instructed him to back a bag for him with enough clothes, which he could manage himself, to last for up to a week. Garner gave him a pained look but went off to fetch his travelling portmanteau without commenting but with an audible sniff. Luke ran a hand through his hair. Garner had only just forgiven him for the last time he had been left behind. Perhaps he ought to be firmer with his staff but it wasn't his style. He hated all the ceremony being a viscount entailed.

Luke ran lightly down the stairs to find his butler hovering in the hallway.

"A footman has just arrived with a message from the Duke of Cathlay, my lord."

Luke accepted the note and wandered into the library. He tore it open and scanned the contents. Excellent, he now had a new man of business who had been informed he was to work with Wallace. He sat down at his desk, behind the pile of documents Wallace had waiting for him, and handed him the note.

Luke sighed with relief as he signed the last document in Wallace's pile. "I can look my tenants in the eye now. Well done, Wallace."

Luke walked across to the sideboard in the library and poured out two brandies. He handed one to Wallace and sat down next to him.

"You can have some time off whilst I'm away, but don't forget about the marriage settlements. I want some money settled on my future wife."

He named a sum that made Wallace stare at him. Wallace started to protest but subsided immediately when Luke raised his eyebrows.

"Quite. I gave you the details for my new man of business, didn't I?"

"Yes, my lord."

"Excellent. I'll bid you good night. I intend to make an early start in the morning."

Chapter Fourteen

A trip to Hatchards bookshop the following morning did much to restore Kitty's spirits. Marriage was bound to take considerable adjustment for any couple. Luke cared for her and he was kind. Once they got to know each other there was a good chance that love would follow. She was far better off than many women. Some girls were sold off to the highest bidder, often men they barely knew, with no thought for their future happiness. She selected a couple of books and joined Grace and Lady Grant at the counter. One of the assistants was wrapping a large tome on ancient Greece. That had to be for Grace.

"You are putting me to the blush, Grace. I've got two novels instead of an improving work like yours."

Lady Grant held up two novels. "It seems we have similar tastes. At last I have someone I can exchange books with. Grace rarely reads anything that isn't about history and if she does it's about politics."

They had a quiet luncheon together in the family dining room. Afterwards Grace left them to meet a party of friends at the British Museum. When she had gone Lady Grant invited Kitty to her sitting room.

"I have to go out in an hour or so. I'm promised to a

group of society hostesses, an engagement that I can't break, unfortunately. I feel that I stand in your mother's place and with Grace out this is the perfect opportunity to discuss your marriage with you." Lady Grant's features softened and she smiled. "Do you know what is involved in the marriage bed?"

Kitty looked at floor. "I do. My aunt was careful to explain it to me when I was quite young."

Lady Grant patted her hand. "That's good, but if you do think of anything you want to ask me I won't mind. Anything at all. You hear tales of young women being married off with absolutely no idea of what to expect. Something I find quite shocking."

"Thank you. You have been so kind to me."

"Think nothing of it. I'm certain your mother would have done the same for my girls. I will leave you now. A quiet afternoon with one of your novels is just what you need."

Kitty fetched a novel and curled up in the window seat. She stroked her mother's pearls and smiled. It was a joy to find such a precious link to her mother wasn't lost to her and she couldn't resist wearing them at every opportunity. What would she have thought of Luke? Her thoughts kept straying to him. Would he reach Northamptonshire tonight or would he break his journey beforehand? She could hardly wait to see Edward. He had taken to Luke after the way he handled the school episode and he was bound to approve. She turned her attention to her book again, this time with more success. The sound of a travelling carriage pulling up had her peering out of the window. There was something familiar about it.

A groom jumped down from the seat next to the coachman and pulled down the steps. The door opened to reveal the squire from Shepley. He stumbled down the steps and scurried to Lady Grant's front door. Kitty watched his progress with mounting concern. Something must be wrong. She was on her feet before the butler opened the door.

"Sir Randolph to see you, Miss Davenport. He says he's your neighbour."

"Yes, he is. He looks seriously concerned about something. Show him in but leave the door open if you please. Oh, and I think perhaps a glass of brandy might be in order."

"Yes, Miss."

Sir Randolph almost ran into the room, breathing heavily. His face was bright red. Kitty looked at him with concern.

"Do please be seated, Sir Randolph. Has something happened in Shepley?"

The butler arrived with a glass of brandy on a silver salver. Sir Randolph accepted it without a word of thanks and tossed it down. Kitty shivered. Sir Randolph was normally such a calm man.

"Dear Sir, what has happened to put you in such a taking?"

Sir Randolph ran a hand around the inside of his cravat. He was looking anywhere except at her. Kitty's breathing quickened.

"It's Sir Edward, Miss Davenport. He's met with an accident and he wants you to come to him."

Kitty covered her face with her hands for a moment. Shock made it impossible to speak. This didn't make sense.

"He can't have. He's at school."

Sir Randolph pulled something out of his coat pocket. "He ran away and came back to Shepley. He dropped his pocket watch in the accident. Let me give it to you for safe keeping I picked it up for him but I forgot to give it him back in all the commotion."

Kitty accepted the watch as if in a dream and placed it on a side table. It was Edward's and he never let it out of his sight. Things must be serious.

"Of course, I'll come. My hostess is out and I don't know how to get there."

Sir Randolph sat back in his chair, much calmer now he had passed on his news. "Our carriage is outside, my dear. We have come to convey you to Shepley." His voice sounded brittle.

"That's so kind of you. I'll run up and get my maid to throw a few things in a valise for me. I won't be long."

He stopped her with a hand on her arm. "Best bring your maid with you."

He couldn't meet her eyes and Kitty's stomach churned. Was Edward's condition worse than he was admitting to? She snapped her shoulders back. There was no point speculating.

"I will since you have no objection. Thank you."

Kitty ran out of the room and charged up the stairs. Fortunately, Annie was tidying her things in her room when she got there.

"Annie, my brother has been involved in an accident in Shepley and a neighbour has come to take me to him. Can you pack the barest necessities for both of us?"

"Of course. Let's get you into a warmer gown first."

Kitty almost hopped with impatience but she could see the sense in changing. The weather had turned cold again and she would be no good to Edward if she arrived half frozen to death. Annie ran off to fetch valises and her own clothes leaving Kitty frantically pulling things out of her wardrobe. Annie's quiet good sense helped to keep her calm and it was less than a quarter of an hour later when Kitty joined Sir Randolph, leaving Annie by the front door with their bags. Sir Randolph was pacing up and down and again he didn't meet her eyes. Kitty's throat tightened.

"At last. Let's be on our way." Sir Randolph rushed into the hall. Kitty followed to find Annie explaining to Harvey what had occurred. He promised to convey Kitty's apologies to Lady Grant when she returned.

Sir Randolph ran past Harvey. "Yes, yes, man. Say whatever you think proper. We must go."

A footman ran forward to load their bags. Sir Randolph bundled Kitty and Annie into the big, old-fashioned travelling carriage. The door had barely closed behind him when the coach took off. Kitty opened her mouth to tell him that if they pushed their horses too hard it would take longer to reach their destination and then snapped it shut. Where was Lady Randolph? Strange that she wasn't with him. Perhaps she was waiting at a hotel for them.

The coach careered through the streets of London at a reckless pace. Annie's eyes were huge as she bounced around on the backwards facing seat opposite to Kitty. It soon became obvious that they were making straight for the road north. Had Lady Randolph stayed to look after Edward? Was Edward dying? She dashed away a tear, crying wouldn't help. Why didn't Sir Randolph say something? The coach slowed down a touch and Kitty turned towards him. Beads of sweat covered his forehead.

"Where is Lady Randolph?"

He mopped his brow with a handkerchief. "In Shepley." His voice was little more than a croak.

Kitty wrapped her arms around herself. "Is Edward dying?" Her breath came in fast pants as she waited for his answer.

This time he did look at her, with a hard, unblinking stare.

"Oh, there will be no need for that." He turned his body away from her. "You'll find out more when we get to Shepley."

Kitty stared at him. What was that supposed to mean? Was the man mad? A glance at Annie's faced suggested she had had the same thought. What did she know of the Randolphs other than that he was the local squire? He and his wife had always been friendly towards her in church and on the odd occasions she had met them at the vicarage. Surely the vicar wouldn't invite them to his house with his large family, some of them quite young, if there was anything untoward about Sir Randolph.

"Sir Randolph, what are you saying? Just how seriously injured is Edward."

He didn't respond and Kitty repeated the question more sharply in her agitation.

"What was that my dear? Oh yes, Edward. We don't know yet. I'm sure you will be able to save him. That is, he is bound to pick up when he sees you. As far as I know he is well enough for now."

He closed his eyes but Kitty was sure he wasn't asleep. A horrible suspicion took hold of her. She exchanged glances with Annie, who looked distinctly uncomfortable. Annie started to say something but Kitty shook her head and put a finger across her lips. Annie stopped immediately. An elusive memory that wouldn't quite materialise teased at her. She must stop trying to remember. At last it came to her. Sir Randolph had been talking to Sir Walter Greenough the last time she had attended church in Shepley and they had seemed very friendly. The squire was friendly to everyone and she had thought nothing of it. They would move in the same social circles after all. She gasped, were they in league?

She felt Sir Randolph stir beside her. He must have heard her gasp. She closed her own eyes, two could use that trick. Her mind whirred. The best thing was to go along with it until she found out more. She was overwrought by the sudden news that Edward was in danger and might not be thinking straight. Annie was quick witted and she was worried something wasn't right. What better way to undermine someone's resistance than by flooring them with news like that? Had she been tricked?

Part her wanted it to be so and for Edward to be perfectly well but there was his pocket watch to consider. How could Sir Randolph have come by that if not from Edward? Perhaps she was reading too much into Sir Randolph's odd phrasing. Chatting to someone at church didn't make you that man's accomplice. If only Luke had still been in London, he would have taken her to Shepley. He would have got more sense out of Sir Randolph as well. Of course Sir Randolph could be in a state of shock. He hadn't said how the accident had happened but he must have been there to pick up Edward's pocket watch. Had the accident been Sir Randolph's fault and he was too upset to talk about it?

They would have to stop for the night and she might get him to open up after he had eaten. The coach was slowing down considerably, hardly unexpected considering the way the coachman had pushed the horses. They came to a village and she wasn't surprised when they drove under an archway into the yard of a coaching inn. Sir Randolph jumped down and the sounds of an altercation came to them.

"These horses won't go no further. If you don't agree you be welcome to drive them yourself."

"Very well, man. Change them if you must."

Annie tapped Kitty's knee. "This is a rum do, Miss Davenport. There's something havey-cavey about Sir Randolph if you ask me."

They both peered out of the window to see Sir Randolph disappearing into the inn. Kitty came to a decision. Her own instincts were screaming that something was wrong.

"I think you're right, Annie. Let's get out and throw ourselves on the mercy of the innkeeper."

They pushed open the opposite door to the one that Sir Randolph had used. Without the steps there was an awkward drop but they managed to scramble down. It was a busy yard and Kitty didn't want to take the risk of Sir Randolph coming back before they were in the inn. There was another coach to their right. She pointed towards it, intending to go around it and skirt the yard to find a back door. The dark shape of the coachman loomed in front of them. He lifted her off her feet.

"Oh no you don't. Back in the coach with you." His voice was a throaty growl.

Annie jumped in front of him. "How dare you do that to my mistress? We're just going to find the necessary house."

"There be a chamber pot under the seat. Get back in or it will be the worse for you."

Annie started to protest. Kitty's captor tucked her under one arm and put his other hand in his pocket. Kitty felt something hard pressing on her hip. The man was carrying a pair of pistols. She kicked out and caught Annie on the thigh. She stopped talking immediately. Thank heavens for the girl's quick wits. Annie scrambled back into the carriage and the coachman threw Kitty in after her.

He pointed a pistol at Annie. "Behave or you'll know about it." He slammed the door shut.

Annie turned frightened eyes to her. "What's this all about, Miss Davenport."

"I'm not sure but I think they're both working for Sir Walter Greenough. It seems he hasn't given up on the idea of marrying me."

But why? She was just an insignificant country miss with no dowry. Why was he so determined? They had to keep calm if they were going to get out of this with her unmarried and Annie still alive. Had they got Edward or was that just a bluff? If they hadn't got him then they could try and escape. If they had got Edward then she would have to marry Sir Walter. She bit back a cry. The thought of not marrying Luke was painful but, if that was the only way to save Edward, she had no choice.

Kitty turned her attention back to Annie who was staring at her with her mouth open.

"I can't see a squire doing someone else's dirty work. I expect they're working together."

"You're probably right." Kitty pointed to the backwards facing seat. "Let's both sit there. If I'm too close to Sir Randolph I might be tempted to hit him."

Annie nodded and leaned close once they were seated. "You must have something that they want, Miss Davenport. If you could think what it is, we might be able to bargain our way out of this."

"I've no dowry, nothing, and yet what you say makes sense. I've seen a man become besotted with a girl and not accept repeated refusals when we lived at Davenport Court. That was what I assumed was the case with Sir Walter Greenough."

"The coachman is in on it. Could they have both been paid to kidnap you?"

Kitty shook her head. "Then why would Sir Randolph have

suggested I bring my maid?"

She slapped her forehead and sat bolt upright. "Of course. The story about a neighbourly gesture to take me to Shepley in a hurry wouldn't have satisfied Lady Grant if I hadn't taken you."

Annie shivered. "That's what I was thinking. If Lady Grant believes the story then there will be no pursuit of us until Lord Enstone returns to London, most probably in company with Sir Edward if you ask me."

The door opened and the coach tipped as Sir Randolph jumped in. His breath smelled of brandy. He said nothing and looked in every direction except Kitty's. They lurched forwards and he crossed his arms in his lap and closed his eyes. It seemed he was determined not to speak to her. There didn't seem much point trying to force him, for now anyway.

She sat with her head in her hands, trying to think. Annie's calm sense was reassuring. A hysterical maid would have been a terrible liability. Annie's reasoning made sense. What could she have that they wanted? Luke had mentioned there was something The Duke of Cathlay had told him about her. Something connected to her mother's trust fund. The drive in Hyde Park seemed weeks ago rather than one day. It had to be to do with that. As far as she knew, her father had never signed any paperwork for it. The income had been paid to her father but hadn't he once said it would be hers one day? Perhaps it belonged to her? The amount hadn't been a great deal, not enough to kidnap someone for.

Once again, the coachman pushed his horses at a furious speed. Were they afraid of pursuit? Kitty stared out of the window when they pulled up at a toll booth. This didn't look like the fastest route to Shepley, which did suggest that they were trying to hide their destination. Were they just being careful or was there a serious possibility that Lady Grant would send someone in pursuit of them?

Sir Randolph stuck his head out of the window and shouted at the coachman. "Get a move on can't you. We'll never get there at this rate."

Kitty couldn't catch his reply. Sir Randolph flopped back onto his seat and mopped his brow. He seemed to be under extreme stress. Now that was interesting. That would make it harder for him to foil any escape attempt they might make. Their pace quickened again until they were rattling along the toll road. The coachman was taking a chance on a quiet road like this. If anything went wrong with the horses, they would struggle to find a coaching inn to replace them. Sir Randolph was a hunting man. He ought to know better.

They bowled along for some time without mishap. Sir Randolph appeared to be asleep again but she shook her head when Annie started to say something. It was as well to be careful. Annie leaned close and whispered in her ear.

"Do you know where we are?"

Kitty shook her head and mouthed the words. "This isn't the main road to Shepley."

The pace barely slackened for some time but eventually it slowed down rapidly. Kitty leaned towards the window as an inn sign came into view. It wasn't one she recognised and the place looked dirty and unkempt. The coach pulled into the yard by the side of it. Sir Randolph climbed down. This time the coachman yelled for several minutes before ostlers arrived to change the horses.

Annie leaned towards her. "Could we escape here, Miss?"

"It's isolated but it might be our only chance. Can you see

where the coachman is?"

At that moment the door was wrenched open and the coach-man levelled his pistol at them. "Behaving ourselves this time are we?"

He leered at her but Kitty refused to let him see she was afraid. The noise in the yard halted and he banged the door closed. Sir Randolph stumbled up the steps of the opposite door and almost collapsed on to his seat. He was carrying a basket, the contents of which rattled until he laid it down beside him. The man was shaking. The coach pulled away and he took out his handkerchief, this time to blow his nose. Kitty looked at Annie. From her wide –eyed expression she had also realised that he was doing this under duress. What sort of hold had they got on him? He was in such a state that he wouldn't be a very good jailer when they stopped for the night.

Chapter Fifteen

L uke was on the road shortly after first light, with Fletcher by his side and his spare curricle following.

"You're sure Ashton will be able to handle the other curricle?"

"Oh yes, my lord. The lad is a brilliant whip."

By dint of changing horses frequently and stopping for the minimum amount of time to eat they reached Northampton-shire by mid-afternoon. Luke made a short detour to Dowling and pulled into a coaching inn. He decided to stop for long enough to drink a mug of ale. He refused the landlord's offer of a private room and settled at an empty table in the bar. The place was quite full and within a few minutes a rather portly but prosperous looking gentleman asked if he would mind sharing his table.

Luke smiled pleasantly. "Not in the least. What brings you to town?"

The gentleman settled into a chair opposite to Luke. "Some commissions for my wife. I don't remember seeing you before Mr?"

"Bamford. I'm new to the area. I'm looking for a local man of business to handle my affairs."

"My name's Preston." Mr Preston held out this hand.

Luke shook it. Mr Preston had a surprisingly strong grip and there was an air of energy about him. Could he be a local businessman?

"There are only two in the area. I recommend Archibald and Pinner. They keep my affairs ship-shape."

"Thank you. A navy man are you?"

"I was but I have some business interests now."

Luke studied Mr Preston as he downed the last of his ale. He had the look of a shrewd business man. Which suggested that Archibald and Pinner was a respectable and efficient firm.

"I might go and speak to them now, if you would be so kind as to give me directions."

"Turn left out of the inn and then first left and you are on High Street. Archibald and Pinner is along there on the right. My wife and I would be delighted to entertain you to supper one evening as a new neighbour."

"Things are not yet decided. I have to report back to my future wife in London before we commit to anything."

That much was true in its way and Mr Preston seemed to lose interest. Luke managed to escape without giving him any more information about himself. He probably had a daughter of marriageable age. In some ways his life would be a lot simpler once he was married. He found the office he was looking for and walked in. A dark-clad clerk occupied a desk set near the door and with a view through the window.

"Good afternoon, Sir. What may I do for you?"

Luke hesitated, he didn't really want to produce his card but if he didn't he was unlikely to get an audience with one of the principals. He pulled out his card case.

"I'd like a quick word with Mr Archibald if I may."

The clerk shook his head. "I'm sorry Mr?" He glanced at the

card. "Ah. Lord Enstone. I'll see if Mr Archibald is able to see you, my lord."

The clerk scurried through a heavy oak door. Luke sighed. He hated the way his title gave him preferential treatment but in a case like this it was useful. The clerk returned and ushered him through the room's rear door into a hallway. An elderly man stepped forward.

"Mr Archibald, my lord. Please follow me," he said in a pleasant voice.

Luke was taken into an airy room, dominated by a substantial, leather topped mahogany desk in the middle. He accepted the seat offered and Mr Archibald took the seat behind the desk.

"Now what may I do for you, my lord?"

"I have recently become engaged to Miss Davenport, the niece of the late Lady Swift."

"I see. I don't wish to give offence but I can't discuss another client's business." Mr Archibald studied him with narrowed eyes.

Luke held his gaze but remained silent.

"However, I might be prepared to stretch a point in this particular case if you could show me proof of your identity."

Luke frowned and then remembered his special licence, for some reason he preferred to keep it on his person. He extracted it from the pocket of his great coat and proffered it to Mr. Archibald.

"Would this be sufficient?"

Mr Archibald studied the document carefully and his expression changed to a smile.

"Yes, my lord. My felicitations, I have met Miss Davenport and she is a sweet young woman."

"She is. Thank you. There are things Miss Davenport has told me about the actions of the new Lord Swift that lead me to wonder if her aunt had fears for their safety."

"Yes indeed, my lord. I believe that Lady Swift was frightened of the distant cousin who inherited when Lord Rupert died. There were grave irregularities in the way she was treated. I wanted to take them up with Lord Swift but she begged me not to. She even refused to give me her new address."

"Really? How did she get her funds then?"

"They were sent direct to her bank and she contacted me through them if she had any queries. Besides her jointure, what Lord Swift passed on of it, she had a few small investments which occasionally produced dividends. Her last message to me was to sell them all up and send on the proceeds, which I wasn't able to do."

Luke frowned. "Why not?"

"I couldn't sell them without her signature and she died shortly afterwards. I paid the last instalment of her jointure into her bank account but I have no idea if Miss Davenport was able to access it. I sent a note to the bank and asked them to pass it on to her but I never had a response."

"I'm not sure, but what concerns me at the moment is why Lady Swift was so worried about the new Lord Swift."

"That had me in a puzzle until I met him once by chance. I didn't take to him at all, a most unpleasant man."

Luke sat forward. "I doubt the name will mean much to you but I believe Lord Swift might have had dealings with Lord Peter Sewell."

"I've come across him." Mr Archibald scowled. "He lives on the fringes of society and catches out the unwary. I've heard that Lord Swift may be associating with him and I suggest you take care."

Luke stopped breathing for a moment. Thank goodness he had resisted the urge to leave this visit to another time. "I will. Sewell sounds a most unpleasant individual. Can you tell me any more about him?"

Mr Archibald rested his elbows on the desk and steepled his hands together. "Sewell ruined one of my clients a year or two back. Fleeced him at cards." He sniffed. "I can't say I've ever understood this aristocratic thing about ruining yourself to pay gambling debts, especially when someone got you drunk to make you lose to them."

Luke let out a breath. Had Sewell found Kitty's father through Lord Swift?

"I tried to recover some of my client's money. I did get a modest sum back. Sewell's man of business said he would agree to my demands to get rid of me as he was working on something big." He stroked his chin. "I didn't like the sound of it."

"Mr Archibald you have been a huge help. I'm sorry I can't tell you more at the moment and I know I can rely on your discretion not to mention what we talked about."

"Of course, my lord. I won't mention your visit at all."

Luke smiled. "Thank you. We will be in touch after our wedding so Miss Davenport can finalise her aunt's estate with you."

"Thank you, my lord."

Luke made his way back to the inn, deep in thought. The pieces of the puzzle were coming together. It was centred on that family trust of Kitty's, unless he had missed his guess. Lady Swift had probably guessed something of what was going on but hadn't known what to do about it. She must have deliberately hidden their new address and foregone the income from Kitty's trust to keep them hidden from Swift and Sewell. Kitty would have presumed that her father had lost the income with the house.

They should get to Edward's school in an hour or two if they pressed on. It was a clear day and the light should last that long. The sooner he could get back to London the better. If Sewell's henchman couldn't be bothered to fight a claim from a small country solicitor then there must be a lot at stake. His army instincts for trouble were definitely starting to niggle at him. Now Sewell had found Kitty's whereabouts what would he do when he found out his plan to marry Kitty off to Sir Walter Greenough had failed?

He debated turning straight back but they were so close to Edward and a few extra miles shouldn't make any difference. They would still have to stay overnight somewhere. If the headmaster wouldn't release Edward straight away the lad would have to make his own way on the mail coach. If they got to the school tonight, they could make an early start in the morning, hopefully with Edward. He arrived back at the inn and found Fletcher.

"I want to get back to London as quickly as possible. We are nearly twenty miles away but I would love to reach Edward's school tonight. It's at Moppington. What do you think?"

"We should make it if we start now. There's not much daylight left but it's a clear night and the moon will be almost full later. I've made sure that we have two good teams of horses."

Luke nodded. "That's what I thought. As far as I remember from my previous visit, there's a good inn at the town before Moppington, leaving about five or six miles to go. We could change horses there and bespeak rooms for the night."

"Right you are, my lord."

Fletcher called to the ostlers to harness up their curricles and went in search of Ashton. They were on the road in minutes. Even with stopping for fresh horses and to bespeak rooms, they pulled up at the main entrance to Edward's school in less than two hours. Luke gave the reins to Fletcher and jumped down. He handed his card to the porter and was directed to the headmaster's study. His breathing felt forced. Kitty would be so disappointed if Edward wasn't at their wedding but he had learnt never to ignore his instincts when safety was concerned. He wouldn't rest until he saw Kitty again.

Mr Brown, a cheerful looking man who was probably younger than his bald head made him appear, stood up to greet him.

"Ah, Lord Enstone. I'm happy to report that your young charge has been doing very well at school since your visit earlier in the year."

Luke smiled. "I'm pleased to hear that."

Mr Brown ushered him to a chair with an answering smile. "Indeed, Sir Edward is a very intelligent boy. However, I feel something is bothering him." He sat back in his chair. "Are there any problems with his home life?" He frowned and studied Luke with a piercing gaze.

Luke sighed. He didn't have time for this but if he didn't humour Mr Brown he was unlikely to get the boy released to him.

"I believe he has struggled to come to terms with the loss of his father and then his aunt but I hope my news will reassure him." Luke felt heat flood his cheeks. "Edward's sister has done me the honour of accepting my hand in marriage."

Mr Brown beamed at him. "Well that is good news."

"Thank you." Luke decided to plunge straight in. "I know it's a few weeks until the summer holidays, but would you release Edward to attend the wedding?"

Mr Brown frowned but then his expression lightened. "We have been wondering whether to prepare him for university entrance next year, but he is so far in front of his fellow students that a few weeks off shouldn't make much different. As long as he undertakes to do some study over the summer."

Luke relaxed. "If I agreed to engage a tutor for him would that be agreeable?"

"I think that might serve. We have a young master here, who Sir Edward has been working well for, who would relish the prospect of summer employment as long as you have a good library."

Luke pulled out another card and wrote Wallace's name on the back. "Tell him to write to my secretary. He will make the arrangements and buy any books he would care to name. I'll send a groom to fetch him as soon as he is free."

"Excellent. There is one other thing."

Luke slumped. He wanted to be back on the road but he waited patiently.

"Sir Edward is not entirely sure that he wants to go to university, which would be a waste for a boy with such a fine brain."

"I'll talk to him. I won't stand in his way if he has another plan for his future which sounds reasonable"

"That's all I ask."

Mr Brown rang a bell on his desk. A dark clad male servant joined them.

"Find Sir Edward Davenport and send him here please."

A few minutes later there was a tentative knock at the door. A nervous looking Edward entered at the headmaster's invitation. His face broke into a delighted smile when he saw Luke but then he sobered. He looked from Luke to Mr Brown and back again.

"There's nothing wrong is there, Sir?"

"Not that I know of. I've come to ask for your permission to marry your sister."

Edward bounced with excitement. "That's capital news."

Luke grinned at him. "I take it that's a yes then. Mr Brown is allowing me to remove you from school early, on certain conditions which I will explain to you later. Can you pack your things ready for the summer holidays in record time for me?"

Edward looked across a Mr Brown who nodded at him. "Off you go, Davenport. His lordship will be waiting for you at the main entrance to the school."

"Yes, sir." Edward hurried out."

Luke smiled. "Thank you, Mr Brown."

Chapter Sixteen

Sir Randolph opened the basket and produced bread and cheese. He held some out to them. Annie went to refuse but Kitty shook her head. They needed to keep their strength up. Sir Randolph seemed calmer after he had eaten. Kitty shivered. Perhaps he was afraid of the coachman? He was a scary individual but she had the feeling that there was something else bothering Sir Randolph. Perhaps she could get him talking.

"What hold have they got over you, Sir Randolph?"

He jumped and turned to look at her. "I'm sorry my dear but they've got my wife. If I don't deliver you to Walter Greenough then they will kill her." His face crumpled.

Kitty gasped. She knew for sure who was behind it now but it didn't help her at all. If they managed to escape then Lady Randolph would be killed.

"Have you any idea why he is so keen to marry me?"

Sir Randolph surprised her with a bark of laughter. "It's not Greenough, he's far more interested in the church altar boy. I expect that's why Sewell picked him to marry you. Not likely to be complications caused by him falling in love with you then."

Kitty was all at sea. "Why on earth does this Sewell you speak of want Sir Walter to marry me?"

Sir Randolph trembled until his chin wobbled. "I don't really know and I've told you more than I should already."

Kitty stared at him. "Have you told me about your wife to stop me trying to escape?"

Sir Randolph stayed silent and turned his head to stare out of the window.

This time the coachman set a more sensible pace, perhaps because the light was beginning to fade. They must surely get back to a main road soon. If she could get her bearings there would be chances to escape when they stopped for the night. Heavens, would they travel through the night? They might be able to if there was a full moon. She peered through the window. The sky was clear and she could just see the outline of a nearly full moon beginning to show. Her stomach churned.

The coach came to a crossroads and forked left onto a road that was little more than a cart track. They bumped along it for a few minutes and then turned into a farmyard. Kitty's gaze skittered all around looking for some sort of sign with a name but found none. Sir Randolph came to with a start. Perhaps he really had been asleep this time. They carriage swayed to a halt by the side of a large barn. The coachman shouted until two burly young men emerged from the farmhouse and opened the barn's huge double doors. She exchanged glances with Annie. The coach door was wrenched open to reveal the coachman pointing one of his pistols at them.

Sir Randolph looked green. The coachman must make him nervous. Could they use his nervousness to their advantage? If he gave them an opportunity to escape here they would have to take it. If these people were as ruthless as they seemed then the chances were the Randolphs wouldn't survive whatever happened. They wouldn't want witnesses to their abduction.

"Now then, ladies." The coachman made the word sound like an insult. "Down you come and no funny business or I shoot the maid."

When they hesitated, he grabbed Kitty roughly by the arm and swung her down. Her shoulder creaked in protest. Annie jumped down behind her. An older man came out of the farmhouse and the coachman handed him a pistol.

"Take this and get these two into the house." He grinned at Kitty. "We want the dark haired one unharmed, more or less, but if they try and make a run for it shoot the other one."

Kitty grimaced and caught Annie's hand. She couldn't risk any harm coming to her. The old man shoved her towards a run-down farm house. She looked over her shoulder to see two young men unharnessing the horses inside the barn. They looked alike and had a strong resemblance to the older man. She tucked the knowledge away in case it was useful later. For now, she had to believe they would escape somehow even though this was such a well-planned operation that she was having doubts.

They were taken up a rickety staircase and pushed into an airless room. The only window was high up and looked as if it hadn't been opened in fifty years. They heard a grating noise.

Annie tried the door. "He's locked us in."

"I thought as much."

Kitty pointed to a small table next to a lumpy looking mattress suspended on a rough wooden frame. A plate of bread and mouldy cheese sat next to a flagon of ale. Kitty bent down to sniff it.

"I think this is drinkable but I'm not sure about the food."

Annie wrinkled up her nose. "I'm glad you made me eat what Sir Randolph offered us. At least that was fresh."

Kitty sighed. "I was hoping that Sir Randolph would slip up and give us an opportunity to escape, but there's not much chance of that with us locked away in here."

"It's not Sir Randolph we have to worry about is it? The coachman seems to be in charge."

Kitty laughed. "He certainly does, since he's the one carrying the pistols."

Annie raised frightened eyes to hers.

Kitty put an arm around her. "Don't worry. We'll find a way to outwit them. Let's see if we can open that window for some air, so we can think better."

They pulled an old wooden framed armchair from the corner of the room until it was underneath the window. Kitty climbed up and studied the catch. It appeared similar to the ones at Davenport Court. It refused to budge at the first attempt. Kitty pulled out a hairpin and picked away at the ingrained grime around it and tried again. This time it opened with a creak. She waited for a moment, listening intently, but there seemed to be no reaction. With it pushed open as far as it would go, she had a view of the side of the barn. She could hear curses coming from it.

One of the younger men came out rubbing his shin. "Those are some wild brutes of horses. Where did you get them from?"

Kitty moved back from the window a little as she heard the coachman speak.

"That's none of your business, you chucklehead. There's nothing wrong with the horses. I thought you used to be a groom."

"That was with proper horses, not vicious old bone-setters like these."

Kitty risked leaning forwards and saw the coachman disappear around to the side of the cottage. The young man carried on complaining to his father and brother.

The older man went across to him. "Give over Seb. It's a pity that horse didn't kick your head. He might have kicked some sense into you. Ignore that fat-wit. The quality cove has a big bottle of brandy he said he'd share with us. Come into the kitchen."

Kitty was about to close the window when they heard a grating noise from below. The window below theirs was flung open. She listened for some time before shutting the window and climbing down.

"Sir Randolph must have bought the brandy with the food in the basket. I think he's intent on getting bosky to dull his anxiety. I can hear four voices but not the coachman."

Annie sighed. "More's the pity. He's the one we have to outwit."

* * *

They spent the night huddled together for warmth on the most uncomfortable bed Kitty had ever come across. She woke with a start as the sun shining through the bare window fell on her face. A splash of cold water, from a jug on a wobbly washstand in one corner, helped to ease the headache she had woken up with. There was no sound of their captors. Eventually Annie stirred.

She sat up and rubbed her eyes. "From the height of the sun it must be quite late. Do you think Sir Walter is going to come here?"

Kitty closed her eyes briefly as she fought a wave of nausea. She squared her shoulders and willed herself to stay calm.

"That's what I'm afraid of. If he does I'll have to throw myself on the mercy of the vicar he's employed to conduct the service. No man of the cloth should force me into a marriage I don't want."

"I wouldn't be too sure about that, Miss, not if they're paying enough."

They heard footsteps outside their door and the sound of a key turning. The door edged open and the old man from the previous evening stood there. He seemed to be swaying on his feet and Kitty was sure the dark shadows under his eyes hadn't been there before.

"What's this all about?" she shouted at him.

Annie stared at her in surprise but the man's wince at the sound of her voice confirmed what she had suspected. He was feeling the effects of too much alcohol.

"Lord, how should I know? I've been paid for housing you that's all I need to know. Come on with you the carriage is waiting."

Kitty took Annie's hand and they followed him down the rickety staircase. He swayed more than once but reached the ground floor in one piece. She gave Annie's hand a squeeze as she spotted the coachman. His face was a furious mask as he helped push Sir Randolph into the carriage. The coachman wedged him into a corner and jumped down. He advanced towards them.

"Don't stand there gawping. Get in that carriage."

They climbed up, with a hand from one of the young men who tapped Kitty's knee.

"Hang on to the seat if you can. Your driver is in a foul temper at the delay." He nodded at Sir Randolph who was singing away in the corner.

The coach rocked forward with little warning and he was obliged to jump away from it before Kitty could thank him. If yesterday's pace had been reckless today's held the terror of being turned over into a ditch. Kitty was surprised when they slowed down a short while later. There had been no indication of one of the horses faltering. They came to a halt. She put her head out of the window and saw a large famer's cart blocking the road as it moved at barely walking pace. She could hear the coachman cursing up front. If he had been angry before he would be in a towering rage after this. Perhaps they would have a chance to outwit him.

The farmer's cart pulled into a gateway to let them through. The coachman shouted at the horses and they heard the crack of his whip. They lurched forwards. In spite of their terrible situation Kitty couldn't help smiling at the sight of the farmer waving a fist at them as they sailed past him. Annie was smiling when she turned towards her once they were past. Annie's smile turned to horror as they picked up a furious pace, with the coachman's curses to his horses reaching them above the rumble of the wheels on the rough road.

"Lawks, Miss. If we meet anything coming the other way we're done for."

"The farmer's son was right about trying to hang on to the seat." Kitty caught at the side of the seat as she said it.

They heard a crack and the coach tilted to the left at the front. Sir Randolph was thrown on to the floor as they slowed up abruptly.

"Hang on tight, Annie. I think a wheel has come off."

The coach listed farther to the left and toppled into the ditch. They couldn't avoid landing on top of Sir Randolph. Kitty pulled herself off Annie and tugged at the right-hand door.

Annie managed to clamber up beside her and between them they wrenched the door open. Kitty gulped at the distance to the ground but the squeals of the terrified horses spurred her on. She lowered herself over the side of the coach by her arms and dropped to the ground.

At a quick glance the horses looked to be intact but the coachman shouting at them wasn't helping. She moved around them, being careful to avoid getting in reach of flying hooves, crooning to them as she went.

The coachman dropped his reins and pulled out a pistol. "Where do you think you're going?"

"To try and save your horses. Hold their heads quietly and let me see if I can calm them. They will be breaking legs if they keep on like this."

Kitty ignored the pistol and walked to the front of the snorting, screaming horses, taking care to stay out of the way of harm's way.

"Come on now, boys. Calm down for me. Whoa there. That's it stand firm for me."

The nearest leader responded to her crooning by standing still and letting her stroke his neck. She checked that his legs were free and edged around him.

"Good boy. Now what's your friend up to?"

His partner was pawing at the ground, with his left foreleg caught up in the traces. She edged her way to his head and caught his collar.

"Steady now boy."

After a few minutes she managed to calm him. She looked up at the coachman, who was staring at her with his mouth open wide.

"Don't just sit there like a looby. Find something to cut this strap with unless you want this poor horse to break its leg."

Annie had managed to climb out and was holding the head of the other leader. She must have been brought up in the country. The two horses behind them had calmed down but it wouldn't take much to set them off again.

"Well done, Annie. What's the condition of the second horse on your side?"

"He doesn't look too bad."

"Good. I don't like the look of the other horse this side. Where's Sir Randolph?"

"He's convinced he's broken his arm when we landed on him, says he can't get out."

A furious looking coachman marched around to the horse Kitty was holding.

"Let's have a look. I'm sure I can untangle him." He grabbed the horse's collar and the animal tried to rear up.

Kitty managed to calm the horse down and the coachman pulled out a pocket knife. Without a word he sliced through the strap that was trapping him. The horse tried to run away and it took all of Kitty's strength to hold him. He looked sound but could they be sure of their guess that Sir Walter didn't have Edward? Someone was bound to come along sooner or later and the coachman could hardly shoot them in front of witnesses if they mounted a horse each and rode off. If it wasn't for the pocket watch she would risk it but surely Edward would have said if he had lost it, he was so attached to it. Even if they did have Edward, they wouldn't harm him if they wanted to force her into marriage.

The coachman had untethered one of the other two horses and tied it to a tree. It was obviously lame. Walking like that it wouldn't be fit for a while. She glanced across at Annie, who had the other leader standing calmly.

She kept her voice low. "Can you ride astride?"

"Yes, Miss," Annie whispered back.

Kitty heard the sound of a cart. "As soon as that cart gets here jump up if you can. We'll try and escape."

Annie nodded and Kitty could see her looking for a suitable rock to help her mount. She edged her horse towards a bank and waited. The cart pulled up and she nodded to Annie. A hand landed on her shoulder.

"Oh no you don't."

Kitty wriggled frantically trying to see the newcomers. She froze when she saw it was the two brothers from their prison of the night before.

Chapter Seventeen

L uke had his party back on the road shortly after sunrise. How could he have ever thought that he didn't love Kitty? The anxiety gnawing at his guts wouldn't leave him, so sure was he that she was in danger.

Edward yawned and stretched as they trotted out of the inn courtyard.

"Lord, you keep early hours. What time is it? I lost my pocket watch the last time I was home." He coloured. "That is the last time I was at Shepley Hall."

"It's just shy of six o'clock." Luke laughed. "Don't tell me they keep Town hours at school these days?"

Edward grinned and shook his head. "I would be getting up around this time, I suppose, but we were quite late to bed."

Edward was a delightful young man and adept with the ribbons. Luke was content to let him do a large part of the driving. He had the feeling that he needed to conserve his energy. They arrived in London by late afternoon. Luke pulled up in front of Lady Grant's house, closely followed by Fletcher and Ashton. Ashton jumped down at a signal from Luke and took the reins of Luke's curricle.

"Thank you. Drive this home for me will you. We'll walk back later."

Luke jumped down and paused long enough to see Ashton settled in the curricle. He ran up the steps to the front door, closely followed by Edward. Harvey himself open the door to his sharp rap.

"Lady Grant is at home, my lord. She's in the drawing room."

"Thank you, Harvey. There is no need to announce us."

Harvey looked at Edward and his eyes opened wide. "But my lord..."

Luke's lungs contracted at Harvey's reaction to seeing Edward. Had something happened to Kitty? He strode across the hall way and almost ran through the door of the drawing room. Aunt Theo was chuckling at something in the book she was reading. Luke relaxed. He was worrying about nothing.

"Allow me to introduce Sir Edward Davenport, Aunt Theo."

Aunt Theo looked up with a start. She stared at Edward as he made her a very correct bow.

"Sir Edward Davenport, but it can't be. That is to say I am very pleased to see you have recovered from your accident so quickly, Edward." She turned to Luke. "Where is Kitty?"

All the strength in Luke's legs drained away. He collapsed into a seat. "I haven't seen Kitty since I left London. Tell me what's happened here."

Aunt Theo waved Edward to a chair. "Grace and I were both out yesterday afternoon. Harvey tells me Kitty was reading in here when one of her neighbours from Shepley arrived, in an agitated state. As far as Harvey could piece together, he told Kitty that Edward had met with a serious accident and he offered to escort her to Shepley."

Luke ran a hand through his hair. "But she knew Edward was at school, why would she believe him?"

A white-faced Edward pointed to a side table, next to him. "That's my pocket watch, the one I lost in Shepley at Christmas. It must have been a trick, but why would Sir Randolph trick Kitty into going to Shepley with him?"

Luke's mind was spinning with possibilities. "What do you know of Sir Randolph, Edward?"

"Not a great deal. He has always been perfectly amiable and he's well-respected. It makes no sense."

There was a knock at the door and Harvey showed in Wallace. Wallace was breathing heavily and wiping beads of sweat out of his eyes.

"Lord Enstone, please forgive the intrusion." Wallace sank on to the seat indicated by Aunt Theo. "I was on my way out when I saw Fletcher. He mentioned Sir Edward Davenport and you were here. I fear Miss Davenport may have been kidnapped."

"We have just come to the same conclusion."

Wallace glanced at Edward and Aunt Theo. "Perhaps I could speak to you in private?"

Aunt Theo jumped up. "Kitty's personal maid went with her but I'll go and question the housekeeper in case she said anything to the other maids."

"Thank you. Would you send Harvey back, please?"

Edward eased himself out of his chair but Luke pushed him back with a hand on his shoulder. "You should hear what Wallace has to say. After speaking to the late Lady Swift's man of business, on our way to your school, I have a good idea what it's going to be. First I need to put arrangements in hand."

Harvey arrived so quickly he must have been hovering in the hall. "My lord, Mr Bright has just arrived. He's waiting outside."

"Send him in."

Bright rushed in at Luke's words. "I arrived back yesterday. I just saw Fletcher. He said you were here. Something very smoky is going on with Lord Sewell. A lady from Shepley, Lady Randolph, has disappeared and I think Sewell has her locked up. I overheard him say something about Miss Davenport and a banking company, which didn't make sense to me but I though you should know."

Luke groaned aloud. "I should have left Kitty under guard. She's been kidnapped. Bright can you round up three good horses and I'll join you in a few minutes."

"Make it four horses, Bright," Wallace said. I should have worked this out sooner and intercepted you, my lord. I'm coming too with your permission."

Edward jumped up. "What about me?"

Luke shook his head at Edward. "Make it four horses, Bright."

"Right you are, my lord." Bright rushed out.

"I'll take Wallace but not you, Edward."

Edward crossed his arms in front of him. "Why not?"

Luke put a hand on his shoulder. "It may come down to a fight. I'll need to focus on saving your sister and keeping you out of Sewell's clutches would be a distraction."

Edward's lips thinned and his nostrils flared. Then he relaxed. "I suppose I can see the sense in that. I'll stay here if I must."

"Thank you, Edward."

"Miss Davenport is the heiress to a large fortune from her mother's family trust," Wallace said, "mostly shares in the family bank and other businesses. We believe that Lord Sewell targeted the Davenports in an effort to get his hands on them."

Luke groaned. "I suspected something like that. Sewell seems to be friendly with the new Lord Swift, who inherited from Kitty's uncle."

Wallace nodded. "That makes sense. Sewell is married but Sir Walter Greenough works for him and he's a bachelor."

Lady Grant entered the room. "The maids can't tell us anything else, but one of the footmen returning from an errand thought he recognised the coachman. He thinks he's a driver for hire who works for one of the big coaching inns at St Alban's but he can't remember which one."

"Thank you, Aunt Theo. If we can find it, they may be able to tell us where the coach was hired to go to. Bright is organising horses." He glanced at Edward whose expression was still mutinous. "Will you put Edward up for me?"

"Of course." She smiled at Edward.

"Thank, you, Lady Grant." Edward sighed. "I wanted to go too."

Luke caught Edward's shoulder. "I'm sorry, but it's for the best. We need to get off. I'll leave you to explain it all to my aunt." His jaw tightened. "Don't worry we'll find her. We'll ride through the night if we have to. If they've married her off to Greenough, I'll put a bullet through him."

Edward stared at him. "I believe you would. If I know Kitty, she'll fight every inch of the way so it shouldn't come to it." His face clouded. "I just hope she doesn't believe them about having me. Kitty would sacrifice anything for her family. I can understand why you don't want to take me."

Chapter Eighteen

The coachman had Kitty, Annie and Sir Randolph loaded into the farm cart. He climbed on to one of the horses that didn't seem much harmed and tied the other relatively unscathed one to it. He left one brother looking after the injured ones and told the other brother to drive them back to the farm in front of him.

"Now remember, I've got a pistol in each pocket so don't get trying to escape will you, ladies."

Sir Randolph nearly fell over the low side of the cart as they started off. It seemed he was still a long way from sober. Kitty slumped at the back of the cart next to Annie. They had been so close to escaping. What were the chances of two of their jailers being the first people to drive past? Her thoughts turned to Luke. What was he doing now? He and Edward would probably be on their way back to London today. She bit back a sob. It was no good despairing. By tonight he would know they had been kidnapped.

The carriage would take a lot of fixing and two of the horses were too lame to carry on. It would be tomorrow at the earliest before they could resume their journey, unless the coachman managed to hire another carriage. If Luke got back to London today then he would be right behind them. A stab of fear ran through her. What if he caught them up and got shot? She fought down nausea. He had been a successful soldier and would be cautious.

Annie tapped her on the shoulder. "Are you unwell, Miss Davenport? You look a bit green."

Kitty forced a smile. "It's the movement of the cart. I'll recover as soon as we stop."

Once they reached the farm they were bundled back into the airless little room. This time they heard Sir Randolph protesting as he too was put into a bedroom. They heard the sound of a key scraping in a lock and Sir Randolph shouting to be let out. Eventually he quietened down.

"Thank goodness for that, Annie. At least now we can think. It's maddening not knowing what's happening. I think Lord Enstone will probably reach London by tonight. He will realise we were tricked and come after us."

"Yes, but will this lot take us to Shepley or somewhere else?"

Kitty dropped down on to the bed. "Oh Lord, I hadn't thought of that. We need to try and delay things as much as we can. I wonder if the coachman has enough money on him to hire another coach."

Annie shook her head. "I doubt it. The farmer wasn't very happy last night. I reckon he would have given him extra to turn him up sweet if he'd had money to spare."

"I hope you're right."

They settled down for a long and tedious wait. A while later they heard the creak of the stairs. The door opened to reveal the farmer with one of the coachman's pistols in his hand.

"Come on you two. You might as well make yourselves useful and cook some of the food my lads have brought back from the market."

They followed him down with something like enthusiasm. Anything was better than sitting around waiting. The brother who had warned them to hold on to the coach seat was unloading sacks of vegetable in a surprisingly spacious farm kitchen. Kitty decided to try and get information off him.

"What's happening?"

The young man looked across at his father, who was sitting in a rocking chair facing them and nursing the pistol.

"He's quite deaf. My brother insisted on fetching our food from market before he would do anything. He's taken our friend to try and hire another carriage."

"I see. My betrothed, Viscount Enstone, is a very rich man. Whatever they are paying you he will double it if you can contrive to delay us as long as possible to give him a chance to catch up. He was out of Town but he will be back soon and is bound to follow us."

The man rubbed his chin. "I reckon I trust you a lot more than that bag of bad barley what calls himself a coachman." He shook his head in disgust. "I can't believe my pa agreed to this. I'll see what I can do. I doubt they'll get another carriage around here." He sniffed. "Our friend won't want to carry you in an open cart for all to see."

"Thank you." Kitty's rumbling stomach reminded her of how little they had eaten. "What do you want us to cook?"

"There's a fresh caught rabbit in the larder. A nice rabbit stew would do me. I'll be off to do some work around the farm once I've fetched the rabbit. Don't try and escape. He's a hard man, my pa. He'll shoot if he has to." He nodded towards his father, nursing a pistol and went out.

Kitty exchanged glances with Annie. "Come on let's get this stew cooked as quickly as we can in the hope we get to eat some of it."

Kitty blanched when the rabbit arrived, still intact. The farmer's son grinned at them but jumped when his father spoke to him.

"You had better skin that, Seb. I'm not letting them have a knife."

"They'll need a knife for the vegetables, Pa."

"Give them a small one for that."

Seb handed them two small knives and expertly skinned the rabbit. Kitty averted her eyes and heard Annie give a soft chuckle.

They soon had the stew prepared and cooking in a large pot over the kitchen fire. The farmer picked up the knives and shoved them in a drawer.

"You two sit by the fire and keep that pot stirred."

They sat on a bench in front of the fire. At least they were warm here. Kitty could see the drive up to the farm from where she was sitting. She kept her eyes focussed on it, willing the coachman to stay away. They were in luck, the stew cooked without any sign of the coachman. Seb doled them both up plates of stew before his father could object and handed them hunks of bread so fresh that his brother must have bought it that morning.

Kitty forced herself to eat slowly and Annie followed her lead. Once they had finished Annie patted her stomach.

"I feel so much better for a good meal, Miss Davenport."

Kitty smiled. "I do too. I'm ready for anything now."

She gave a little cry and wished the words unsaid. The farm cart was back. The coachman jumped down and hurried towards the farm. The kitchen door was thrown back so forcefully it creaked in protest. The coachman stormed in with a thunderous expression.

"What kind of a place is this? Not a coach to be had anywhere. There's only one thing for it. Get me some sacks. We'll harness up the two good horses to the cart and cover the three of them up with sacks." He jerked a finger at Seb's brother. "You'll have to come with us if you want your cart back."

"You'll have to wait with food on the table. I'm eating first."

The coachman retrieved his pistol from the farmer and pointed it at Seb. "You'll do then."

He gestured to Kitty and Annie to get up. Within minutes they were loaded onto the farm cart and a protesting Sir Randolph was thrown in beside them. One arm was out of his coat sleeve and he must have sobered enough to fashion a sling for his arm from a cravat. Kitty couldn't imagine that anyone else had done it for him. After an altercation the coachman agreed to let him sit with his back to the driver's seat so he could nurse the arm.

"You two, lie down on the floor."

They lay down where the coachman pointed and he covered them with a layer of sacking. Kitty managed to pull one off and roll it up to cushion her head and did the same for Annie. Even so it was an uncomfortable ride and the sacks over them smelt musty. Kitty prayed that she would keep her dinner down. She needed all her strength to find a way out of this.

After what seemed like a lifetime, the noise from the wheels changed. Kitty caught Annie's hand.

"We're on a toll road now I would say."

"I hope so, Miss. I'm sick of this."

Within a few minutes they jolted over cobbles and came to rest. They heard someone jump down. The sacks were pulled off and Seb helped them into a sitting position. They were around the back of an inn yard but there was no one in sight. Seb winked at her.

"They stopped hiring out horses and carriages here a year or two back, when a better toll road opened on a more direct route. We'll have to either go back the way we've come to pick that up or carry on for at least five miles." He winked again. "The horses are tiring so it will take ages either way."

He climbed back onto the driver's seat. The coachman joined them.

"What are you, the village idiot? They don't hire out horses let alone carriages no more."

"How was I to know? We ain't been this way in a twelve-month or more."

"So which way now?"

Seb shrugged. "Back the way we've come?"

"It might be quicker but the innkeeper says The Red Lion should be able to help us and it's not far."

Seb nodded. "Right you are."

The coachman roared at them to cover up and they set off. They soon slowed down. Kitty spread the bags a little so she could hear what the coachman was saying.

"They don't look lame to me."

"Not yet, but I tell you they will be soon if we don't take it slowly."

"Well try and speed them up a bit."

They picked up speed slightly but it wasn't fast enough for the coachman.

"Faster, dammit."

"If you say so but this be a quiet stretch from what I remember, if they break down we'll be stuck."

"We should reach the Red Lion soon."

"About five miles to go I should say."

"What?"

The coachman roared so loud that Sir Randolph started shouting too. "I can't stand another minute of this."

The coachman ignored him. "He said it was close by."

"Not a countryman, are you? Now do you want to get to the Red Lion or do you want the horses to break down along the way?"

The coachman grunted something and the cart slowed down. They trundled on for what must have been at least two hours. Seb was doing his best for them. Kitty gasped at the angry expression on the coachman's face as he pulled the sacks off them.

"Sit up now. We can pretend we begged a lift with a farmer for the start of our journey." He jerked a thumb at Sir Randolph. "If anyone asks, he's your uncle, Miss Davenport. Don't speak to anyone if you can avoid it."

Kitty glared at him. "So what part are you playing, his jailer or his long-lost best friend?"

The coachman raised his hand as if to hit her. Annie cried out which seemed to bring him to his senses. His face contorted into a snarl.

"You'll pay for that Miss High and Mighty."

He grabbed Kitty's arm and held it so tightly that tears came to her eyes. She fought them down. She wouldn't give him the satisfaction of seeing her cry. A vision of Luke swam before her. Would she ever see him again in the flesh?"

The coach stopped and the coachman yanked her to her feet.

"You can come with me. I'll have that pretty necklace off you if I haven't got enough money."

Kitty fingered her mother's pearls. What had possessed her

to wear them in the day time? The possibility of losing the link with her mother was like a physical pain, but it wasn't as bad as the thought of never seeing Luke again.

The coachman let go of her arm when they neared the inn.

"Get rid of that Friday face. We need to get a carriage and horses from here or we're sunk. If I can't get you to Shepley, I'll shoot the pair of you and disappear. You're tangling with dangerous men. Don't say I didn't warn you."

Kitty shuddered and pasted a smile on her face. She believed him, but at least he had let slip that they were indeed going to Shepley. A gust of wind shook the sign hanging in front of the inn. Kitty's gaze was drawn to it. A pink lion, which must have once been red, stared down at her. The Red Lion had seen better days. They went in and found the coffee room. The coachman assumed a sickly smile when the landlord answered his summons.

"My lady and her uncle are on the way to visit relatives and our coach has lost a wheel. We need to hire a travelling carriage and four horses."

The landlord, a giant of a man, stared at him. "A carriage and four horses you say?"

"That's what I said."

The coachman's struggle to hide his impatience would have been funny if her situation wasn't so dire.

"We're low on carriage horses. Not so much call for them these days with the new road over the way. Our trade is mostly riding horses. Suppose that's no good with the lady in your party. I'll go and find out what we've got." He lumbered off.

Kitty took a seat. She glanced around but the coffee room was deserted. It was a good few minutes before the landlord returned and addressed the coachman.

"Best we can do for you is a coach with two horses and I'll be in trouble if the squire wants to hire it this week. So just you get it back to us as soon as you can."

Two men entered and the coachman studied them before answering. He looked like he wanted to argue. The men weren't taking any notice of them but an altercation would draw attention and from the stubborn set of the landlord's jaw Kitty didn't think there was any better to be had. She wasn't surprised when the coachman capitulated. The landlord named a very reasonable price and he handed it over. Her mother's pearls were safe for now but whether the Red Lion would see their coach again was a moot point.

The coachman jerked his head towards the door and she followed him out towards the inn yard. An ostler in a torn and grubby uniform harnessed two horses that her father would have had no hesitation in calling bonesetters to an outmoded coach. Annie helped Lord Randolph to climb in and Kitty joined them. There was no sign of Seb. If she escaped Sir Walter's clutches, she would have to make sure that Luke paid him a decent sum. She heard the coachman shout at the horses and they set off.

It soon became apparent that the horses had two paces, slow and stop. She heard the sound of a whip but even that made no difference. A few splashes of rain hit the coach window. There was no way they would reach Shepley tonight, especially with the weather closing in. If he was following, Luke would have a good chance of catching up at this sort of speed, for they would have to re-join the main road at some point. She smiled at Annie.

"We won't get much farther at this rate with this sort of weather," she whispered. Sir Randolph appeared to be fast asleep but she wanted to be sure he didn't hear.

"With horses like the ones we've got I doubt if we'll manage more than another ten miles before it goes dark."

Annie leaned towards her. "I heard the coachman talking to Sir Randolph. He used to drive mail coaches. He said he would drive in the dark as this coach has lamps fitted."

"It might have lamps but there's no protection for the coach driver. He'll get wet through if this rain keeps up." Kitty laughed. For the first time since they had stopped at the farmhouse with Lord Randolph she felt confident they would be rescued. "I'm sure Lord Enstone will be on our trail soon."

Annie shook her head. "I hope so, Miss, but he could be days in Northampton."

The coach slowed down and Kitty risked putting her head out of the window. The dark clouds overhead blocked out the early evening light but she could just about make out the outline of the horse on her side of the coach. The poor animal had gone lame. The coachman had an impressive command of curses. Some of them she had never heard despite often working with the horses at Davenport Court and hearing the grooms talk.

They proceeded at a snail's pace with the rain now drumming at the sides of the coach. They would have to stop at the next inn. Kitty allowed her mind to wander to dreams of marrying Luke. Heat flooded her cheeks at thoughts of their wedding night and she was glad of the gloom enveloping the interior of the coach. Her thoughts returned to the horse. Lord, if the coachman pushed it on much farther the poor thing would be ruined for good.

The rain seemed set in for the evening. Whether it was that or the condition of the horses, the other one probably wasn't in much better case, they pulled into an inn quite quickly. The yard was clean and tidy and what she could see of the inn was well kept. Sir Randolph woke up as they jolted to a stop. He sat up and nursed his arm in the sling with his other arm.

"Damn and blast my arm. It's agony. What's going on, where are we?" A smell of brandy on his breath suggested he had manged to find another supply at the Red Lion.

"I couldn't see the name of the inn but we must be back on a main route, probably one leading to the main toll road," Kitty said.

The coachman wrenched the door open and lifted her down before she could protest. She shivered as water from his dripping coat spread through her clothes, where he held her against him as he turned to put her down. Her hand found its way to her mother's pearls. This place looked expensive and she didn't doubt that the coachman would carry through on his threat to use them to pay their way.

Chapter Nineteen

L uke's party rode until failing light and growing cloud cover necessitated an overnight stop. Perhaps he should have had the big family travelling carriage with its lamps out but that would have drawn too much attention. His plan to arrive stealthily was sound, which conclusion didn't help him to cope with the tightness in his chest at the thought of Kitty in the power of the likes of Greenough. He tried shrugging his shoulders but it did nothing to reduce the tension coiled throughout his body. He ached with it.

He turned in the saddle and called out to the other three. "I can see an inn coming up. We had better put up for the night."

They were soon ensconced in a sizeable coffee room with a blazing fire and a jug of ale in front of them. Now he had made the decision to stop, Luke's brain seemed clearer. He glanced around the room as they waited for their supper. He was under the impression that they were the only occupants and then the rustle of a newspaper alerted him to a gentleman seated in an armchair near to the fire. Even sitting down the gentleman's fine physique was obvious and marked him out as something of a Corinthian. He looked up as if he sensed Luke's scrutiny.

Luke produced an easy smile and received a polite nod in acknowledgement. He turned back to his companions with his mind whirring. There was something about the man which jarred but he couldn't work out what. Had there been a glint of recognition in his steely grey eyes? If so, why hadn't he mentioned that they were acquainted? Fletcher and Bright started talking about horses. Luke smiled at Wallace who was sitting by the side of him and leaned a little closer.

"Don't look now. The gentleman in the armchair may have recognised me," he said, keeping his voice low. "I can't place him. Have a look if you get a chance without him seeing you. There is something about him that troubles me. Perhaps I'm imagining shadows where there are none but I'm uneasy."

"I've noticed Bright and Fletcher have been careful not to use your name in here." Wallace raised his voice. "I wonder how long we will have to wait for our supper."

Bright rose. "I'll go and find out." He glanced over his shoulder and leaned forward. "Avoid him in the armchair."

The blood roared in Luke's ears and the tight feeling came back in his chest. So Bright knew the man and it wasn't good news. It took all his willpower to avoid looking across to the armchair. Instead he kept up a stream of inane chatter. Bright returned a few moments later.

"They say it won't be long now. It smells like it will be worth waiting for."

The man in the armchair rose and made his way out of the room. Luke risked a glance at his retreating back. He was everything that was elegant. His clothes clearly from a master tailor and his boots shining with a gloss that only a first-rate valet could have achieved.

Bright leaned back in his chair as far as he could without tipping it up. "He's gone now. Fletcher, have a scout round and see where he is now and where he goes, if you can without being seen."

"That's Lord Sewell. I tracked him down living in Davenport Court. I was very careful not to be seen." He looked at Luke. "He might have recognised you, even though you've dressed in old clothes."

Luke grimaced. "I'm pretty sure he did, but couldn't place me. He can't have seen me more than once or twice. We don't move in the same circles. At least we know we're going in the right direction. How far is Davenport Court from Shepley?"

"Less than an hour. The house Greenough is living in is just outside Shepley village. They could be taking them to either place."

Fletcher returned. "He had a word with the landlord, who told him we were Mr Wallace's party. Then he set off in a smart curricle."

Luke stroked his chin. "He isn't sure who I am but it may come back to him. He'll stick to the main routes if he's on his way to wherever they are holding Kitty. Is there any way to avoid them without losing too much time, Bright?"

"There's an almost parallel route for a good stretch of the way. It's not such a good road but that won't matter on horseback."

The landlady arrived with a young maid and they laid a large pie and a cooked chicken in front of them.

Luke sniffed the air and smiled at the landlady. "That smells delicious."

The landlady dimpled up at him. "I do enjoy having my food appreciated. We'll be back in a moment with the rest."

Luke thanked her and called to the landlord for another jug of ale. The ale arrived at the same time as two dishes of buttered carrots. Eating was the last thing he felt like but he had learned in the army to eat whenever a meal was available and it stood him in good stead.

Finally, Luke leaned back in his chair. "This is good food for a country inn. I wonder why Sewell didn't stop here. We should press on or we might be too late." His stomach lurched at the thought. He went to stand but Wallace put a hand on his arm.

"Your new man of business told me that Sewell has an aunt this side of Leicestershire. He has expectations from her. It's possible he's visiting her but didn't want to disturb the household for a late meal."

"Maybe." His brain started functioning again. "He doesn't strike me as the sort of man who wants to be personally involved in this sort of business and yet would want to be reasonably nearby. He may be giving himself a witness as to his whereabouts."

"I expect you're right, my lord," Fletcher said. "He knows the landlord pretty well from what I managed to see."

Luke nodded. "Ideally, we should split up and have Bright track him but would we find this route without you, Bright?"

"Do you mean the road to the Red Lion at Carsby?" Wallace asked.

Bright nodded.

"I can find that. My father was the vicar in the next village when I was a boy."

"Good. I'll be off then." Bright pushed his plate away but Luke shook his head.

"Finish your food. You don't want to get too close to him to start with."

The window rattled. "There's a storm brewing," Wallace said. "I don't think our man will go far in this. His aunt's house was called something like Ridgeacre Grange. There's a village called Ridgeway about five miles along this road."

Rain started beating at the window. Luke picked up his knife and fork. "Eat your meal, Bright. Perhaps we had better all stay here."

Bright pursed his lips. "You three should but I know somewhere I can borrow a horse and catch a few hours sleep. Not that far from Ridgeacre. I know the paths around here pretty well and my horse should be good for a few more miles after a rest."

"Then we all should go."

"It's a farm. They won't have four horses. Besides I'm much fresher than you. I'll find out what I can and meet you by Shepley Church in the morning."

"What if they go to another church?" Luke tried to focus his tired brain. "Greenough lives in Shepley. They would need a bishop's licence for anywhere else."

"If only I had worked out what it meant I could have checked in Shepley if Greenough was having the banns called."

"True, but if I hadn't told the Spencers to keep away from him they would have been in church to hear them. I can't think of a better plan. We'll get to Shepley as early as we can."

Chapter Twenty

L uke roused his party before dawn and they were on the road at first light. Even with the hold up of a flock of sheep blocking their way at one point they reached Church Lane, Shepley at around half past eight. They hid the horses in a spinney near to the church. Luke's pulse thundered in his ears at the sight of an old coach drawn up by the church and two rough looking individuals standing by the main door. He signalled to Fletcher and Wallace who captured and tied up the two guards with the minimum of noise.

Luke ran into the church and came to an abrupt halt. Kitty was standing at the altar with Sir Walter Greenough beside her. Her green travelling dress was crumpled and she had no bonnet. He would murder Greenough if he had harmed her. He gulped for air and edged forwards. Had their frantic chase all been for nothing? He heard the words, 'Will you take this man...' as if in a trance.

Kitty's voice rang out loud and true. "No. I will not. I am betrothed to another and have been brought here by force."

The clergyman stood immobile watching Greenough. No help there by the looks of it. Luke crouched low and edged his way around the unoccupied side of the church.

Greenough grabbed Kitty's arm. "You'll do as you're told or

we'll kill your brother."

"Produce Edward and I'll marry you."

"Make your vows now or I'll shoot your maid." Greenough's red face was a mask of fury.

Kitty pushed him off. "Shoot my maid and I'll know you don't have Edward."

Luke sprang into action, trusting that Fletcher and Wallace had his back, in case there were any more of Greenough's men besides the two they had already tied up. He ran towards the altar and came to a full stop when Greenough raised a pistol to him.

He stared at the clergyman, who refused to meet his gaze. "She doesn't want to marry Greenough. Stop this farce immediately."

The clergyman looked at Greenough and then at Luke. "Everything is perfectly in order. I suggest you leave. I don't want any bloodshed in this church."

Greenough glanced at Kitty. Bright appeared from behind a pew and grabbed the pistol from him.

Luke left Bright to grapple with Greenough and blocked the path of the clergyman when he tried to run out of the church.

"Where do you think you're going? You have a lot of explaining to do."

The man dodged through an empty row of pews but Fletcher grabbed him. Kitty screamed and Luke twisted around in time to miss a blow from a large, red-faced man, wearing groom's clothes. Luke floored him with one punch. Fletcher and Bright soon had Greenough and the clergyman tied up. They turned their attention to helping Wallace subdue Luke's adversary, who tried to get up but failed.

Luke's legs somehow obeyed his instruction to move to

Kitty's side. He threw an arm around her.

"Luke, that's Mr Peters, the new curate. I think they have the vicar tied up somewhere, probably in the crypt." She pointed to a door at the side of the church.

Luke signalled to Fletcher who slipped through the door.

"My darling, I'm so glad to have you safe. When I realised you had been kidnapped ..."

Luke buried his head in Kitty's hair. It had escaped its pins and was hanging down her back. Lord she must have put up a fight.

"Who's there?" Wallace's voice came from behind him.

Luke spun round to see a young woman wearing the clothing of a maid and an elderly man with his arm in a sling, who looked distinctly foxed, sitting up in a pew. "The witnesses I presume."

Kitty caught at his arm. "That's my maid, Annie and Sir Randolph. Sir Walter has Sir Randolph's wife somewhere and he was forced to trick me into coming with him on pain of her death."

An elderly gentleman in clerical robes limped through the door from the crypt.

"Thank you for releasing me." He turned to Kitty. "I hope your rescuers arrived in time, my dear."

"Yes, Mr Fisher." She smiled up at Luke and his heart missed a beat. "Fortunately, Lord Enstone arrived just as I refused to make the vows. Are you badly injured?"

"I've escaped with nothing worse than a sore leg from being thrown down the crypt stairs. I fear Mr Peters will have to be reported to the church for agreeing to officiate at a forced marriage. He seemed such a suitable young man too." Mr Fisher shook his head.

Luke felt his pocket and found the reassuring bulk of his special licence. There was no sign of Sewell. He wouldn't feel safe until Sewell was under lock and key but without direct involvement it would be difficult to prove anything. He squeezed Kitty's hand.

"You're a rich young woman, Kitty. That's what this is all about. Does that make you change your mind about marrying me?"

He studied her face, watching every change of expression. Did she have feelings for him or had she agreed out of expediency?

She stared at him for a long moment and smiled. "I haven't changed my mind unless you have."

Luke thought he would faint with relief. He couldn't imagine life without Kitty. He took a great heave of a breath.

"I want to marry you more than ever. If Mr Fisher feels up to it, let's get married now. I've got the special licence with me. Once we're married, I can keep you safe with me. I thought I would lose my mind with worry on the journey here."

Kitty looked stunned for a moment. "I can see why you suggest it but it's a shame not to have our family here."

The church door opened and Mrs Spencer ran in. She enveloped Kitty in a tearful embrace.

"Spencer has gone to fetch the magistrate, Colonel Sheppard," Bright said. "I tracked Sewell to his aunt's house last night. I managed to hide by the stables for a bit and overheard a groom complaining about having to go to Davenport Court this morning. I expect Sewell is waiting there to meet up with Greenough. It could get interesting when Sewell doesn't hear from him."

A distinguished looking man with a military bearing entered.

"Ah, Enstone. Pleased to meet you. I knew your father well and I would have recognised you anywhere. Mr Bright has told me about Sir Walter Greenough, bad business trying to force a respectable young woman to the altar." He looked across at Sir Walter's trussed up figure, lying in front of the pulpit. "Can't say I liked the fellow from the moment he arrived. We'll soon have everything right and tight for you. You can rely on my discretion."

"Thank you." Luke could contain his impatience no longer. "If Mr Fisher will marry us now it should keep Miss Davenport's reputation safe."

Mr Fisher grinned at him. "I shall be delighted to do so, my lord. I believe you are worthy of our Miss Davenport. First though, let us repair to the vicarage. My wife will be wondering where I am and Miss Davenport will surely be grateful for a chance to tidy her hair."

"Capital." Colonel Sheppard beamed at them. "I'll have my men load these villains up and take them away so you can have a proper ceremony."

* * *

Everything seemed so unreal Kitty expected to wake up at any moment. A bubble of happiness made her smile. Luke loved her. It had been plain from his expression as he waited for her to say if she still wanted to marry her. She was going to have the love match she had always wanted. Luke reached out for her hand and she instinctively held it out, forgetting the rope burns on her wrists.

Luke stared at the red wheals. "Who did this to you?" His voice came out as a roar that had Mr Fisher limping towards them.

Kitty pointed to two of the colonel's men, staggering under the weight of the coachman. "The coachman did. My maid is still tied up."

Luke signalled to Fletcher to free Annie.

"We tried to escape so he tied us up. When we tried to get away earlier he threatened to shoot Annie, so we waited until we were in Shepley. We nearly made it but one of the men who joined us in Shepley spotted us." Kitty bit back a sob. "Annie told me she would rather be shot than see me married to Sir Walter. We agreed that she would duck down in the pew as soon as I refused to make the wedding vow to give me time to try and brazen it out with Sir Walter, to buy some time. I had a feeling he didn't have Edward."

"That was clever, demanding he produce Edward."

"My defiance would have crumbled if he had looked like shooting Annie, whatever she said."

Luke pointed to the coachman. "Hanging is too good for him. Is he the man who drove the carriage from London?"

"Yes. I'm glad to say he was an awful driver." Kitty felt a laugh bubbling to the surface. "This is the first time I have ever been glad of someone treating his horses badly. If he had looked after them properly you wouldn't have caught us in time."

"My poor girl, you were so brave. Let's get you over to the vicarage."

A tearful Nella was standing nearby.

Kitty managed a smile for her. "I'm quite safe now, Nella."

"I'll go and talk to Colonel Sheppard before he goes. He needs to know how you were treated. Go to the vicarage with Mrs Spencer and have her look at your poor wrists."

Kitty nodded and watched Luke leave the church. Nella hugged her again.

"I'm perfectly well, Nella. Somehow I knew that Luke would get here in time." She laughed. "I didn't expect him to leave it quite as late as he did. Where's Annie? She was knocked to the floor and she's badly bruised."

Nella let her go and scanned the church. "There she is, in the second pew from the front. Oh, the poor dear, she looks dreadfully pale."

Nella ran across to Annie and Kitty followed at a more sedate pace. Her legs still felt wobbly. Lord, what an adventure. The relief of Luke's arrival had soon turned to horror when Sir Walter aimed a pistol at him. She shivered and breathed hard. They were all safe now and Luke still wanted to marry her, even though there was no longer any need. He loved her. She hugged the thought to her. Her secret dream, the one she had barely been able to admit even to herself, had come true. Marriage to a man who didn't love her would be her worst nightmare.

Kitty came to a halt next to Annie's pew. Nella helped Annie to her feet and led her out into the aisle. She exclaimed over the rope burns on Annie's wrists. The sound of her voice seemed to galvanise Sir Randolph, who had been the other side of Annie. He pushed past them.

"My wife, where is she?"

He ran around the church as if she was hidden somewhere within it and then howled when he couldn't find her. Even though he had tricked her, Kitty felt sorry for him.

"Have you any idea what's happened to Lady Randolph, Nella?"

Nella put an arm around a shivering Annie.

"Mr Bright might know but let's get you two into the vicarage before you catch cold."

A short, stocky man, with twinkling eyes called out to them. "Lady Randolph is quite safe. Colonel Sheppard's men rescued her earlier."

Sir Randolph fell to his knees in front of the altar and started praying. Kitty heard him say something about forgiveness and Kitty went across to lay a hand on his shoulder.

"We forgive you, Sir Randolph. You must love your wife very much."

Sir Randolph nodded and burst into noisy sobs. Nella asked Bright to look after him and chivvied her charges out of the church and across to the vicarage. Mrs Fisher was standing at the open door waiting for them.

"You poor dears. Come in and get warm. I've got some milk warming up for you. There are some freshly baked biscuits as well. I can't believe I was happily baking away with so much drama going on in the church."

Kitty and Annie sat side by side on an old settee in the kitchen and allowed the two ladies to fuss over them. Once they had eaten and drunk their fill, Mrs Fisher produced some salve for their grazed and bruised wrists. Kitty heard Annie wince when she turned to hold up her wrists.

"I think Annie has bruises on her body where she was pushed over, Mrs Fisher."

There was a knock at the door. Mrs Fisher opened it and Bright came in carrying their bags.

"I thought you might like a change of clothes, ladies. Are these yours?"

A spurt of joy ran through Kitty. She would have a clean gown for her wedding. "Yes they are. Thank you so much, Mr

Bright."

"My pleasure, Miss Davenport."

Mrs Fisher locked the door behind him. "This is the warmest room in the house. Let's strip you off."

Annie jumped up. "It's my job to dress you Miss Davenport."

Kitty hugged her. "I know it is, Annie but you need looking after too today. Mrs Spencer helped me dress at Shepley Hall even though she's the housekeeper. We shall manage very well. Let Mrs Fisher look at your bruises."

Kitty winced when Mrs Fisher peeled off Annie's clothes to reveal a huge bruise spreading over one thigh and hip. She put a hand to her wet cheek and realised that she was crying.

"You were so brave, Annie."

"Not half as brave as you, Miss."

Mrs Fisher reached for the pot of salve and gently spread some over Annie's bruise.

"This will help but you will be sore for days. I don't think there will be any long lasting damage though."

Once they were dressed in clean clothes, Annie insisted on tidying up Kitty's hair. Her deft fingers soon had it in reasonable order. Mrs Fisher stood back and looked at Kitty.

"That's much better, Miss Davenport. I can see London style in your gown. It's lovely."

"Thank you. Yes, this was bought in London recently."

Kitty glanced down at the pretty cream sprigged muslin. It seemed a lifetime away since she had first gone shopping with Lady Grant and Grace. She took a deep breath and closed her eyes. How would she have felt then if she had known she was to marry Luke? He had seemed quite arrogant and uncaring at first but now she knew him better his personality was much closer to Grace's sunny nature. She opened her eyes to see

Nella smiling at her.

"Oh, Miss Davenport, I'm so happy to see you settled with a good man who will look after you." Nella dabbed at her eyes.

Kitty's own eyes felt suspiciously damp. "Thank you for everything, Nella. We would have never managed without you and Robert."

There was a knock at the door and Mrs Fisher opened it. Mr Wallace entered.

"Lord Enstone sent me to tell you that everything is ready for the wedding, Miss Davenport. Allow me to escort you into the church."

"Thank you." Kitty placed her hand on Mr Wallace's arm and allowed him to lead her across the churchyard. Nella was right. It was wonderful to have someone to look after her, at least for some of the time. She had looked after her father and brother ever since mother had died. Then latterly her aunt had needed all her care.

Nella, Annie and Mrs Fisher followed behind them. Robert Spencer was already in the church, sitting towards the back with Mr Bright. Kitty allowed her gaze to travel to the man standing at the altar. He had found a clean neck-cloth but he was still in his riding gear. Her breath hitched. He would look wonderful in a sack but the buckskin breeches showed off his powerful thighs to perfection. His smile when he first saw her was breath-taking. How could she have ever thought him anything less than handsome?

She smiled back at him as she reached the altar and took her place next to him. At last she had found the sort of love that her parents had enjoyed. It was a dream she had long given up on, expecting to spend the rest of her life being useful to Edward. It was hard to believe that she could be so lucky. The vicar beamed at them and the service began. This time she had no hesitation in making her vows. Afterwards Luke tucked her arm through his and led her out of the church. The contact with him sent shivers through her.

Surprisingly, a small crowd had gathered outside. Kitty couldn't help smiling.

"News travels quickly in the country."

"Indeed. Once we've given them time to look at the bride we had better get you into the warm, you keep shivering."

Nella bustled up to them. "I've kept all the rooms at Shepley Hall aired, my lord. It's too late for you to be travelling now."

"Mrs Spencer you're a gem. I believe Mrs Fisher wants us to go back to the vicarage for a while and then we will make our way there," he glanced down at Kitty, "if that is agreeable to you."

"Of course."

The vicar and his wife led the way back to the vicarage. Mr Fisher was still limping and had a hand on his wife's shoulder for support. Kitty watched with concern. They were shown into the dining room where Mrs Fisher had laid out a cold collation.

Kitty stepped forwards. "This is so kind of you Mrs Fisher. Should we send for the doctor to look at Mr Fisher's leg?"

Mr Fisher shook his head. "It's of no matter."

Luke answered before Kitty could. "I agree with Kitty. I'll send Bright to fetch the doctor and I insist on paying his fee."

Luke slipped out to find Bright and Nella followed him with Annie. He was soon back and they took their places around the table. There was a knock at the door and Mr Wallace joined them.

"The Spencers are on their way to Shepley Hall with Fletcher and Miss, sorry, Lady Enstone's maid. I'll follow them."

Luke glanced at Mrs Fisher who nodded. "I would prefer it if you joined us Mr Wallace."

"That's very kind of you."

Luke grinned. "Not at all. It means you and Bright can escort us later. There is always the possibility that Sewell might try and join the party."

Chapter Twenty One

Kitty lay awake in the big bed listening for the sound of anyone arriving. The light from the candle by her bed sent shadows dancing around the room. She heard the huge grandfather clock in the hall chime twelve times. This was not how she had dreamed her wedding night would be. Fear left her gasping for breath. She couldn't bear it if Luke was injured, or worse. Why couldn't he have left Colonel Sheppard to wait for Sewell to make an appearance? A laugh escaped her and her breathing eased. She ought to know by now that Luke was a man who led from the front.

Even if they caught Sewell, would Greenough's testimony be enough to put him behind bars? She shivered. Neither she nor Edward would be safe with him at large if what Luke had found out about their family trust was true. Oh where was Luke? She would happily give Sewell her share of the fund to keep Luke safe but men didn't see it that way.

Kitty jumped out of bed and ran to the window at the sound of hoof-beats. She counted the horses and let out a huge sigh when the fourth horseman appeared. Luke, Mr Wallace, Mr Bright and Mr Fletcher were all safe. Thank goodness. Her thoughts turned to Luke and her body tingled. Luke would be tired but the excitement of the chase would have kept him alert.

She glanced at the connecting door into his room. Strange to think that Luke's mother had slept in this very bed, with his father next door. Would he come to her tonight? Should she let him know that she was still awake?

She hesitated but climbed into bed. There was so much she didn't know about him and she didn't want him to think that she was too forward. Her breathing quickened as she lay listening for his tread on the stairs. Their snatched kisses had been so exciting, especially the day he had pulled her onto his lap. Heat pooled between her thighs at the memory. What would it be like to be joined with him? He seemed a tough man on the outside but he was a kind man underneath. Of that she was sure. He had mentioned his father being cold-hearted. Perhaps his tough shell was his way of protecting himself?

She was half asleep by the time he finally came through the connecting door. Her eyes flew open and she sat up in bed. He was wearing a simple nightshirt, open at the neck to show a dusting of light-coloured hair. Her heart raced and she held out a hand to him. He sat on the side of the bed and gently kissed the inside of one of her rope damaged wrists. It stung at first but then the aching pain seemed to ease.

"I've been so worried about you, Luke. Did you catch Sewell?"

Luke moved closer and stroked her hair. "Yes, we did. You're safe now." He shuddered as he said it.

Kitty licked her lips. He was so close she could feel his breath on her cheek. She closed her eyes and stretched her lips up towards him. The warmth between her thighs was so insistent that she longed for something more but didn't know what. Her whole body felt heavy. Luke's lips played with hers and she arched her back to get closer to him. He groaned and took her in his arms. Her arms found their own way around his neck. His tongue teased her lips and she opened for him. The kiss made her senses reel. Waves of heat shot through her and settled deep in her abdomen.

Luke sat up and she stared at him in surprise. He smiled at her and pulled his nightshirt over his head. She gasped at the shadows playing on his chest muscles from the candlelight. Her own nightgown found its way over her head, with help from Luke. He tossed it on top of his nightshirt on the floor. Her pulse raced when he lifted the covers and climbed into bed with her. He nibbled at her ears and then feathered little kisses all the way down her neck and onwards until he reached the valley between her breasts. She gasped as he tasted one rosy nipple and then the other. His hand played with the curls at the apex of her abdomen and then found its way between her thighs.

Luke leaned forward so his mouth was by her ear. "Let's see if you are ready for me." His finger teased at her entrance and sank deep.

She squirmed with pleasure. "Oh, Luke."

His hips bucked as he lay beside her. Kitty remembered the feel of his erection underneath her when she had sat on his lap.

"It's my turn to explore. Now might be the time for me to find out why sitting on your lap wasn't a good idea."

"Are you sure?" Luke withdrew his finger and chuckled at her gasp of protest. His finger started circling around the little nub it landed on. "There is that better?"

Kitty arched her back. "Much better but you're not going to deflect me. I want to play with you."

Luke sighed. "If you must, but I warn you be careful or you

will spoil our fun. Too much stimulation and I won't be able to last."

"How do you mean?"

"If you don't find out I'll explain later."

Kitty ran her hand down his chest and stopped as she reached his abdomen, suddenly shy. "Are you sure you don't mind?"

"Why on earth should I when I'm doing this to you?" His finger slipped back inside her and he added a second one.

For a moment Kitty was completely lost in the wave of sensation that shot through her. Then curiosity got the better of her and her hand swept lower to find its target. Heavens he was huge. She ran her hand over his length. It felt like silk over an iron core. Her hand closed over it and she squeezed gently. Luke's hips lifted off the bed. He raised himself on one elbow and kissed her. So this was what girls risked everything for. His lips moved lower and found one of her nipples and then the other. Her hand closed round him seemingly of its own accord.

"Enough. You're ready for me. Do you know what that means?"

For a moment Kitty was too lost to answer him. "Yes I do. Yes I'm ready for you."

Luke groaned and lifted over her. He placed himself at her entrance and a quick spurt of pain was replaced by a feeling of exciting fullness. Luke entered and retreated again and again, gently at first and then with more urgency. He reached between them and played with her nub. Waves of pleasure washed over her as her abdomen contracted in a rhythm of its own and she cried out. Luke sank deeper into her and gave his own cry before collapsing on top of her, panting.

He rolled off her and fell asleep. Kitty pulled the covers,

which had somehow been thrown off, back over them. She wanted to talk to him, to tell him how wonderful it had been, but he must be tired after such an eventful day. She was exhausted herself. He had been so patient with her that she couldn't doubt that he loved her. It was a wonderful feeling to be loved and cared for.

* * *

Luke woke up with a start. Where was he? He sat up in bed to see Kitty curled up next to him. The events of the last few days came back to him. He was a married man now. The gnawing anxiety of not knowing if he would be able to save her from the clutches of Sir Walter Greenough had come close to oversetting him. Oh Lord, he was just like his father. What had he done? Kitty might be bearing his child after only one night of pleasure. His teeth began to chatter. He rolled out of bed, grabbed his nightshirt from where it lay on the floor and threw it over his head as he made his way to the connecting door. He needed time alone to think. Kitty muttered something but she seemed to be fast asleep. He eased the door open and fled to the sanctuary of his own room. His whole body was shivering.

Light was creeping around the edges of the curtains. He pulled the drapes around the bed, something he rarely did after years of camping out in the army and burrowed under the covers. He hadn't been able to resist Kitty when she was so obviously waiting for him. If only he had gone straight to bed. Merciful sleep claimed him and the room was bathed in light when he woke up. He eased into a sitting position. It was tempting to try for more sleep but his mouth was dry from thirst, it must be late. There was a knock at the door and Mrs

Spencer entered, carrying a tray.

"It's nearly noon, my lord. I've brought you some tea."

"Mrs Spencer, you're a lifesaver. I didn't get much sleep on the way here and it's caught up with me."

Mrs Spencer avoided his gaze and bustled forwards to lay the tray on a side table. "A nice cup of tea will set you to rights."

Luke felt himself blush. His sleep had been disturbed last night as well as Mrs Spencer had no doubt realised. "Thank you, Mrs Spencer. A drink is just what I need. Then I had better think about getting dressed."

She pointed to a bell. "Take your time. When you're ready ring that and I'll send Robert up to help you dress."

Luke felt a lot better after two cups of tea. It was time he paid a courtesy visit to Colonel Sheppard, which gave him an excuse to avoid Kitty for a bit until he had sorted out his feelings. Kitty would be enjoying spending time with the Spencers and he could send Bright or Fletcher on ahead to let Aunt Theo and the others know they were all safe. How was he going to cope with being a husband? One day at a time, like a military campaign, that was how.

Lord what had possessed him to get married straight away like that. The urge to protect Kitty had been so overwhelming all he could think about was keeping her safe from another attempt to marry her to one of Sewell's cronies. With Greenough out of the way there was no threat to Kitty's reputation. With time to think about it Kitty might have had doubts too. They hardly knew each other after all. He sighed. That wasn't the point though, was it? He couldn't see how he could ever be a good husband when he was so terrified of being a poor father. What madness had come over him to think about marriage at all?

He had let lust rule his head. He had wanted Kitty ever since the day she had fallen into his arms in the library here. It was too late to worry about it now. There had to be a way to manage. If all the formalities of the arrests were tidied up today they could start the journey to London tomorrow. He could make some excuse to ride. Sharing a carriage with Kitty would make it very difficult to sort out his thoughts. He would have to keep his distance for a bit until he felt more comfortable. It would be easier when they were in London and there were more things to distract him.

There was a tap at the connecting door and Kitty put her head around. "Are you well? You've slept for hours."

Kitty sat down on the edge of his bed, uninvited.

Luke pulled the covers up under his chin, almost as if they were a shield. "I didn't get much sleep on the way here. It's not surprising if I'm tired."

Kitty smiled at him, she must be thinking the same thing as Mrs Spencer. He loved the way her smile lit up her lovely grey eyes. Lord he mustn't think about that. His body was urging him to repeat last night's performance. She moved a bit closer until he could smell her perfume. It was the exotic scent he had noticed the first day he met her. It wasn't lavender or rose or anything he could name. It was light, yet heady and it suited her. She was lovely and his body wanted her but his mind was in turmoil. Memories of his childhood despair at his father's cold rebuffs came back to him and successfully dampened his ardour.

"When will we go back to London, Luke?"

Kitty's smile seemed to falter. He was probably scowling at her.

"Not until we've made sure Sewell and his men have all been

detained so he can't harm you again."

"I can understand that and I'm happy to spend some time here but Edward and your family will be worried."

He bit back a sharp retort. It wasn't Kitty's fault that he was feeling blue-devilled. "I've already thought of that. I'll dress straight away and see if either Bright or Fletcher is here. I'll send one of them on ahead."

Kitty put a hand over one of his. "You could send a messenger."

"There's no time for me to linger. If you'll excuse me I had better get dressed." He snatched his hand away and this time he was sure he could see hurt in her eyes.

Kitty stood and bent over him. She kissed him gently on the lips and it took real effort not to respond. "I'll let you get on."

She sailed out of the room and didn't look back. He felt like a complete bounder but if he couldn't bear to love her then it was better for her to find out now. Although in fairness to her he had to try and make their marriage work at some level. Things would get better. He pulled himself out of bed and rang the bell for Spencer. Once he was shaved and wearing his only set of fresh clothes he went downstairs. He found Wallace in the library.

"Ah good, I'm glad you are here. I was afraid you would all be out. I need to send either Bright or Fletcher on ahead to get a message to my aunt."

"It's in hand, my lord"

"Wallace you are a treasure. Remind me to increase your salary. I don't want anyone stealing you from me."

Wallace grinned. "No need to worry about that, my lord. I haven't enjoyed myself so much in ages."

"What's happening about Sewell, do we know?"

"We've heard from Colonel Sheppard. His men are escorting him to the nearest suitable jail and Fletcher has gone to help. Bright said to tell you he felt it best if none of Sewell's people saw him in case his surveillance skills are needed again. We agreed he would go on ahead in the carriage used to bring Lady Enstone here and return it to the Red Lion on his way to London."

"That's a good plan. I'll go and have some breakfast and then we can head out to see the colonel. Once we hear Sewell is safely detained, along with any of his men Colonel Sheppard can make a case against, we'll go back to London. I don't want to risk travelling if he's still on the loose."

Luke found he had a surprisingly good appetite. He had eaten a plate of ham and eggs when Mrs Spencer came in. She laid a plate of biscuits in front of him.

"Those smell heavenly."

"They are fresh from the oven." Mrs Spencer beamed at him. "Lady Enstone has gone for a walk with her new maid. I'm so glad to see her in her rightful place as a gentleman's wife. The first time I saw you I thought you would be perfect for her.

Luke grinned, in spite of himself. "I've often wondered if you were trying to throw us together at the start."

Mrs Spencer studied the floor with a tell-tale pink glow in her cheeks. "Well I might have done, I suppose, but you would have been hard pressed to find a better wife, not if you searched the length and breadth of England."

"I'm sure you're right, Mrs Spencer. It would be better if she stays inside until we know all of Lord Sewell's men have been caught. I'll go and find them."

The day was much warmer and he decided to forego a coat. He wandered along the drive to the main road. The road was drying out quite well and they should be able to start the journey tomorrow. The walk cleared his head and he went back towards the house to look for Kitty feeling more relaxed. He spotted Kitty and Annie walking around the herb garden and went over to them. Kitty looked his way and gave him a smile but it seemed strained. The muscles behind his neck tightened and he tried to shrug them loose. Kitty had already sensed he was troubled it seemed. She was far too perceptive for comfort.

"I'm going over to see Colonel Sheppard. It will be safer for you to stay inside for now until we are sure that all of Sewell's men have been caught or at least left the district."

Annie looked nervous but Kitty caught this gaze. "There is no need to worry about us." She pulled a small muff pistol out of her reticule and held it up. "I found these. There's a pair. They were a present from my father when I was twenty one. Robert has cleaned them up for me and they're ready to fire. It's a shame I didn't take them to London with me."

Luke stared at the pistol and chuckled. He couldn't keep the amusement out of his voice. "I don't suppose I need to ask if you know how to use that but you would oblige me by staying indoors nevertheless."

He caught a mutinous look on Kitty's face but turned away and marched off towards the stables to find Wallace. Fletcher was by the stables polishing up a sturdy looking travelling carriage.

"That's a good coach. Where did you find it?"

"Colonel Sheppard has lent it to us. He said to tell you he's not sure if he can make any charges stick but he'll make sure Sewell is kept under lock and key for the next few days so you can travel back to London. He's lent you this and some carriage horses for the first stage."

"That's very good of him. Where's Wallace?"

"Colonel Sheppard asked me to send him over to organise the details of Sewell's arrest. He said he would like to see you if you can spare him some time this afternoon."

His team were working wonderfully well together it seemed. "I'll go over now. It's the least I can do. Is it far? I'm wondering if we will need fresh riding horses for tomorrow."

"He's only about three or four miles away. The horses we've got should manage the first stage. Bright has tied his behind the carriage but that will still leave an extra one if you go in the carriage."

"I've a mind to ride rather than be cooped up." He glanced at Sheppard's carriage. It was in good condition but it wasn't in the first flush of youth. "Getting shaken up in that doesn't appeal." Nor did spending two days in close company with Kitty, truth be told.

Fletcher stroked his chin. "As long as neither of the horses you and Mr Wallace ride today is injured we'll manage to the first posting inn. My horse is in good shape, even after a bit of a ride this morning with the colonel's men. I'll ask Spencer if he knows of any farmers who could lend us a horse if we were to be unlucky."

"Good thinking. Lady Enstone and her maid are in the garden. Can you keep an eye on them just in case there are any of Sewell's men still around?" He had no reliance on Kitty returning indoors. She could be quite headstrong. He should have remembered that from his first visit to Shepley Hall.

"Will do. I'll saddle your horse for you first."

Luke helped Fletcher with the horse and memorised Fletcher's directions to Colonel Sheppard's house, Natby

Manor, in the nearby village of Natby. When he arrived he was shown into the library, where Wallace and Colonel Sheppard were deep in conversation.

Colonel Sheppard smiled at him. "Come on in and sit down, young man, if I may call you that. The last time I saw you was before you went away to school."

Luke accepted the high-backed leather seat he was offered. "Good Lord, I remember now. It was the year before Mama died. I think it was probably you who gave me the idea of going into the army."

"Oh dear, was it?" Colonel Sheppard gave him a conspiratorial grin. "I remember that your father missed you dreadfully but he was very proud of your achievements."

Luke couldn't think what to say. How could his father have missed him when they had hardly ever spent any time together since he was eight and virtually none since that incident when he was twelve?

"I see modesty forbids a reply. I understand you sold out when your father became ill but didn't make it home in time."

He was on surer ground now. "I'm afraid so. I was on the continent and it was quite a journey back."

"If it's any consolation to you he wrote to tell me you were on your way and how happy he was that you had agreed to manage the family estates."

Luke's throat tightened. It was surprising that the colonel's words made him feel so sad. He sighed. "There always seemed plenty of time to learn what I needed but suddenly there wasn't. I've been lucky to find a good secretary in Mr Wallace here and an equally good Land Agent."

"At least he knew you were on your way and he had every confidence in you. Mr Wallace has been a great help. He's sent a message to the Duke of Cathlay for help in contacting the other shareholders in Lady Enstone's family businesses. Between them they have a lot of influence I believe. I'm hopeful we shall be able to keep Lord Sewell out of circulation."

Luke accepted a glass of port and it was another hour before he and Wallace were able to take their leave.

"We must be careful with the horses. We'll need them tomorrow."

"We're going back to London then?"

"Yes, it should be safe enough. Fletcher will drive the coach and you and I can ride as guards. I have pistols with me. Lady Grant won't rest until she sees Lady Enstone with her own eyes." It felt strange to refer to Kitty as Lady Enstone and it brought back memories of his mother. "You seem to have made an extremely good impression with Colonel Sheppard."

Wallace went pink and started to protest until Luke held up a hand. "I shouldn't tease you. I'm lucky to have found you. I'll set you to helping sort out the Davenports' affairs once we're in London. I'm hoping to get Davenport Court back for Sir Edward eventually."

"I shall look forward to that. Your new man of business is excellent to work with."

They arrived back at Shepley Hall and Luke stayed chatting to Wallace until it was time to dress for dinner, guiltily aware that he should be spending time with his new bride. Mrs Spencer came in to ask if he wanted Robert's assistance to dress. He declined and made his way upstairs. She had worked wonders with his mud-spattered breeches and somehow managed to wash and dry his neck cloth and linen shirt of the day before. There had been no room to carry anything other than the most basic necessities on horseback, certainly not evening clothes. He spent some time arranging his clean neck cloth into something acceptable for a dinner table and shrugged himself back into his riding jacket.

It was time to face Kitty. Part of him wanted to spend all his time with her and yet the other part was terrified. He was being totally illogical but it seemed that emotions defied logic. He sighed in frustration. All his adult life he had avoided facing up to his problematic relationship with his father. If he had resolved that he might not be in such a sorry state now. Colonel Sheppard's revelation of his father being proud of him, and even the fact of Father talking about him at all had surprised him. Looking back, there had been times when his father had offered opportunities to try and heal the breach. He couldn't regret going into the army straight from university, but he could see now that it had been his way of avoiding the issue.

He made his way down the stairs. His eyes fastened onto peeling wallpaper and threadbare carpets. The place needed such a lot of work. Kitty was waiting for him in front of the fire in the parlour. His cheeks felt hot at the memory of his first interview with her in here. Lord, he had really put her through it. Not that he ought to blame himself for that. If anyone was to blame it was his father. Although, if he had been in regular contact with him before his death he would have known all about it so he could not escape some blame. He felt, rather than saw, Kitty take his hand. She smiled up at him. How hadn't he noticed what a sweet smile she had.

"Come and sit down, Luke. What happened about Sewell?"

He let her lead him to a sofa. "Colonel Sheppard has him under detention for now. He's sent to London for advice from the Duke of Cathlay on how to proceed. His being a peer makes it awkward but we should be able to travel safely tomorrow."

Wallace entered and he waved him to the seat opposite to them. "A word around the clubs from the Duke of Cathlay should be enough to scupper Sewell. There are plenty of rumours about him already."

Kitty put a hand on his shoulder. "What about the coachman who drove us here? They haven't let him loose have they?"

Luke felt her shiver next to him. Being kidnapped by stealth must have been a terrible experience for her.

Wallace answered. "He's on his way to London. He was a mail coach driver but he was caught stealing from travellers and they turned him off. Remember, one of the footmen said he recognised him and thought he was a coach driver? Colonel Sheppard had been warned to look out for him. It seems he has family in this area."

Kitty shivered in earnest and Luke felt obliged to put an arm around her. He didn't like to see her upset.

"Don't worry we'll soon have you safely back in London. What should we do with this place? Renovate it and turn it into a stud to breed our own horses?"

"I would love to do that. I managed to be happy here, with the help of the Spencers, even with our family problems."

He smiled. "I'll give it to you as a wedding present. It sounds as if you will have plenty of your own funds to renovate it."

"Thank you. I don't understand this family trust. If it all belongs to me, can I share it with Edward? It doesn't seem fair otherwise."

"I don't really know much about it. Wallace will sort it all out for you with the help of my new man of business."

"I shall enjoy doing so. Your man of business told me that the family trustees had been looking for Lady Enstone and her brother for ages. It's an intriguing story. Did you know you have a Scottish cousin?" Wallace smiled at Kitty, looking like a conjuror who had just pulled a rabbit out of a hat.

She shook her head. "I wasn't aware of any relations, let alone Scottish ones."

"Your cousin is the next in line to the family trust, on his mother's side, after you and your brother. His father was very well connected and the family has other interests. Although I suspect there might have been some sort of family rift keeping them aloof. The other owners of the various companies you have an interest in were partners with your mother's family. They run the businesses now and they want to meet you and Sir Edward."

Kitty puffed out her cheeks. "It's strange that father never mentioned it but then he probably would simply take Mama's income at face value. It's typical of him not to take the time to understand the details of it." She sniffed. "If he had known it was still mine he might not have sunk into a decline and caught that fatal chest infection."

She looked so woebegone that Luke squeezed her hand. He couldn't help himself.

Robert put his head around the door. "Your dinner is ready."

They followed him into the dining room with Wallace close behind. Luke wanted to keep a distance between him and Kitty so why did he wish Wallace at Jericho? He had been too absorbed to notice how hungry he was until he smelt the roast beef Robert laid before them. The rest of the meal was equally good and he tucked in with enthusiasm. Wallace proved to be a well-mannered dinner companion and yet he wanted to continue his conversation with Kitty, alone. Somehow, he was going to have to broker a truce with himself if he was ever going to cope with his newly married state.

CHAPTER TWENTY ONE

The meal came to an end and Wallace addressed Kitty.

"There are a few things I want to work on before I retire this evening, if you will excuse me, Lady Enstone."

She glanced at Luke and he nodded. "Of course we will, Mr Wallace."

Wallace bowed and withdrew. Now that Luke was finally alone with Kitty he was at a loss for what to say.

"You look tired, Luke. Perhaps we should retire too." A smile played around her lips.

The invitation in her gaze had his body jumping to attention. The urge to take her into his bed was almost overwhelming. He closed his eyes in an attempt to shut her out so he could think. Lord, that damned exotic perfume of hers was trying to overwhelm him with the promise it held out. He opened his eyes quickly and smiled at her but he couldn't meet her gaze.

"As much as I enjoyed last night, perhaps we should try and get some sleep now. We have a lot of travelling to come," he said in a firm voice.

"Of course, if you wish."

She sounded disappointed and even a little hurt. He looked at her face but she had lowered her gaze and her expression was blank. Perhaps guilt was making him imagine things. He stood and bent down to kiss her cheek to find her nearness enhanced the smell of her perfume even more. He seemed peculiarly sensitive to it. His resolve faltered for a moment but he dropped a second kiss on her forehead and went out. What sort of a coward was he to run away? Somehow, he was going to have to conquer his fear of emulating his father's actions if he allowed himself to love Kitty and something happened to her.

Chapter Twenty Two

Kitty retired to the library and read for a while. There was something about reading a good book that helped put problems into context. She ought to be ecstatically happy now and yet she could feel all was not well with Luke. He seemed to have backed away from her. It didn't make sense. With Sir Walter Greenough unable to cause mischief he had no longer needed to marry her. So why had he been so keen to marry if he didn't love her? It seemed she was in possession of a considerable fortune but from what she had seen of Luke that wouldn't have influenced him.

Luke had put himself in danger to rescue her and he had seemed so genuine in his desire to marry her there and then that she had convinced herself that he must love her. The chill of the room seemed to seep through her clothes. Had he married her out of a sense of chivalry and regretted it later? If he had, it was too late now. She would have to work hard at being the best wife she could. Her shoulders drooped. Many couples married out of a sense of family duty and lived reasonably happy lives. She knew that, but it was hard to go back to accepting second best when she had held her dream of a love match in her hands.

It hadn't felt so bad when she had overcome her resistance

to a marriage of convenience and accepted Luke's proposal in order to secure Edward's future. He had sounded sincere in assuring her that it helped him to avoid the matchmaking mamas. She had hoped he would grow to love her but had accepted he might not. It was only when they had seemed to get on so well that her dream really came alive. He had seemed to cool towards her later on, but he had a lot on his mind and she had dismissed her worries then. She closed the book and stood up, squaring her shoulders. Only time would tell if her dream was made of sand, ready to slip through her fingers.

* * *

Kitty woke early the next morning after a restless night. She strained her ears but could hear no sound from Luke's adjoining bedroom. There was already a fire in her room when Annie arrived.

"Would you like me to fetch you some chocolate before you dress, my lady?"

Heavens it sounded so strange being called 'my lady'. She wrinkled her nose.

"Hmm. I expect we'll be making an early start. I may as well dress and go down for breakfast. The food will be better than anything we'll get at an inn."

Annie smiled. "I'm sure it will. Mrs Spencer is good at everything. She's shown me how to get awkward stains from clothes. We've managed to get every trace of mud out of your travelling gown."

Kitty was soon dressed in the now-clean gown. She wrapped a woollen shawl around her shoulders.

"It's hard to believe that summer is just around the corner

with this cold, wet weather. It's time for me to find out what there is to eat. Off you go and get your own breakfast."

Kitty's heart beat uncomfortably fast by the time she reached the door to the breakfast room. She pushed it open and walked in, trying to look confident. She wasn't sure whether to be relieved or frustrated to find it empty. Two used coffee cups and plates were still on the table. She couldn't have missed Luke and Mr Wallace by much. Robert came in carrying a plate of hot toast.

"Here you are, Lady Enstone. There's cold meat and eggs too. Nella was determined to see you well set up for the journey." He beamed at her. "We're so happy for you."

Kitty smiled back. She didn't know if she would ever have Luke's love but she did have her position as his wife now and he had promised her Shepley Hall.

"Thank you, Robert. You and Nella have been so good to me. Shepley Hall is to be my wedding present. I'll have it renovated and you can get some more staff, stable staff too. We may breed some horses here. What do you think?"

Robert's face lit up. "It'll be right good to see the old place come alive. Nella will be pleased when I tell her."

Kitty smiled at his retreating back. At least somebody was happy. She ate her breakfast in solitary splendour; half hoping that Luke would come to find her. When she could delay no longer, she went back to her room to find Annie waiting for her.

"Mr Wallace says we are to start as soon as you are ready, Miss Davenport." Annie laughed. "My lady, I should say. It's going to take me ages before I remember every time. I've got everything packed up."

"Thank you, Annie. We had better put our outdoor things

on. Then I'll go and say goodbye to Mr and Mrs Spencer."

Once they were ready, Annie helped Fletcher carry their scant luggage to the coach. Kitty went downstairs and found the Spencers waiting for her in the hall. Nella enveloped her in a hug and expressed her delight at the planned renovation of Shepley Hall. Eventually a tearful Kitty made her way to the coach to find Luke waiting. She managed a smile.

"Thank you for giving me Shepley Hall. The Spencers are thrilled at our plans to renovate it and give it a new purpose with horse breeding."

Luke seemed to look through her. "That's good. You can do what you like with it. Wallace will give you advice and help on hiring workmen and servants for it." His voice sounded distant as if he was thinking of something else.

He didn't give her any time to reply but lifted her into the carriage. Annie was already inside. "We must be off. I want to get as far as possible today."

He walked off and mounted a horse and rode up to Mr Wallace. Fletcher was driving the carriage. Kitty tried to hide her disappointment from Annie and kept up a steady stream of chatter for some time. Then she relapsed into silence and finally fell asleep. She was dimly aware of the coach stopping and Luke saying something to Annie, before slipping back into sleep. She had no idea how long she had slept when she woke to the noise and bustle of a large posting inn.

Several ostlers were unharnessing the horses from their coach but she couldn't see any fresh ones being brought forward. The door swung open and she turned towards it. A rush of anticipation made her pulse race. She held her breath but it was Fletcher who appeared in the doorway, not Luke.

"His Lordship said to tell you he has secured a private room.

We are going to rest here for a short while. Let me help you down."

Kitty smiled at him. "Thank you, Fletcher."

She waited for Annie to be helped down and then made her way into the inn. The landlady was waiting for them. She knew a moment's panic, she was hardly dressed as a viscountess, but then drew back her shoulders and followed the woman down a narrow corridor. After all, who wore their best clothes when travelling? The landlady led them into a sizeable room with a window facing east. With the morning sun finding its way through the two windows along its length it was reasonably warm.

"There you are, my lady. Make yourselves comfortable and I'll bring you some tea."

"What a charming room. Thank you."

The landlady smiled at her and dipped a curtsy. "I may have some cakes ready to come out of the oven too."

Kitty felt stiff from sleeping in an awkward position and walked around the room to loosen up. After a couple of circuits, she was drawn to one of the windows. Luke walked past deep in conversation with Mr Wallace. Her pulse raced. Shortly afterwards footsteps sounded in the corridor. She held her breath as they drew nearer but the footsteps carried on past and slowly disappeared from her hearing. She kept a smile fixed in place and moved over to the table. It seemed that Luke was determined to avoid her as much as possible.

The same pattern was repeated for the rest of the day. Luke barely exchanged a word with her. It was twilight when they pulled into a comfortable looking inn. Made of stone it looked solid and inviting. Fletcher informed them that they were to stay the night when he helped them down from the carriage.

Kitty rolled her shoulders to loosen the tension in them.

"Thank you, Fletcher. I'm sure you will be glad of a rest after so many hours on the box."

"It's very kind in you to be concerned, my lady, but I didn't do all the driving. His Lordship can drive any sort of carriage and he took over for some stretches." Fletcher led them into the inn.

Yet another landlady was waiting to escort them to a private parlour. This one was short, stoutly built and had a tendency to chatter incessantly. The only useful information she imparted was her name, Mrs Gander. Kitty hid a smile. She could imagine Mrs Gander shooing off any undesirables just like the geese they had kept as lookouts at Davenport Court. She gave polite answers in all the right places. The landlady was nervous, judging by the way she was wringing her hands together as she talked. Heavens, it was strange having people nervous at her presence. She must remember to ask Luke how he coped with it, if he ever deigned to speak to her.

Mrs Gander ushered them into a room with several chairs around a good-sized table at the far end. Kitty's insides quivered. Surely Luke would join them for dinner. A fire burned in the hearth and spread a cosy glow over the comfortable chairs set before it.

"If you ladies would like to take a seat in front of the fire, my maids will soon have a tasty dinner ready for you. It's still quite chilly in the evenings so I like to have a fire lit for my guests." Mrs Gander curtseyed and walked out. She kept her head turned so she could smile at them until she reached the door, which made her progress somewhat erratic.

Annie's shoulders were shaking. "Mrs Gander's well named isn't she, the way she went out then."

They collapsed into giggles.

"She had already reminded me of the geese we used to have guarding Davenport Court before she walked out." Kitty sank into a chair by the fire. "We shouldn't be rude. This room is really comfortable. Let's hope the food lives up to the same standard."

They didn't have long to wait to find out. A maid arrived to lay the table and Kitty's hopes were dashed when she only laid two places. Two more arrived with dishes of beef and vegetables. Mrs Gander herself followed with a carafe of wine and two glass goblets, which she placed on the table by Kitty.

"You must be in need of this after a full day travelling. There is fresh-made lemonade if you would like some as well."

Kitty willed herself to smile. "That would be most welcome, thank you. The meal looks excellent and the smell is delicious."

Mrs Gander beamed at her and withdrew, to return a few moments later with a flagon of lemonade and two tumblers.

"There you are, my lady. I'll leave you to enjoy your meal."

Kitty filled their goblets with lemonade and drank deeply. Annie filled a plate and handed it to Kitty.

"This looks delicious, my lady. I'm so hungry."

Kitty managed to eat most of hers. Once the worst of her hunger was assuaged, she put down her knife and fork and filled the two goblets with wine. What Luke was about she had no idea but wine might take the edge off her anger. She sipped cautiously. It was elderberry and made by an expert.

"This is really good. Try some, Annie. You've earned it with all this travelling in a few days."

Annie hesitated. "I don't rightly know, my lady. I've never had wine before, only small ale."

"It's time you tried it then."

Annie had a few sips but didn't look convinced. Kitty laughed.

"Don't give up too easily. Wine is an acquired taste and elderberry is quite strongly flavoured but it happens to be one of my favourites."

She drank hers down and re-filled her goblet. It might not be wise but she felt in need of fortifying. She would have to say something, if Luke carried on ignoring her, even if she had to make an appointment with his secretary. She applied herself to the rest of her food and then drank up her wine. It was tempting to have a third goblet full but Luke wasn't worth giving herself a headache over. She poured another tumbler of lemonade instead.

After they had eaten she suggested they retire early. Mrs Gander showed them up to the best guest bedroom and offered to send a maid along to escort Annie to her chamber as soon as she was ready. Half an hour later there was a tap at the door and Annie opened it to reveal a young maid.

"Off you go, Annie. I can manage now."

Kitty debated locking the door behind them but that would be too petty. It was just possible that Luke might have a reasonable explanation for his neglect of her. The inn seemed quiet and she would leave it open. If she was found murdered in her bed then Luke would be sorry. She lifted her portmanteau to put it out of the way. It felt quite heavy. Of course, the book she had been reading the afternoon Sir Randolph called was in there. With the side table pulled close to the bed she should be able to read. If Luke thought he could sneak in after she had fallen asleep he would get a surprise.

* * *

Luke dropped into an easy chair and stretched his feet out towards the fire in the coffee room, ignoring Wallace's quizzical look. They were the only inhabitants. The door opened and the landlord came in with the brandy he had ordered. The landlord poured them both a glass and withdrew, leaving the decanter on a small table by Luke's side. He sipped at his brandy. He had tasted better but it was reasonable for a country inn. He held his glass up and watched the play of the firelight alter its colour from brown to amber and back again. He had always considered himself a solid, reliable sort of person. Now he felt as changeable as the colour of the liquid in his glass, in the presence of a source of light.

Life had seemed so simple. He had intended to find a pleasant, suitable sort of wife once he was ready. They were going to live a comfortable life of mild-mannered companionship with children to brighten his days. Then he met Kitty. Warm, courageous, determined Kitty who made his pulses race and had set his world on end. It had felt so right to marry her and keep her safe from Sewell. He had been swept along in a rush of relief that she was alive and well. He had swept her up with him and she deserved better than a lukewarm husband. Wallace said something and he tried to concentrate.

"What was that? I was thinking of something else." Luke felt heat rush to his cheeks. Wallace would assume he had been thinking of someone else. Which, of course, he had but not in the way Wallace would expect.

"I was just saying that we hadn't finalised the marriage settlements, my lord. Do you want me to leave that until we have ascertained the full extent of Lady Enstone's fortune?"

"I'm not sure how these things work but I expect you will have to. Everything that Lady Enstone brings to the marriage I want settled on her." He had taken her innocence he couldn't take anything else from her. "She told me she wants to share that with Sir Edward, although I think there may be a certain amount that will belong to him. I want to get Davenport Court back for Sir Edward as well, even if we have to go to court."

Wallace grinned. "I'm in for an interesting time of it."

Luke tossed back the rest of his brandy. Wallace really would think he was odd if he stayed here much longer.

"I'm glad you think so. All these legal details seem deadly dull to me. Perhaps you should go into the law."

Wallace's cheeks turned a deep shade of red. "I think I would tire of the law but I do hope to go into politics one day." Luke grimaced. "I knew you were too good for me to keep you forever. It will take a year or two to get my affairs in order. After that, if you are still of the same mind, I will see what I can do to help you.

Chapter Twenty Three

K itty woke up with a start to the sound of a cock crowing. Her candle had burnt to the bottom and her book lay on the bed next to her. She had avoided being murdered but there was no sign that Luke had ever been in the room. She should have realized he had no intention of joining her when he bespoke two rooms, even if they were adjacent. What would he think if she went to his room? It was tempting but she wouldn't demean herself. Why had he rushed her into a marriage ceremony if this was the way he was going to treat her?

The answer eluded her and she drifted back into an uneasy sleep until the sound of her bedroom door opening woke her. She gave a satisfied sigh. Luke had come to her at last. She sat up in bed only to see Annie stirring the fire into life and adding logs. Her delight faded and she tried to school her expression into something neutral. She followed Annie's quick, assessing glance around the room. It was far too tidy for Luke to have visited her and from the look of concern in Annie's eyes she hadn't succeeded in hiding her disappointment. Next time Luke avoided her she must remember to untidy the room if she wanted to keep her marital difficulties private.

There was no sign of Luke when Kitty and Annie entered the

private parlour set aside for their party. She had expected as much but she could have been forgiven for wondering if Luke had married her for her money after all. She twisted a tendril of hair around her finger. Instinct told her it was something more personal coming between them. Had her enthusiasm on their wedding night disgusted him? How mortifying if it had. A tremor ran through her. She went to the breakfast buffet table to hide her hot cheeks and filled her plate with toast and egg.

A maid entered with a fresh pot of coffee. Kitty thanked her and sat down next to Annie. She poured two cups of the steaming brew and handed one to Annie. Luke had seemed happy at the time, it couldn't be that, surely. Aunt Theo, as she thought of her already, had mentioned a troubled relationship with his father and to give Luke time. Perhaps something connected with that was troubling him? Which was all very well, but if he wouldn't talk to her how was she ever going to be able to resolve things. She chewed her way through her breakfast, barely able to taste what she was eating. All her life she had put everyone else first, was it too much to ask that her new husband might at least consider her feelings?

The next few hours in the coach seemed to stretch on forever. Stops were short and there was no time for conversation with Luke until they halted for a drink and light meal in the middle of the day. Fletcher helped Kitty and Annie down from the coach in the yard of a busy posting inn. Ostlers scurried everywhere and Luke arrived to escort them through the throng.

"We would have gone on a bit further but one of the leaders was showing signs of going lame. It's a nuisance as the inn is so busy it will be some time before they can provide us with fresh horses." He grimaced. "We might as well eat here whilst we wait. Wallace has managed to secure a private parlour."

Luke threaded her arm through his before she could reply. The feel of his warmth next to her lifted her mood, especially when she felt him lean towards her as if he too was affected by the closeness. Perhaps he was simply exhausted after all that chasing around and needed a lot of sleep. He had slept late at Shepley. Things would be better when they had settled down together. Wallace was waiting for them, outside the inn. The parlour he showed them into had barely enough space for a round, scrubbed pine table with four chairs and a small side table.

Luke led Kitty to a chair and squeezed into the seat next to her. "This must be their third or fourth best private room" He made a wry face. "At least it's clean and has a view of the garden."

Wallace grinned. "I presumed you would prefer to be inconspicuous so I used my own name. I've checked and I don't think there's anyone here you're likely to know."

"Excellent thinking. Kitty, I imagine you will want to see Edward before we go home?"

Kitty nodded, momentarily rendered speechless at the reference to home. Luke would spend more time with her when they were back at Enstone House. She shivered at the prospect.

"Yes please. I imagine Lady Grant and Grace will have something to say to us too."

Luke laughed. "They won't be very happy that they've missed our wedding. We can make it up to them with a ball." He hesitated and then rushed back into speech. "If that's what you want, of course."

"Yes, we owe them that, although I will need some time to

become used to the household before I am ready to prepare for a ball."

"Of course. Wallace is the man to help you with the invitations and so on."

Wallace had taken a seat next to Luke. He looked up at the mention of his name. "It would be my pleasure, Lady Enstone."

"Thank you." Kitty chewed at her bottom lip. "How do we explain the absence of our families at the wedding to other people?"

Luke rocked back in his chair and slapped a hand to his forehead. "Oh Lord, where have my wits gone begging? I don't want you besmirched by scandal because of Sewell and Greenough. You will have to stay with Aunt Theo for a few days and we'll place an advertisement in The Times announcing a private wedding has taken place."

Wallace nodded. "I assumed you would do something along those lines, my lord. Fletcher and I have been really careful to conceal your identity." He glanced at Annie, sitting next to Kitty. "I'm sure Lady Enstone's maid can be relied upon to keep the secret."

Annie went bright pink. "Of course." Her voice rose to a squeak of indignation. "No one will hear of it from me."

Kitty squeezed her hand. "I know that, Annie. I couldn't wish for a better maid."

Two serving maids arrived and there was no chance of any more private conversation. After a hurried meal of cold meats and fresh bread, Luke went out with Wallace. Kitty couldn't look away from his retreating back. It was true they didn't want a scandal but a few days apart from Luke was the last thing she wanted at such a difficult stage in their relationship.

* * *

It was late afternoon before they arrived at Lady Grant's door. Luke ran up the steps and came back to help Kitty down.

"Aunt Theo is at home. I'll come in with you. She'll want to know all the details of our adventures."

Harvey opened the door to the family drawing room. Kitty let go of Luke's arm and rushed in at the sight of Edward standing by the window overlooking the road. She threw her arms around him. Edward shuffled his feet but allowed her to hug him. He stepped back and studied her.

"You look good for someone who was kidnapped, Sis. I'm glad you're safe. If only I had told you I'd lost my watch at Easter you wouldn't have been fooled. I dropped it in church and was pretty sure that Greenough had picked it up. I saw him watching you in an odd way and didn't mention it in case you decided to confront him about it."

"Don't blame yourself. They would have found some other way to trick me."

"I had a feeling he was trouble." Edward glanced at Luke, chatting quietly to his aunt. He lowered his voice. "I can't be sorry at the end result though. Luke is a great gun. When will the wedding be? I have a particular reason for asking."

Luke chose that moment to join them.

"Wedding did you say, Edward? I must apologise to you. I still had the special licence in my pocket and deemed it expedient to marry Kitty straight away to keep her safe from Sewell's machinations."

Edward grinned at him. "Oh good. I wasn't looking forward to it above half, knowing Kitty would want me to stand in our father's place."

"At least one person isn't annoyed with us then!" Luke threaded Kitty's arm through his. "Kitty, Aunt Theo wants to talk to you." He looked anxious.

Edward laid a hand on Luke's free sleeve. "Can I just tell you I've met my mother's family's business partners and I'm going to have dinner with them tonight?"

Luke smiled. "Excellent."

"The thing is they've invited me to stay with them until my tutor is free for the summer. When shall I tell them I can join them? They're only in London for a few days."

Luke exchanged glances with Kitty. "That all sounds exciting but there is a bit of a complication. We want to avoid a scandal and don't intend to announce our marriage for a few days. We need you to remain in London with Aunt Theo until then, so it's hard to say."

Edward sighed. "Never mind. They weren't expecting an answer tonight. I had better go and get ready."

"Edward." Kitty raised her hand to get his attention. "Remember not to mention that we are already married."

Edward rolled his eyes. "I know how to keep a secret. We told them you were out of town visiting friends."

Kitty smiled at him. "That was well done of you but I know nothing about these people. I ought to meet them before letting you go off."

Edward waved a hand towards Lady Grant. "Luke's aunt knows all about them. She said she was sure you would be happy for me to stay with them."

Kitty would have protested further but Luke shook his head at her and she let Edward go. Aunt Theo was smiling at them and she pulled away from Luke to sit next to her.

Luke followed. "I don't think you need to worry about

Edward going with your family's business partners. Wallace tells me they are well thought of. Have you met them, Aunt Theo?"

"Yes, they called the first day you were away and again yesterday with their wives, to introduce them to Edward." Aunt Theo gave Kitty a reassuring smile. "I liked them. Their wives are both from sensible families. The aunt of one was a friend of mine years ago, before she buried herself in the country."

Kitty wrinkled her brow. "What puzzles me is why they are so keen to have Edward to stay with them."

"They were very open about their intentions. Neither couple have sons. They are hoping he will be interested in learning the insurance and banking business with a view to taking over one day. Edward is enthused by the idea."

Kitty's mouth dropped open. "He is?"

"It turns out that your brother has already made up his mind he wants to be a businessman after spending time with a friend's father. I think Edward's new friends will be a good influence on him." Her eyes twinkled. "They have persuaded him that going to university will be an advantage for their business and he is determined to gain entrance when he is seventeen."

Luke laughed. "I wondered why Edward didn't suggest we dispense with the tutor altogether now he has this invitation. He tried hard to persuade me he didn't need one."

Aunt Theo laughed back. "Edward is a delightful boy, full of energy. I think banking will suit him." She raised her eyebrows at Luke and her voice became brisk. "Now tell me how you came to arrive back already married."

"Kitty, I'll leave you to explain what happened to Aunt Theo.

I have a lot to do." Luke rose and bowed to his aunt. "I'll see you all tomorrow."

Luke walked off without giving Kitty time to answer. She tried to hide her dismay as she watched his disappearing back but surprised a concerned expression on Lady Grant's face when she glanced her way.

Lady Grant patted her hand. "I imagine you've had quite an adventure. Would you rather leave the telling of it until later?"

"I'm happy to tell you now." The alternative was to be alone with some uncomfortable thoughts. Thoughts she was tempted to share, but her relationship with Luke was something she had to work out for herself.

* * *

After an early bedtime, which yielded an indifferent night's sleep, Kitty woke up feeling jaded. Her troubled dreams had always seemed to end with her watching Luke's retreating back. She couldn't get away from the conviction that he had done what he saw as his duty and was pulling away from her. Annie offered to bring her hot chocolate but she opted to dress straight away and breakfast downstairs. Activity was what she needed and with luck she would be in time to talk to Edward.

Kitty walked in to the breakfast room to find Edward consuming a large plateful of cold meat and eggs. He was chatting away to Grace in between mouthfuls. They both looked up and smiled at her.

Edward waved his fork in her direction. "You look well, Sis. I can see married life suits you."

Kitty forced a smile. "I haven't had time to find out yet but knowing your future is secure is a huge weight off my mind."

"I told you not to worry about me." Edward gave her a lopsided grin. "I said at Christmas that my friend Cartwright is determined to go into the army and his father offered to take me on as an apprentice in his business."

"I remember now and I told you then that it wasn't suitable for you to work in a manufacturing business." Kitty walked over to the breakfast buffet. She was surprisingly hungry and filled her plate.

Grace pointed to the coffee pot. "This is a fresh pot, let me pour you a cup."

"Thank you." Kitty sat next to Grace and opposite Edward.

Edward swallowed his last mouthful and sat back. "I don't see what was wrong with Mr. Cartwright's offer. I can't be doing with all this snobbish stuff about trade being beneath a gentleman. Trade is the future. Anyway, I knew that would only be temporary. I have a feeling Cartwright's young brother will follow his father into the business. Which is why I don't feel bad about telling him I'm going to go into insurance instead."

Kitty took a deep breath. Edward was often hard to move when he got an idea into his head. "I'm not at all sure about you accepting that offer either."

Grace laid a hand on her arm. "I don't think you need to worry, Kitty. It's a prestigious firm with banking interests. I think Edward is right. Things will soon be different. Besides Aunt Theo said going into that business would be perfectly acceptable for Edward."

Aunt Theo walked in. "I did indeed, a well-respected company." She joined them at the table and a footman arrived with a fresh pot of coffee.

Edward gave Kitty a triumphant grin. "There, you see. I'll

apologise to Mr. Cartwright, although I hadn't got as far as agreeing anything. I'm looking forward to going to university and studying mathematics."

Kitty sighed. "I can see there is no changing your mind. I had a genteel profession like law in mind for you."

Grace shook her head so hard a lock of hair escaped its pins. "No, no and thrice no. The law wouldn't suit Edward at all. I know quite a few lawyers and they are all soooo boring. He'll do much better as a banker."

"I'm sure I will. I'll talk it over with Enstone later, he's bound to agree," Edward said, looking pleased with himself. "Both partners have had to go out of town for a couple of days on business. I promised to let them know when I'll be free to join them as soon as they're back."

Kitty made an excuse and went back to her room after breakfast. She needed some solitude. The lengths she had been prepared to go to for the sake of giving Edward a good future - and all along he had his own escape route from poverty planned out. Lord she had seriously considered accepting a carte blanche, if Luke had offered it, for Edward's sake. Instead she had married a man who had done his duty but wanted nothing more of her. She had no way out, since they had consummated the marriage. Was that what that first blissful night, at least for her, had been about? No! She wouldn't settle for a cold, loveless arrangement. It was time she put her own needs first and fought for a love match.

Chapter Twenty Four

Luke pushed the last piece of beef around his plate with his fork. He needed to attack the pile of paperwork waiting for him in the library but he couldn't work up any enthusiasm for the task. A night's sleep had done little to restore his equilibrium. He poured himself another cup of coffee and sipped it absentmindedly. It had been an eventful few days, to say the least of it. He put his cup down and lowered his head into his hands, with his elbows resting on the table. If his desire to punch Wallace every time Kitty had spoken to him on the journey back to London was anything to go by, love was something he couldn't control.

He should have realised sooner what his fierce desire to protect Kitty at all costs meant. He was deeply and irrevocably in love with his wife and he was terrified. How could a man who had led his troops into battle more times than he cared to remember be so scared of an emotion? It made no sense and yet his instincts were screaming at him to distance himself from his lovely wife. His early fears that she was trying to entrap him seemed ridiculous now he knew her better. He smiled despite his agitation. Had she agreed to marry him for Edward's sake?

Kitty was so conditioned to look after everyone else she

may have done so, initially, without even realising it. She had noticed his withdrawal from her. The look of hurt and confusion he had seen in her eyes, more than once, suggested that she was well on the way to loving him. She had enjoyed his lovemaking and had every right to expect it to resume. His body tingled at the prospect. He wouldn't be able to live with her without resuming a physical relationship. If only he had arrived back in England in time to make his peace with Father it might have helped. This fear of loving someone had to go back to the trauma of the countless rejections from him after Mama's death.

None of Aunt Theo's assertions that his father had loved him dearly could take away the pain of those rejections. If Kitty had developed feelings for him already, and heaven alone knew how quickly he had fallen in love with her, he was inflicting that sort of pain on her. His worry had always been treating any children he might have in the same way his father had treated him, if he loved his wife and anything happened to her. Wasn't pushing Kitty away after he had tied her to him even worse? What was he going to do?

He ought to at least go and talk to Kitty. The paperwork could wait. He went upstairs to check his appearance and found Garner tidying his room.

"What clothes do you need today, my lord?"

Luke wasn't fooled by Garner's innocent expression; he was trying to find out what was going to happen next. Kitty wasn't the only one who must be wondering about his strange behaviour of late.

"I'm going out this morning to my aunt's."

Garner picked up Luke's travelling valise. "I'll have a footman tidy this away. It will be the work of a moment to find you something more suitable."

Luke lifted a hand to stop him. Father's letters were still hidden in the secret pocket. "Leave that a moment and go and see if any messages have been received for me. In case there has been any change of plan."

As soon as the door closed behind Garner, Luke fished out the letters and dropped them onto the bed. A quick glance through the rest of the correspondence between Father and Lady Swift revealed nothing of interest. He stashed them away in a private drawer and picked up the other pile he hadn't had time to look at when he was at Shepley Hall. The ribbon moved as he grasped the bundle to reveal his own name on the letter at the top. A muscle twitched at the corner of his eye. He should have made time to have another look at the letters before this, but he felt compelled to read this second bundle now.

Luke ran lightly down the stairs, past a surprised looking Garner. He gave a footman orders to ensure he wasn't disturbed and shut himself in the library. He opened out the letter addressed to him with shaking hands.

* * *

Dear Luke

I hope you are home in time for me to try and put things right between us but I've written down some of what I want to convey to you in this letter in case you are not. I have been the worst kind of father to you and if I explain a little of how I let that happen I hope you will find it in your heart to forgive me. I'm thankful that I have at least made a better job of being a father to Grace. As my relationship with her has grown, I understand now what Theodosia tried so hard to explain to me in those awful years after your Mama died.

My mistake with you was to think that an aunt and her husband, good people that they were, could ever be a substitute for a boy's father. You have to understand that my whole world collapsed in on me after losing your mother. I was no fit company for anyone, especially an impressionable young boy. I saw you playing happily with your cousins and felt you were better off with them. The last time you ever asked me to take you with me I thought you were just being a dutiful son. Yet something about your expression that day when I refused worried me.

Theodosia said to take you with me even if it was just for a few days but my courage failed me. You looked so like your mother in those days. I was afraid I would break down in front of you if we were alone together in the house where she brought so much joy into our lives. You kept yourself at a distance from that day on. I fooled myself into thinking that was bound to happen once you were at school and university. How could I complain when you preferred to spend your holidays with your cousins? When you went into the army, I was so proud of you. Here was a young man of substance and yet it was then I realised I had lost your regard completely. I found out you had turned down the chance of a few weeks at home before your first posting. I wish I had had the courage to write to you then.

Theodosia told me how much Grace blossomed when I took more and more notice of her as she grew up. I'm sorry I didn't do the same for you. I think to some extent I have turned Grace into the son I was missing so much. She knows more about foreign affairs, politics and the plight of the poor than I do. I know you will do your best to help and guide her as I fear she will find it difficult to settle down to the life of a proper young lady. The best I can hope for is that she will marry a reforming peer of the realm and be allowed to carry on her good works. At least she is in good hands with Theodosia.

None of my difficulties excuses my failure to be a proper father to you, I should have tried harder to connect with you once I was more myself, but I hope it goes some way to explain. At least then if you have children of your own you will understand how important a father is to them and be able to avoid my mistakes. Whatever you do, don't let my example stop you finding a wife of your own. I say this not with any thought of the succession but because I want you to be happy. You have proved yourself to be a courageous soldier so use that courage and have a good life.

When it comes to finding a wife, you don't need me to tell you to be careful of traps to ensnare you. Pick someone kind and caring. You could do worse than take a look at Kitty Davenport. A lovely young woman and she takes such good care of her aunt. If she is not to your taste, I trust you will take over my promise to look after them and young Edward Davenport, Kitty's brother.

Your loving father.

* * *

Luke dropped the letter onto the desk and ran the back of his hand across his eyes. If only he had spent some time with father before he went into the army it might have spared him a lot of pain. At the same time would he have truly understood before he had fallen in love with Kitty? Probably not. If he had read this letter before he met her, his father's recommendation that he look at Kitty as a prospective wife would have had exactly the opposite effect to the one intended. He shuddered at the prospect. Father was right about one thing. Only a coward would run away from a proper marriage with her.

First of all, he had to make sure there was no scandal. Wallace's idea of trying to get a private blessing of the marriage in a London church was a good one. The arrival of Kitty's family's business partners on the scene was an added complication but if they could find a way of not inviting them to the blessing it wouldn't matter. Their invitation to Edward to stay with them would make his idea of a bridal trip to Shepley Hall much less complicated. He hated to keep imposing on Aunt Theo and she would be spared the necessity of entertaining Edward. He heard Wallace's voice in the hall and went out to greet him.

"Come into the library."

Wallace followed him in looking pleased with himself. "My curate friend has a space this afternoon to perform a blessing."

Luke grimaced. "That would be perfect if it wasn't for Edward's prospective business partners."

Wallace grinned at him. "I took the liberty of calling on Lady Grant before I came here. They have had to go out of town on business for two days. Everything is in place."

Luke slapped him on the back. "Well done, Wallace. Whatever rise in your salary I promised you, double it!"

* * *

Edward handed Kitty into the waiting coach and climbed in after her. Kitty sank back against the squabs. She gripped her hands together tightly. It was a clever idea of Mr Wallace's to have a church blessing but pretending to be happy for Grace and Aunt Theo, when she was so churned up inside, was going to be difficult. Neither of them missed anything. How would Luke handle it? Perhaps he wasn't even aware that there was a problem between the two of them? The scenery ran past the window of the coach in a blur. They pulled up outside a small church, in a quiet street. Her pulse raced as Edward helped her down.

Kitty walked down the aisle on Edward's arm. They passed Aunt Theo, Grace and Mr Wallace who were sitting at the front, wreathed in smiles. Aunt Theo and Grace had dressed for the occasion and their brightly coloured outfits relieved the gloom of the dark wooden pews. Would she and Luke return to his home tonight? It was her home too now and she would have something to say about it if they didn't. The smile Luke gave her when he turned to greet her at the altar was everything she could have hoped for. Perhaps things would work out after all, or was Luke putting on a show for the others? Kitty smiled back and shivered when Luke took her hand as she joined him.

Kitty was glad Aunt Theo and Grace had been able to enjoy dressing her in a frivolous confection of cream satin with a gold spangled gauze overdress. She felt more like a bride this time. The service seemed to go on for nearly as long as their original wedding. At last Luke placed a proper ring on her finger, which fitted perfectly. The earnest young clergyman gave his blessing with Luke holding her left hand, his thumb caressing her finger and the ring. Kitty closed her eyes and enjoyed the sensation of togetherness it gave her. Perhaps it was a good omen.

Finally, the service was over. Luke threaded her arm through his and they joined the others. Aunt Theo was drying her eyes with a lace edged handkerchief. She took Kitty's free hand.

"What a lovely service. I hope you will be very happy

together. Luke, your father would have been so proud."

Luke nodded but didn't meet his aunt's gaze. "I think we've been in here long enough to convince any interested observers that we've been through a private marriage service. Mrs Cater should have a wedding breakfast prepared for us now."

"I hope she's not upset at such short notice." Kitty watched Luke's expression relax. He always seemed tense whenever his father was mentioned.

"Wallace warned her yesterday to be ready at a few hours' notice. I told her not to ask cook for anything too elaborate."

Kitty exchanged a wry smile with Aunt Theo. The whole household would be on their mettle. They were no doubt in for a banquet. Luke helped her in to the first coach drawn up in front of the church and jumped up after her. Kitty caught her breath as he sat next to her. Of course, the others would be expecting him to do that. Grace waved at them frantically from the pavement until Wallace led her to the coach lined up behind them.

Luke grinned. "With Grace behaving like that it won't need the announcement I've sent to The Times to let the world know that we're married."

Their coach moved off and Luke clasped her hand. "Kitty, there is a lot I need to explain to you but it will have to wait until later. I intend to be a good husband to you no matter what." His voice was thick with emotion.

He drew her closer and kissed her. She could feel his body tremble until he released her. They pulled up outside Enstone House before she had time to reply. Something was troubling him but that sounded promising. Didn't it? All the staff were lined up in the hall to greet them and there was no time to question him further. Mrs Cater looked tired but triumphant.

Kitty walked up to her.

"I'm sorry we weren't able to give you more notice of our plans."

Mrs Cater dipped a curtsey. "Think nothing of it, my lady. We have an excellent staff who are equal to anything." She smiled at Kitty and glanced along the line of servants. "They have enjoyed the challenge."

Kitty relaxed. Mrs Cater looked welcoming and the staff all seemed happy. She wouldn't have too many problems with overseeing the London house.

"Thank you, Mrs Cater."

Luke joined them. "Let me add my thanks to that. I knew we could rely on you, Mrs Cater."

He led Kitty along the line, introducing the staff to her and stopping to chat with every employee. It was obvious he was a popular employer. They reached the end of the line just as they heard the unmistakable sound of the second coach pulling up. The butler threw open the front door to admit Aunt Theo, Grace, Edward and Mr Wallace.

* * *

The wedding breakfast fully justified Mrs Cater's confidence. Every dish was exquisitely prepared. Even so Kitty struggled to eat even small portions of the dishes she tried. Grace's steady stream of excited chatter helped to keep the conversation alive and she was able to sit back and listen most of the time. Grace was so obviously fond of her brother and seemed to have extended that to her. It was lovely to have a good female friend. Now all she had to do was to sort out her marriage. Luke was smiling and laughing in all the right places but she could sense the tension in him.

Aunt Theo caught her eye. "I think it's time we called for our carriage." She signalled to the butler who was hovering in the doorway. He nodded and disappeared.

"Thank you for a lovely day. I think Grace and I will agree that we will remember this as your wedding celebration, even if we missed the real service."

Grace sighed. "Absolutely, but I suppose we have to say goodbye for a while now. I expect you will be off on a wedding trip."

Luke squeezed Kitty's hand. "I do have something planned if Kitty is agreeable." He smiled down at her.

Suddenly breathless, it was a moment before Kitty could answer. "Yes, I would like that."

"Good, we'll talk about it later. Wallace, I think you deserve a few days off, we can take Fletcher with us on our journey. Why don't you go and visit your family for a week or two? You can take my second coach and one of the grooms."

"That's very generous. Thank you. If Lady Grant will excuse me, I'll take my leave of you now." Wallace bowed to Lady Grant and slipped away.

The carriage was announced and Lady Grant shepherded her party out of the dining room. She turned back to Kitty. "Your maid should have put all your things away for you by now." She patted Luke's arm. "Be kind to Kitty, won't you."

Kitty felt the heat rise to her cheeks. Lady Grant smiled at her and followed the others to the front door. Luke put his arm around Kitty and they too followed. They waved the party off, standing in the front doorway. Kitty felt suddenly shy. What should she do now?

Luke answered the question for her without being asked.

"Come into the library with me." He pulled her into the library and shut the door behind him.

Kitty stared at the floor unable to meet Luke's gaze.

"I think it will be perfectly acceptable to close the door now we are married, don't you?"

"True, even Nella couldn't complain." A laugh bubbled up to the surface but Kitty still couldn't look at Luke. Her heart hammered so hard her legs felt weak.

Luke put a finger under her chin. "There is no need to avoid me, although heaven knows that's what I have been doing to you. If I promise to try harder will you look at me?"

Kitty's eyes flew to his. "I wasn't imagining it then?"

"No, you weren't. I have an awful lot of explaining to do, but do you mind if we postpone that until later? I find myself in urgent need of feeling my wife in my arms."

"Only if you promise to be truthful with me. I thought you were offering me a full marriage, in the widest sense, in Shepley, not a marriage of convenience. I would have said no if that was all that was on offer."

"I promise you I mean to offer you much more than a marriage of convenience."

"In that case I don't mind at all." His face was filled with emotions Kitty couldn't quite identify. Her breathing quickened. Perhaps she wasn't going to have to fight for the love match she wanted.

Luke bent down and kissed her. Kitty hesitated for a moment and then joined in enthusiastically until he pulled away breathing heavily.

"May I join you in your room once we've shed these infernal clothes?" Luke tugged at his cravat. "I swear Garner has put twice the normal amount of starch in this neck-cloth."

CHAPTER TWENTY FOUR

Kitty stood on tiptoe and whispered in his ear. "Yes please."

"I'll escort you to your room." Luke clasped her hand and led her upstairs. He opened the door to a light filled room. "This is your room when we're in London."

Kitty gazed at the blue, cream and gold colour scheme. Cream and gold striped paper covered the walls. Her gaze was drawn to one end of the room where a light blue chaise longue sat at the foot of the huge four poster bed. The bed was draped with gold damask hangings the colour of the gold stripes on the wallpaper.

"It's beautiful."

"My mother had wonderful taste. You would have liked her." His expression became wistful.

"I'm sure I would," Kitty said softly.

Luke smiled. "Your maid should be on her way up to you." He dropped a kiss on her forehead and walked out, leaving Kitty feeling bereft.

* * *

Kitty dismissed Annie as soon as she had changed. She sat down on a blue brocade sofa placed near a window, wearing nothing more than a silk robe. Luke knocked and entered barely a minute later. Kitty tried not to smile. He must have been listening out for Annie to leave. Luke was wearing a brocade dressing gown. Excitement fizzed through her. She was going to enjoy this and not worry about whether she was being ladylike enough for Luke. He would have to learn to accept her as she was. She was done with trying to please everyone but herself.

Luke sat next to her and feathered kisses along her neck

and jawline. Kitty shivered with anticipation. Their lips met and she gave herself up to the sensations ripping through her body. Luke's hands explored her over her robe. She freed her hands and pulled his dressing gown open to the waist. He was all solid, lean muscle. She ran her hands over his chest. Luke groaned and lifted her onto his lap. She threw her arms around his neck and pulled him down for another kiss. A tremor ran through him when she wriggled closer.

Luke groaned and sat back. "This is torture. Let me carry you to the bed."

He scooped her up as if she weighed no more than a small child and laid her gently on top of the covers. His dressing gown fell to the floor. Kitty blinked. He was magnificent. She wriggled out of her robe and tossed it to one side.

"My gorgeous girl." Luke lay down beside her.

One hand cupped her breast and the other one slipped between her legs and caressed her. Kitty rolled into his arms. She pulled him close and kissed him until he pulled away, panting.

"Are you ready for me, Kitty?"

"Mm yes!" She tingled from head to toe. She was more than ready.

Luke rolled her onto her back and she opened for him. Their lovemaking started out slow and gentle. The pace picked up and Kitty gave of herself freely. They tipped over the edge together. Luke rolled to the side of her and threw an arm around her waist.

"Kitty, I love you so much. I hope you enjoyed that as much as I did?" His breath tickled her ear.

Before Kitty could reply his deep, steady breathing told her he had fallen sound asleep. She felt almost weightless as she cuddled up to him. She had worried about nothing. He wanted her to enjoy herself.

"Oh Luke, I love you too."

Chapter Twenty Five

Luke came to with a start, shivering. He was lying on top of Kitty's bed with her fast asleep in his arms. At least that part of his married life seemed to be going well. He carefully moved away and pulled the covers over her. The fire needed feeding so he threw on a couple of logs and poked it into more energetic life. He pulled his dressing gown on and went to his own room. He had no idea how long they had slept but his stomach suggested it was for some time. Garner had the rest of the day off and the drapes were open. It was nearly dark outside. He heard the grandfather clock strike nine. Lord, they must have been tired. He went out into the corridor and found a footman to order supper to be brought up to his room.

Once the meal arrived, Luke found the key to the connecting door and stepped through it. Kitty was awake and blinked at him owlishly.

"Where did you appear from?"

Luke pointed to the door into his rooms. "There is a connecting door. We could leave it open from now on if you agree."

Kitty laughed. "I should have realised. By all means leave it open."

The smile she gave him almost had him forgetting about supper but he had promised her an explanation of his odd behaviour and he had best get it over with before his courage failed him. He placed her robe on the bed beside her.

"Supper awaits us in my room. Would you like a glass of wine?"

"Yes please. I was too nervous to drink more than a few sips earlier."

They ate their supper largely in companionable silence. Luke refilled their glasses.

"This reminds me of when I was first at Shepley. I thought then that you were a restful sort of female at mealtimes." He hesitated for a moment." I apologise for my boorish behaviour when I first met you."

He got up and wandered around the room before sitting back down. "My father and I had a poor relationship. I thought I had come to terms with what I saw as his rejection of me. Then when I had to step into his shoes it brought it all back. I found myself reliving the past, to the extent it was almost an obsession. Anything connected with Father made me angry. It's no excuse but I'm sure it affected my attitude towards you."

Kitty blushed scarlet. "Did you think I was trying to entrap you?"

"I did wonder after you sagged against me on that first meeting, just before Mrs Spencer came into the room."

"I was afraid you were Sir Walter. I overbalanced trying to see into the hall. The relief when I realised you weren't him made my legs give way."

"I know now that such deception isn't in your nature." Luke grinned. "Mrs Spencer might have been a different matter."

"I did wonder at one point if she was trying to force you into marrying me. Don't think too badly of her. She never had children and she was so protective of me and Edward."

"I'm grateful to her and her husband for their efforts to keep you safe. Would you like to could visit Shepley Hall as part of our bridal trip? We could set off tomorrow if you like."

Kitty hesitated then gave a firm nod. "Yes, I would like that. Part of me thinks I ought to wait to meet these new people Edward is enthusing about, but I decided a few days ago that it was time I put myself first some of the time." She wouldn't meet his gaze.

"Did that have anything to do with me?" He couldn't keep a tremor of anxiety out of his voice.

Kitty licked her lips and put a hand on his arm. "I thought I could cope with a marriage of convenience for Edward's sake."

Kitty looked away and Luke's stomach tightened. He heard her take a deep breath.

"Then I realised that I had always dreamed of a love match. At first you were so attentive I was hopeful it would work out. I sensed you withdrawing from me and felt cheated."

"I'm sorry, Kitty. I had this stupid idea of keeping you at arm's length in case anything happened to you and I treated any children we had in the same way my father treated me. Then I realised it was too late for that because I was already in love with you. I've found a letter Father left for me in case I didn't make it home in time to talk to him. I'll let you read it when you feel ready, it explains a lot."

The sound of sobbing caught his attention. "Kitty what's wrong?" He gathered her in his arms.

"Oh Luke. I've been in love with you for weeks. I just didn't realise it. Although a part of me did. I nearly refused you and I think that was the reason why."

Luke found a handkerchief and dried her eyes. His own felt suspiciously damp. He rocked her in his arms.

"I'm so glad you didn't. I might not have been brave enough to ask you again. This feeling of rejection has never left me. I love you Kitty and I promise to do my best to be the husband you deserve. It won't always be straightforward, I'm not going to get over it easily, but I'll try my best."

Kitty threw her arms around his neck. "That's all I ask. I'll help you."

* * *

Nella and Robert were outside waiting for them when they drew up after a leisurely journey to Shepley Hall. The weather had changed and it was a glorious day. Kitty could hardly wait for Luke to help her down from the carriage. She blinked a couple of times at the brilliant sunshine and then ran across the grass into Nella's arms.

"It's so good to see you Nella." She would have to learn to be the grand lady when she was in London but here, in the country, she could be herself. Eventually Nella let her go and she greeted Robert.

"How are you faring, Robert? You look well."

"Never been better, milady." Robert's eyes twinkled. "We've got some lovely horseflesh for you to see."

Kitty jumped when Luke coughed and gave Robert a pained look. Robert was looking at the floor but she could still see his grin. "What is it, Robert? Have you found a magnificent stallion or something?"

Robert shook his head. "It's not for me to say, milady."

Luke grabbed her arm. "Do you want to get changed first or shall we go straight to the stables so you can see for yourself?" His eyes were sparkling.

Kitty looked from one to the other. "You both seem really excited about something. Let's go to the stables."

Two horses were led out of the stables for them to inspect.

"I hope you don't mind, Kitty, but I had Bright find you some horses to start off the stud. He is a splendid judge."

"I can see that. Have we taken on any grooms yet?"

Robert stepped forward. "I've started training three local lads, milady. I've told them it's up to you if we keep them on."

A third young man came out leading a magnificent chestnut mare with a star on her forehead. Kitty's mouth dropped open. It couldn't be, could it?

The horse whinnied and Kitty ran forward to throw her arms around her neck. "Oh Star, I've missed you so much."

Luke joined her. "I had Bright search high and low to trace her. He wrote that she had been well treated but her new owner had married and agreed to let him buy Star back. At a good price of course."

Kitty let go of Star and threw her arms around Luke's neck instead. "You are the best of husbands. I couldn't have had a better wedding present."

Nella broke into a satisfied smile. "I knew as soon as I laid eyes on you, my lord, that you were the perfect man for Miss Davenport."

"I rather suspected as much at the time, Mrs Spencer." Luke's severe tone was spoiled by a spontaneous laugh.

Kitty laughed back at him. "I'm sure Mrs Spencer will be the perfect housekeeper from now on."

"Hmm. Somehow, I doubt that but I don't care as long as I

have the perfect wife."

THE END

Afterword

If you loved 'The Viscount's Convenient Bride', I would really appreciate a short review. This helps new readers find my books.

This is Book 2 of my Reluctant Brides series of stand-alone novels linked by character.

Other books in the series:

Book 1 A Good Match For The Major.

Book 3 The Marquess's Christmas Runaway.

Book 4 The Duke's Bluestocking.

For more information please visit my website:

https://josiebonhamauthor.com

You will also find me on:

Facebook @josiebonhamauthor

Twitter @BonhamJosie

Instagram @josiebonham

Printed in Great Britain
by Amazon